BEAUTIFUL SIN SERIES BOOK 2

Beautiful Sinners

JENNILYNN WYER

I

II

CONTENTS

COPYRIGHT

text, including without limitation, technologies that are capable of generating works in the same style, trope, or genre as the Work, is STRICTLY PROHIBITED.

Cover Design: Angela Haddon

Photographer: Ren Saliba

Copy Editor: Ellie Folden @ My Brother's Editor

Formatting By: Jennilynn Wyer

Reader's Note: Intended for mature audiences due to sexual and mature content. Beautiful Sinners is dark reverse harem that contains scenes that may be triggering for sensitive readers (scenes depicting torture, violence/abuse/blood, foul language and f-bombs, praise kink, light bondage, and MF/MFM/MFMM scenes).

Connect with the Author

Website: https://www.jennilynnwyer.com

Linktree: https://linktr.ee/jennilynnwyer

Email: jennilynnwyerauthor@gmail.com

Facebook: https://www.facebook.com/ JennilynnWyerRomanceAuthor/

Twitter: https://www.twitter.com/JennilynnWyer

Instagram: https://www.instagram.com/ jennilynnwyer

TikTok: https://www.tiktok.com/@jennilynnwyer

Threads: https://www.threads.net/@jennilynnwyer

Verve Romance: https://ververomance.com/

app/JennilynnWyer

Goodreads: https://www.goodreads.com/
author/show/20502667.Jennilynn_Wyer

BookBub: https://www.bookbub.com/
authors/jennilynn-wyer

BingeBooks: https://bingebooks.com/
author/jennilynn-wyer

Books2Read: https://books2read.com/
ap/nAAgBb/Jennilynn-Wyer

Amazon Author Page: https://www.amazon.com/
author/jennilynnwyer

Newsletter: https://forms.gle/vYX64JHJVBX7iQvy8

SUBSCRIBE TO MY NEWSLETTER for news on
upcoming releases, cover reveals, sneak peeks,
author giveaways, and other fun stuff!

**JOIN THE J-CREW: A JENNILYNN WYER
ROMANCE READER GROUP**

Join link https://www.facebook.com/
groups/190212596147435

SYNOPSIS

Beautiful Sinners is the highly anticipated second book of the Beautiful Sin Series.

Blurb contains spoilers from book 1, Beautiful Sin. You've been warned!

***

I went to Darlington Founders filled with hopes and dreams. What I found were three men from a past I didn't want to remember. Tristan Amato, Hendrix Knight, and Constantine Ferreira. Three dark and possessive men who saw me as beautiful and not as the scarred, damaged, broken woman I had become.

After a decade of loneliness and feeling like I didn't belong because of my scars, Tristan, Hendrix, and Constantine showed me what it was like to be desired. Wanted. Loved. They claimed me. Made me theirs. Protected me. And unknowingly thrust me back into the life I forced myself to forget ten years ago. A life filled with lies, manipulations, and betrayal.

But they weren't the only ones keeping secrets.

As my past and my present collided, I was forced to make a difficult decision. One born from the fire and the knife that marked my body. One of vengeance for myself and for my parents.

Our enemies wanted Aoife Fitzpatrick? They got her. And they would regret ever bringing her back.

Beautiful Sinners is a full-length why choose romance with dark themes and possessive MMCs. It is book two in the Beautiful Sin series and ends with a cliffhanger. Recommended for mature readers. Please check Reader's Note in the front matter of the book for potential TWs.

Beautiful Sin Series
#1 Beautiful Sin
#2 Beautiful Sinners
#3 Beautiful Chaos

DEDICATION

To all the good girls who love bad boys.

DEAR READER

Thank you so much for picking up my book baby, Beautiful Sinners. It's the second book in my new reverse harem/why choose series. Is this your first RH? Just know that why choose romances mean that the woman is in a relationship (yes, this also includes sex) with multiple men. Trust me, once you read your first RH, you will become addicted.

So, about that sex. It's so hard to determine spice levels because each reader is subjective and has their own scale. For example, one reader may give a book 5 chili peppers, while another says it's a 1.5. I wrote Beautiful Sin in the same vein as I did Savage Princess when it came to building the relationships between the characters. If you're looking for pure porn starting from chapter 1 where all the guys wham-bam the FMC from the get-go, then this book isn't for you. With that being said, Beautiful Sinners does contain sexually explicit scenes (MF, MFM, and MFMM).

As with most works of fiction, authors do their due diligence when researching topics to make the story as realistic as possible, but we also have to bend the rules a bit to get things to conform to the story we want to write. If you're asking yourself after reading book 1, Beautiful Sin: Does Syn have amnesia? The answer is... kind of. What she has are repressed memories (also known as dissociation/dissociative amnesia and include state-dependent remembering, motivated forgetting, and retrieval inhibition). It's an ongoing controversial theory first introduced by Sigmund Freud where a person dissociates and represses traumatic memories and experiences as a survival mechanism. I hope this helps explain why Syn doesn't fully remember the guys or her past. It's because she has repressed the first ten years of her life.

Please keep in mind that because this is book 2 in a trilogy, I'll continue to delve into those open plotlines and characters that I introduced in Beautiful Sin. I won't just come out and say, "This is this, and that is that." Nope. I want to keep you guessing and asking questions until the very end.

And if you're wondering, yes, Andie, Keane, Jax, Liam, Rafael, and other minor characters from my Savage Series will show up in this book. I hinted about it in book 1. You do not need to read the Savage Kingdom Series in order to read the Beautiful Sin Series. If you're curious about the characters from Savage Princess, Savage Kings, or Savage Kingdom, you can find those books on Amazon, Kindle Unlimited, or grab the audiobooks (audiobooks are available wide at most retailers, including your local public library).

Are you ready to continue Synthia (a.k.a. Syn, pronounced "sin"), Tristan, Constantine, and Hendrix's story? Oh, whenever you see the name Aoife, it's pronounced "eefa." ;-) And don't forget to look for those Easter eggs I love to put in every one of my books. The journal (About That Night, Savage Princess), the knife (Savage Princess), and the middle name Penelope (The Fallen Brook Series) are three of them.

Shoot! Almost forgot about those triggers. The Beautiful Sin Series contain scenes depicting torture, violence/abuse/blood, foul language and f-bombs, praise kink, light bondage, and sexually explicit MF/MFM/MFMM scenes.

Love and happy reading,

Jennily Wyer

RECAP

In case you forgot that cliffhanger from Beautiful Sin… (not sorry one bit!)

Constantine follows me as I meander from one blooming shrub to another. The morning sunshine lights the gardens in crisp detail, making the colors seem more vibrant and the smells stronger.

"What's this one called?" I ask, touching the bright indigo pinwheel made of flowers.

I must be driving him crazy with all the questions. The man has the patience of a saint.

"Scaevola."

"That sounds made up. How in the heck do you and Tristan know all the names to things?"

He plucks one of the small flowers from the bush and adds it to the five others he's tucked into my braid. The romance of it isn't lost on me.

I do a quick reconnaissance to see if anyone is looking. We lost sight of Tristan and Hendrix standing under an archway a while ago.

Snipping a flower off its stem with my nails, I push it behind the helix of his ear and laugh when his eyebrows shoot up with amusement.

This moment right here—this is happiness. It's simple and silly. This is what I always hoped falling in love would feel like. Effortless.

"You're so pretty." I giggle, and he grins. I live for his smile because they are so rare. Often when he's near, I find myself longing for his eyes to seek me out, hoping to be graced with one of his beautiful smiles.

Constantine looks around, then snags the belt loop on my jeans and hauls me toward him. He drops his mouth on mine, and my arms tighten around him, my fingers digging into his back. His hands go to my ass, lifting me until my feet barely touch the ground. And when our tongues touch, glide, stroke, savor, all other thoughts dissolve from my mind.

"I love the way you kiss me," I sigh when we break apart.

Tristan's kisses are all power and possession. Hendrix's are filled with wicked seduction. But Constantine kisses me slowly, like I'm the air he needs to breathe.

He presses our foreheads together, then loops his pinky finger around mine and continues walking.

When we get to the center of the garden, there's an old-fashioned maze made from hedgerows of dark green boxwoods.

With childlike enthusiasm, I grin up at Constantine. "Hey, do you want to—"

Pop.

I freeze at the familiar sound I remember all too well

from the alley. So does Constantine.

With a quickness that defies logic, he has me flattened to the ground with his body over mine. Tiny, jagged pieces of rock cut into my palms, cheek, and stomach.

"Don't make a sound," he whispers, and I nod to let him know that I heard him.

With his heavy weight on top of me, I can only take shallow breaths, and the lack of oxygen with my heart beating so rapidly makes me woozy.

He lifts up on his arms, his black gaze darting all around.

Snick.

"Hello, Constantine."

Aleksei's cold words stab through the air like a steel blade as two other men appear on either side of us.

"One wrong move and Miss Carmichael will get a bullet through her pretty little head." Aleksei none too gently digs the nozzle of his gun into my skull, leaving no doubt that he wouldn't hesitate to pull the trigger if Constantine didn't comply. "On your feet," he tells Constantine.

Fear shakes me to the core when Constantine does what he says and slowly lifts off me. I watch in horror as the two men grab him by the arms and cruelly kick out his legs, forcing him to his knees in front of Aleksei.

Aoife. Wake up.

"Do you know how much I'm going to enjoy killing you?" Even though he says it to Constantine, he points his gun straight at me.

"Fuck. You," Constantine growls.

In a flash of movement, one of the men lashes out with a brutal heel-kick that slams Constantine face-first to the ground.

Aleksei cocks his shaved head and laughs. "Death can speak! It's been a while. Honestly, I prefer you mute."

I try to think of a way to distract him. Give Constantine time to figure out how to get us out of this situation. Tristan and Hendrix will come for us. Unless...

"Where's Aleksander?"

Aleksander seems to be the more rational twin. He may be an asshole, but he treated me with a semblance of respect when I went to the bell tower. He could have done anything to me while I was there, but he didn't. Maybe I can convince him—

"Busy with your other boyfriends."

Aleksei squats down and forces my head up with his gun under my chin. The acrid stench of cordite crawls into my nostrils, and the heat radiating from the metal barrel singes my skin, indicating that it was recently fired.

"Aleksander wants you alive, but he never said in what condition."

A white-hot searing pain shoots through my skull when he slams the butt of his gun into my temple. My vision wavers, but Constantine's angry, raspy shouts promising death snap me back into focus. My ears fill with the sickening thuds of boots on flesh and bone as the two men kick him with sadistic fury in the side, the legs, the back, the head.

"Stop!" My fingernails break as I claw at the ground, scrambling to crawl to Constantine.

Time slows to a flicker, each second stretching into eternity. Aleksei aims his gun, the metal glinting malevolently in the stark sunlight. My mind races with terror as I watch him take aim at Constantine, his finger curling around the trigger.

"Please! No! Aleksei, please! Please, don't do this!" I sob. I beg. My cries of desperation reach up to the heavens where even God himself would hear them. *Don't take him from me. We just found each other.* "Constantine!"

A sickening trickle of crimson liquid drips from Constantine's mouth to the ground from the gashes littering his face. His pained eyes meet mine, sheer agony pouring out of them like an open wound.

No.

No.

"*Você é meu coração*," he chokes out.

My feral scream shatters my voice and echoes across miles. "*Gheobhaidh mo chroí do chroí! Gheobhaidh mo chroí do chroí!*"

AOIFE! WAKE THE FUCK UP!

...

...

Bang!

"IN ORDER TO RISE
FROM ITS OWN
ASHES, A PHOENIX
FIRST MUST BURN."

-Octavia Butler

PROLOGUE

Ten Years Ago

AOIFE

"I hate you!" I scream at my father when he rips the letter I'd been writing and tosses the pieces into the fireplace. The flames turn them to smoldering black ash in seconds.

I don't hate him. I'm just angry at him and Mama for taking me away. They won't let me talk to Con, Hendrix, and Tristan. No phone call, no email, no text message. Not even a letter—which I had been in the middle of writing before Papa discovered me. Every attempt I make to contact the boys fails. I miss them so much.

"Aoife, apologize to your father," my mother scolds, hands on her hips and her mouth pursed in a disapproving line. She's fed up with my belligerent behavior and daily temper tantrums.

We've been in Ireland for months now. I'm not allowed to go outside or go to school or do anything. They won't tell me why. Only that it's too dangerous.

I glare at my mother, refusing to back down. She throws her hands up in the air in infuriated exasperation, then hits me with a hard truth that stops me in my tracks just as I start to storm off.

"You are so bloody ungrateful! Everything we've done has been for you! To protect you and keep you safe. Do you think your father and I want *this*?" she shouts, arms spread wide in gesticulation of the new house we're currently living in. A house in the middle of nowhere that is much smaller and less opulent than the one back home.

I actually like it better than our old house. I love the verdant pastural land that stretches as far as my eye can see. The thatched roof, pot-marked wood floors, wood-burning fireplace that fills the air with the pleasing smell of crisp cedar, and thick window glass that makes the world outside look wavy and distorted.

"Caroline," Papa harshly clips, sending her an admonishing shake of the head.

She whirls on him, all anger and righteous fury. "No, James. I'm sick and tired of her pouty, obdurate attitude. We gave up everything for her!"

Papa's face contorts into something horrible. It's a look I can't describe in words, but one that sends ominous shivers down my spine. He takes a menacing step toward her, hands curled into tight fists at his sides. Mama stumbles backward at his approach, her usually rosy-tinted cheeks pallid with fear.

"Are you willing to trade our daughter's life for—"

Her eyes dart from him to me in censure as she cuts him off. "That's not fair! You can't expect me to choose between—"

I jump when Papa's arm strikes out like the biting

attack of a fanged snake, his punishing grip around her neck preventing her from speaking further. With a brutal jerk, he pulls her to him.

"Even after I discovered your betrayal, I stayed. I loved you. So don't you fucking dare—"

"*James*," she hisses.

I don't understand what they're talking about, and the way they keep interrupting each other makes it clear that they don't want me to know.

"Papa?" I query, coming closer. I've never seen him so angry with Mama before. I don't like it.

As if coming out of a trance, he shoves her away and drops to his haunches, opening his arms wide for me to walk into his embrace.

"I'm sorry, *a stór*," he says, his beard snagging strands of my hair as he nuzzles his cheek against my face. "Everything's okay. I didn't mean to—"

I cry out when window glass shatters into a million, knife-edged pieces, slicing across my back, neck, and arms. Papa protectively curls his big body over me just as shouts and screams intermix in a confusing cacophony that I can't understand. The air clogs with tiny particulate matter as loud pops of gunfire puncture holes through the wall, leaving behind perfectly circular peepholes.

"Caroline!" Papa's bellow makes my ears ring.

When Mama doesn't answer, I twist around to see her dragging her body across the floor toward us, a line of thick crimson trailing behind her. She's hurt.

I claw at my father's arms, wanting to get to Mama.

With a deafening roar, the front door crashes inward and splinters as two men storm into the house, their guns drawn.

"Aoife! Run!"

But my feet won't budge. My legs have become stone pillars, refusing to bend. I struggle to hear anything over the thunderous beat of my heart. I see one of the men's mouths move as his cold green eyes find us, but no sound carries to my ears. And then a wave of fury, unlike any I've ever experienced, consumes me, scorches through my blood until my veins sizzle.

"Aoife, no!" Papa calls out.

But it's too late.

Rage burns my vision as I launch myself at the green-eyed man. Everything becomes pure instinct when my training takes over as primal energy crackles through me with unstoppable force. Muscle memory flares to life and manifests into a wild, deranged violence that I unleash upon the intruder. My only coherent thought is to protect my parents. It pulses like a siren in my brain, blocking out everything else.

Kill them all.

"Fuck!" the guy shouts just as I wrench his arm to the side when his finger pulls the trigger. I don't react to the loud bang when it discharges near my ear or the heat that burns my left hand when I grab the barrel.

With an animalistic savagery, my fist punches into the underside of his arm, and he releases the gun completely when his hand goes numb. There is no mercy in my gaze as I turn the gun in my hand, point it at his chest, and fire. Point-blank range to the sweet spot straight through his heart. Thick bloody droplets shower down on me, decorating my pale skin with its sticky warmth.

"Aoife, move!"

I drop and roll just as a blur flies by me when Papa

barrels into the second man. They crash over the small coffee table and tumble to the floor with a jolting thud. Mama whimpers as she pulls herself into a sitting position with her back against the wall. There's so much blood, her clothes are drenched in it.

I don't have time to go and help Papa because another man runs into the room. He must have come in through the back door. He hears Mama's raspy cry and turns toward her, a sick smile spreading across his face.

Kill them all.

Thigh and calf muscles bunch like spring-loaded coils, then release as I run at the man. Falling to the floor, I elongate my thin body and slide between his legs, grabbing at his right ankle. My momentum pulls him off his feet, and he timbers like a tree to the floor. There's a satisfying crunch of bone when he slams face-first onto the hard wood. My body collides with the baseboard, and I use my legs to kick off it and scramble up. I grapple onto the man's back in an instant.

His head explodes like a gory piñata when I pull the trigger, and his legs and arms twitch violently for a few seconds as phantom electrical signals from what remains of his mind fight to communicate with his corpse.

Holding the large, heavy pistol with a steady, white-knuckled grip, I take merciless strides toward my father and his assailant. Papa lets the man pin him to the floor, which gives me a clear and unobstructed line of sight to unload the rest of the magazine into his skull. The man becomes dead weight and collapses forward on top of Papa.

Our gazes meet across the carnage and pride fills my father's eyes. That pride quickly transforms into a warning that comes too late.

My father's enraged shout disintegrates in my ears as pain detonates across the back of my head and dark oblivion quickly follows.

I'm not here.
I'm not here.
I'm not here.
I am no one.

The scream that fills my ears is unworldly, like the gates of hell have opened up, letting loose the demons to rip flesh from human bone. My hands grip the sides of my head until it feels like I'm trying to crush in my own skull.

Block out the sounds.

Block out the screams.

But the screams are coming from me. And they won't stop.

"Shut the fuck up!" the man snarls in my face, his spit splashing across my nose and mouth.

A harsh hand grips my long hair and wrenches my head back. I couldn't look anymore as the man, the other one with a jagged red line down the left side of his face, defiled my mother in the cruelest of ways.

When my eyes find her again, her body is unnaturally contorted, bent at an odd angle on the living room's red floral Château rug. Her head is turned in my direction, her once beautiful, clover-green irises are black, like a doll's soulless eyes. I think she's dead.

They already killed Papa. They killed him first. And

I'm next.

Because the Society demands it. That's what the guy with the constellations drawn on his neck said right before he shot my father in the head.

A strange odor, both acrid and sweet, assaults my nose, but I'm not able to process it over the searing pain of the knife being shoved in my side. The pain comes again and again, each time hurting a little less until there's no pain at all.

A whoosh whispers in my ear as a bright light erupts behind my closed eyelids. Heat scorches all around me, tiny licks of fire dancing across my body like magical forest sprites.

I wonder if I'll become a phoenix once the fire burns me to ash, like the one in the story Papa reads to me at bedtime. I'd like that. I'd like to be able to spread my wings and fly.

I feel like I'm flying now. Higher and higher toward a bright light. It's beautiful. Peaceful. I am the phoenix.

Right before the light surrounds me, I'm pulled back down to earth, my wings clipped and useless. As life courses through my body once again, the pain comes. My torn, damaged vocal cords cry out a sound much like that of a kitten's strangled mewl.

I don't want to come back. I want to be the phoenix and fly into the bright light like Icarus did the sun.

But I can't because the person who saved me won't let me go.

"You're safe now. You're safe. I've got you."

CHAPTER 1

Present Day

Standing under an arbor of climbing roses, I watch Con and Syn as they stroll through the garden, stopping once in a while for Syn to look closer at a flower. Every so often, their hands gravitate together for brief touches as they walk. Con tucks a flower in her hair, and whatever he says has her smiling broadly and laughing.

"That's a damn beautiful sight."

"It is," Hendrix agrees, not able to keep his eyes off her. "Even if she's pissed at us."

I pick a rosebud from its thorny vine and tear the petals off one at a time. As a child, Aoife fought against the status quo of our world in her own way. She greeted every lower member and servant by their name and treated them as equals. She would bring them gifts, little things like a flower garland she'd make herself out of wild clover or honeysuckle or cupcakes she would bake with the help of her governess.

"How are you feeling about last night? That she chose him to be her first and not us."

I suck in a jagged breath and let it out slowly. Aoife loved all three of us, but her connection with Con was different. Deeper. But I get what he's saying. For Syn, Con will always hold a unique space in her heart because he took her virginity.

"We need to tell her who she really is."

Hendrix hits me with icy, glacial eyes. "Will you fucking get over that already? You know we can't. At least not until we clean house."

Such a simple euphemism for what we have planned.

We both look over when two men in dark suits walk by. Armed guards. The house and grounds will be teaming with them in an hour. Extra security since the highest-ranking members of the Society will be here.

"I don't like this. Syn's going to notice and ask questions."

"I'm pretty sure she already has noticed." Hendrix follows my line of sight. "Dad was more vague than usual last night when we spoke. Fuck. I forgot to tell you. He's giving his vote to the Stepanoffs."

The brief calm of serenity I was having watching Syn and Con together gets blown all to hell. I back him up until we're hidden from view under the arbor.

"You better have a fucking good explanation why you didn't tell me immediately last night." I tighten a leash on my anger to counter the insurmountable urge to punch him.

He swipes my hand off his upper arm. "Because I knew you'd lose your shit, and there isn't a damn thing we can do about it."

"There you are," a voice calls out from nearby.

I smooth out my features when Eva materializes on the courtyard. As soon as she steps off the stone patio and into the grass, her ridiculously high heels sink into the ground as she walks, making her canter like that of a newborn giraffe. Syn was smart when she took hers off to walk barefoot in the grass.

Eva hasn't had the same amount of plastic surgery as my mother, but she's just as fake. And hidden behind her expensive nose job, polished, glossy veneers, and diamonds is a woman just as ruthless and power-hungry as her husband.

Her oversized designer sunglasses hide half her face, making it hard to tell who she's looking at.

"Your father would like to speak with you."

Hendrix waves her off. "He can wait."

"Not yours. Tristan's."

Knots twist in my gut. I hadn't expected him for another hour.

"He's here?"

"He and your mother just arrived. They—"

There's a hollow *pop* just as blood and brain matter eject sideways out of Eva's head, and she crumples like a rag doll that's lost its stuffing.

"Mum!"

Hendrix and I have no time to react before several men come out of nowhere, guns trained on us with lethal accuracy. Two of them I recognize as the armed guards who'd been patrolling the grounds. They'd been here the entire time in plain sight.

But my murderous fury is locked on the gray-eyed Russian who comes forward, a malicious smile spread across his face.

"I did warn you that you had no idea what was

coming for you."

Hendrix stands motionless beside me, but I can feel the intensity vibrating through him. We both know what's about to happen. Neither one of us will be walking away from this unscathed. Not the best odds when there are five guns aimed at our heads.

With a severity as cold as the demise I will bring him, I promise Aleksander, "I'm going to kill you."

His eyes glint with amused incredulity as he throws his head back in a throaty laugh. "I'd like to see you try, Amato."

With deliberate slowness, he strolls over to Eva and pokes her in the thigh with the toe of his Timberlakes. Hendrix doesn't even care to look. He won't shed a tear that his mother is dead. Aleksander actually did us a favor. And if miracles do happen, he would have made sure that my father is greeting Eva Knight in hell.

"Syn," Hen mutters under his breath with urgency, and I go stone-cold rigid as alarm overtakes my anger. *Fuck!* I have to hope that Con protects her and gets her the hell out of here.

I'm not a praying man or an overly religious one, but I find myself pleading with the higher power upstairs to keep Syn safe, even knowing there will be no divine intervention for men like me. But I would sacrifice myself a thousand times over for her. *For Aoife.*

Please, baby. Please be okay.

"Where's your uglier half?" I ask after my gaze pings every detail of my surroundings. There's no one else out here other than Aleksander and the four men circling us. No movement or noise coming from the house. Where is everyone?

His victorious smile grows, and any hope I had dies

execution style when he replies, "With your woman."

"You fucking bastard!" Hendrix roars just as Syn's agonizing scream tears through my heart like shrapnel.

Dear God, no.

Three of Aleksander's men immediately subdue Hendrix and tackle him with brute force to the ground before he can take one lunging step.

"That was a really stupid thing to do, Knight," Aleksander *tsks* and flicks the safety off his Glock.

Every muscle in my body twitches with the overpowering need to do *something*. Not just stand here and accept the fate Aleksander has chosen for me.

Syn's cries reach my ears over the distance of the gardens and desperation sinks its serrated talons into my flesh.

"Call Aleksei off!" I demand. "Aleksander! Call your brother off!"

He cocks his head my way, intrigued. "You want to beg for her life? Do it on your knees."

His challenge is clear. Abject humiliation in exchange for Syn's life.

Amatos are kings. We bend to no-fucking-one.

With my hands raised in supplication, my knees hit the soft ground in front of him. "Don't let him hurt her. Call him off."

I feel Hendrix's stare from his prone position. He thrashes about like a wild animal, spitting out venomous curses, but Aleksander's men have him in a vise grip, their hands like iron shackles, pinning him down.

With a bewildered expression, Aleksander approaches me but makes sure not to get too close. Never underestimate your enemy, even when they are begging you on their knees.

"You would die for her? A woman you just met?"

"Yes." No hesitation.

He looks down at Hendrix. "I thought she was yours."

"Fuck you," Hendrix growls, blood coating his bared teeth.

"I think I'll let your pretty little thing do that once Aleksei is through with her."

He gives an imperceptible nod, and the men pull a pissed-off Hendrix to his knees.

"Aleksander, don't do this. Let her go. You don't understand."

Hendrix must hear something in the despair of my voice. His eyes bore into me with a ferocity that sends a clear warning. One that I won't heed.

"Don't you fucking do it! Don't you tell him a goddamn thing!" he snaps at me, but I'd do anything at this point to ensure Syn survives.

"On the contrary, please, Tristan, tell me. Just know it won't make a damn bit of difference on the outcome." He shoves the blunt end of his gun against my forehead.

Our gazes lock, a silent battle being played out on the verdant grassy turf of the Knight's backyard garden.

"Aoife."

Her name is a scorched stone in my throat, almost impossible to get out.

"T, shut the fuck up!" Hendrix bellows, then grunts from the kick delivered to his side.

The metal of the barrel scrapes my skin when Aleksander drops his hand. "What did you just say?"

"Syn... is Aoife," I grit out just as the echo of a gun discharging has my blood flash-freezing in my veins. "Aleksander! Do something!"

We can't lose her. Not now. Not after we just got her back. I can't fail her again, even if it means I give her to my enemy.

My head whips back as he strikes me in the face. Again and again, until a liquid red haze occludes my vision. He balls my hair in his fist and yanks my head back. Sunlight temporarily blinds my blurred vision until Aleksander's enraged face looms over me.

"You're fucking lying! I would have known!"

The other men struggle to hold Hendrix at bay as he tries to get free. Then just as suddenly, he goes completely still, his attention on something in the distance.

With Hendrix's whispered, *"Fucking Christ,"* Aleksander and I turn our heads just as a whizzing noise flies past our ears.

The first shot tears through the man on Hendrix's right, and he flies sideways as if tethered to the bullet on a string. In a fraction of a second, the other three men topple in perfect unison, their bodies collapsing like dominoes. Aleksander roughly pulls me to my feet and uses me as a human shield as he prepares to fire back. But doesn't.

Like one of the macabre nightmares she described in her journal, Syn materializes from the gardens, her chin dipped to her sternum so only the pale blue of her eyes shine behind her waterfall of scarlet hair. She's painted red with blood from her face to her bare toes, but her movements are steady, so I'm not sure if she's injured or not. Her blood or not. Where in the hell is Con? Aleksei?

"Oh, god, firefly."

Like a wraith from hell, Syn advances forward with measured steps, arm outstretched, finger pressing the trigger, the continuous clicking of the hammer like that of a grandfather clock ticking off time. The magazine is empty. No more bullets.

"*Aoife?*" Aleksander says in disbelief. She snarls at him in response.

In the next blink and with no warning at all, the ground beneath us trembles violently. A deafening boom shakes the earth, followed by a concussive shockwave that slams into us like a giant invisible fist when the house explodes.

CHAPTER 2

"Please! No! Aleksei, please! Please, don't do this!"
No.
No.
Please, God, no.
Take me! Not him!
I love you. I love you.
"Constantine!"
I come awake with a start.

And freak the fuck out because I'm inside a coffin.

Wait. Not a coffin. I'm under a bed. Eight years have passed since the last time this happened. Maybe seeing Hendrix sleeping on the floor triggered me somehow. But why would...

A pounding ache reverberates through my skull. My vision swims with hazy fragments of memories. And then everything comes back to me in a sudden, soul-wrenching deluge of heartbreak.

Aleksei. Guns. Blood. Aleksander. An explosion.

"Constantine!" I cry out hoarsely.

Pain tears into me as I scramble out from my hiding place as stiff, bruised muscles refuse to move. A roar fills my ears, and an inferno of emotions engulfs me as my mind is barraged with image after image, a slideshow made of horrific nightmares. New ones that have me gasping for breath, and old ones that I never wanted to remember.

"Constantine!"

Every bone and joint scream as I clamber to my feet. Dizziness spins the room around me, and I stumble and crash into the side of the bed. My stomach lurches with nausea that leaves an acrid, nasty taste in my mouth, and I gulp down the vomit that wants to rise. Breathing deeply in through my nose and out my mouth, I try to fill lungs that don't want to cooperate. With a shaking hand, I cup the back of my head. *Thud. Thud. Thud.* It pounds to the same throbbing agony as my heartbeat until it feels like my skull wants to split wide open.

I struggle to blink away the disorientation as my tear-crusted eyes frantically search the dimly lit room. A room that is unfamiliar. Not mine or Constantine's or Tristan's or Hendrix's.

The walls are adorned with faded paintings, and even though I don't see a bookcase in the room, there's a musty scent of old books that hangs in the air and mingles with the ashy aftermath of the explosion that clings to my skin and clothes.

"Constantine!"

My limbs feel heavy with invisible iron chains shackled around my ankles. Ignoring the discomfort, I stumble toward the door, my legs unsteady beneath me. Light spills into the room when I throw open the door, and I cover my eyes with my forearm to block out the glare.

My voice quivers as I quietly call out, "Constantine? Tristan? Hendrix?"

My words seem to vanish into the vastness of nothingness, swallowed by the house's eerie stillness. Where am I?

Cautiously venturing into the corridor, a shiver of unease trickles down my spine. The dark hallway is cloaked in silence, broken only by the sound of my own faltering footsteps. Shadows dance along the tapestried walls, appearing to twist and contort as if alive.

The hairs on my arms and neck raise when a noise at the end of the hallway catches my attention. There's someone else here. Flattening my back against the wall, I bite the whimper of pain that wants to escape my lips when every part of my body protests the sudden movement. I'm in no shape to fight, but that doesn't mean I won't. My thoughts are single-minded and focused on one purpose. Find Constantine.

I never got to say goodbye. I never got to kiss him one last time. Touch him. Have one more morning of waking up in his arms. Hear his beautiful, broken voice. I never said the words...

I cover my mouth when a sob breaks free, the agony unbearable as it beats down on me.

I can't breathe. I can't breathe.

"Syn?"

I respond to the name I've been called for the last ten years spoken by a vaguely familiar voice that isn't the one I want so desperately to hear right now.

I look up from my grief. Dark hair. Hazel eyes. Black-rimmed glasses. Clark Kent looks.

"*Evan?*"

I react without consideration.

Framed paintings fall off the walls and crash against the unforgiving hard wood when my body collides with his, and we tumble to the floor. A surge of pain jolts through me at the impact, and Evan grunts as the wind is knocked out of him, momentarily stunned by the unexpected attack. I use it to my advantage.

Our bodies thrash and twist, limbs entangled in a messy struggle for dominance. Using nothing but pure adrenaline, I lock my legs around his torso when we roll, then jerk my forearm under his neck in a debilitating chokehold.

"Syn, fuck. Stop!"

He tries to flip our positions, and I bring my knee up from under his arm, clipping the side of his jaw. His glasses fly off his face and skitter across the polished wood boards.

Arms wrap around me and pull, but I fight it, too lost in the darkness. They took Constantine from me. My broken angel with the dark eyes. My safe place. My heart.

"Syn, baby, let go."

A Bostonian lilt teases my ears as I increase the pressure against Evan's neck.

"Red, let him go."

Evan's blunt nails dig into my skin, his face turning a purplish shade of red.

"Firefly."

The subtle British accent I used to hate whispers to me, however, it's the guttural, raspy "Aoife" that has my head jerking up.

Tristan and Hendrix are lowered beside me on the floor, their hands pulling at my shoulders and arms, urging me to release Evan. But it's the one man standing in front of me who I thought I had lost forever that has me bursting into tears.

Constantine is beaten and bruised, his face and left eye swollen, his lip puffy where a dark scab mars the corner. I've never seen anything more wonderful in my entire life. I'm off the floor like a hurricane and hurtling myself into his arms, a mess of uncontrollable, ugly sobs.

He catches me easily. I bury my face in his neck and wrap my entire body around him.

"I thought I lost you."

"Never," he whispers, holding me tight.

"Get away from her," Hendrix says and pins Evan to the wall.

Tristan's hand settles on the back of my neck as he walks around Constantine, and I peer up at him, not able to see him clearly through the tears, but I do make out several bruises on his face. His head tilts in a contemplative manner as he stares into my eyes, searching for something. Searching for *her*. It's something I can't deal with right now. It's too raw. Too real. Too painful. And I've had enough heartbreak for one day.

"I had to piss. I saw her leave the room, and when I tried to—"

"Don't give a shit. You don't fucking touch her. Ever."

Evan coughs when Hendrix shoves him away, and I hear the scrape of his glasses across the floor as he picks them up.

I don't question why my lab TA is here, still not knowing exactly where in the hell here is. Evan's mysterious presence is on the bottom of my list of things to ask about.

"Cotton will want to check her out," Evan says.

Hendrix nudges Tristan out of the way and runs his thumb under my eye to catch my tears.

"No doctor," I say.

"She really needs to let someone—"

I jump when Hendrix booms, "When she's fucking ready!"

"Jesus, fine, fuck. I'll let Cillian know she's awake."

Muffled footsteps pad down the hallway until they disappear completely.

"Red." A hand smooths down my hair.

"What happened?" I murmur against Constantine's skin as he carries me back inside the bedroom.

Aleksei was going to shoot Constantine. His finger was about to pull the trigger. Everything after that moment is a whirlwind of confused madness that I can't quite wrap my mind around.

Constantine sits down on the side of the bed, taking me with him since I won't let him go, but he doesn't seem to want to let me go either. I lean back in his embrace, and his eyes fall shut as I tenderly kiss every mark on his face.

Tristan situates himself on the bed at Constantine's back, facing me, his expression stern but his whiskey eyes remain soft when our gazes meet.

"Stop."

Tristan's fingers play with the ends of my hair. "Stop what?"

"Stop looking at me like I'm fragile."

His full lips briefly curve in a small smile before they pull tight into a grim line. "You are far from fragile, Red, but right now, I am."

Oh. I reach a hand over Constantine's shoulder and caress Tristan's handsome, worried face. He covers my hand with his and holds it to his cheek.

"Was there an explosion?" I ask.

"Yeah, baby, there was," Tristan says sadly.

Hendrix moves to the window and pulls the curtains to allow the waxing gibbous moon's light into the room. He doesn't turn around, just stands there, a silhouette of despondency as he peers out into the night.

Night, not morning. How much time has passed?

"Fucking Irish blew up my goddamn house."

What?

"Those fucking Irish are the reason we're still alive. And you hated that house," Tristan replies.

That's what the explosion was? His house? Dear God. All the people. His parents. The staff I saw in the kitchen. "Was anyone hurt?"

Hendrix shrugs a shoulder, and my brow furrows at his casual brushoff about people's lives like they aren't important.

I carefully slide off Constantine's lap and back up a step. My legs shake with the exertion of keeping me upright, and I'm reminded of the bruises and injuries I also carry. The adrenaline is wearing off, and every ache and pain is making itself known.

"Was anyone hurt?" I repeat and back up another step as the walls start to close in on me.

Constantine stands up, and it kills me to do it because I'm so fucking ecstatic that he's alive, but I hold my hand out in front of me to stop his advance.

"Yes."

"Who?"

Tristan slides his legs over the side of the bed. "We'll

talk about it later. Let's just make sure you're okay first."

I'm about to insist that I'm fine when a recognizable sour, metallic smell hits me, and I look down at myself. At the dried blood that covers my clothes and skin. I'm a nightmare matted in gore and destruction. A nightmare that I never wanted to remember. Was it me? Did I kill them just like the words I wrote in my journal?

I don't want to be her. I don't want to hurt people.

I'm not here.

I'm not here.

I'm not here.

I am no one.

"Aoife, baby, please," Tristan implores when I start to fracture apart.

My fingers fist in my hair at my scalp, and I scream, "Don't call me that!"

"It's who you bloody are!" Hendrix yells.

I shake my head obstinately. No. I refuse to be her. She's the reason I was taken from them. She is why Papa hid me away in Ireland. She is the reason why we were tortured for hours, my mother raped, my parents killed, my body mutilated. She is the cause of every bad thing in my life, and I made sure she died that night along with them.

Don't remember. Don't remember.

My hands fly up to my eyes in an attempt to block everything out, but I can't control all the memories that flood back. I desperately try to hold on to the last remaining shreds of the new reality I created, but it's no use. Every detail of the massacre comes back to me.

My legs buckle beneath me as my mind spirals into the oblivion of the girl I used to be, and I fall to the floor in agony as anguish settles over me like a blanket of death.

CHAPTER 3

CONSTANTINE

I watch Aoife collapse in on herself, and seeing how much she's hurting breaks my goddamn heart. I don't know what to do, and I feel fucking helpless. More helpless than I felt when Aleksei had his gun on me, and I knew I wouldn't be able to save her.

But *she* saved *me*.

I'm still trying to wrap my head around what I saw, what she did. There will be repercussions. She has no idea what's coming for her. The things she unknowingly set into motion today. The power balance in the Society has shifted, and civil war is imminent. However, our first priority is her. But which *her* will she be? Syn or Aoife. She repressed that part of her life for a reason, and who the hell knows what kind of psychological damage she's dealing with now that she remembers.

"What do we do?" Tristan's hands clench and unclench at his sides as he hovers over her, wanting to touch her but unsure if he should.

I bend down to scoop up her crumpled body where she lies broken on the floor. "I've got her."

"The fuck you do," Hendrix replies, but the cold stare I send him as I gather Aoife into my arms has him pausing in his attempt to take her from me.

Not fucking happening.

Tristan grasps his shoulder in a futile attempt at calming a fuming Hendrix.

"I'm not leaving her."

She burrows into me, wetting my shirt with her tears.

"I'm not asking you to. But it's not about you or what you want right now," I reply sternly and carry her into the bathroom, quietly pushing the door closed with my foot.

The en suite only has a walk-in shower, but it's big enough to easily accommodate four people.

When I catch our reflection in the mirror and see how small and vulnerable she looks in my arms, I have a moment of uncertainty if I'm doing the right thing.

Turning the handle on the shower, I step inside.

She yelps when the spray of cold water hits her, but it seems to do the job of bringing her back, and I almost smile at the sour scowl she gives me, one I remember very well because it's something Aoife would do. How could I not know when I first saw her at the Bierkeller who she really was? The guilt that I didn't will stay with me for a long time.

But that one small scowl eases the tightness in my chest and tells me everything I need to know. My beautiful, fierce girl is a force to be reckoned with. She's a survivor. So unbelievably fucking strong.

"That wasn't very nice," she mumbles through chattering teeth when I flip the shower handle up to get the water warm. The stall instantly fills with a foggy cloud of billowing steam.

"Better?"

"Much," she says, but she hasn't stopped trembling, so I just hold her under the spray, neither one of us caring that we're fully clothed and drenched to the bone.

"Aleksei's dead."

Not a question but a statement of fact. I nuzzle the top of her wet head and hum a non-answer.

Aleksei never saw her coming. It was sudden and over with before any of them knew what was happening. I will never tell her how magnificent she was or how absolutely resplendent she looked covered in that motherfucker's blood.

"Aleksander? Did I... the explosion... I don't remember what happened after—" She takes a deep breath and shakes her head as she struggles to recall exactly what transpired.

Cillian McCarthy saved our asses for reasons still unknown, but Aleksander escaped before Cillian's men could get to him.

Aleksander will be coming for her, and not because she killed his twin.

"Soon," I answer, and she nods, understanding, even though what I said would make no sense to anyone else.

Aoife and I, *Syn and I*, could always have a conversation without speaking a single word. It's another clue I should've picked up on but somehow missed.

Her cheek caresses my neck, and she presses her lips to my skin, holding them there at my pulse point.

"I was so scared that you..." Her arms tighten around

me. "*I'm sorry,*" she whispers.

"For what?" My voice cracks, and her lips go to the knot of my Adam's apple.

She doesn't answer my question but instead says, "I want to be clean."

Whatever she needs, I'll give her.

"I'm going to set you down. Hold on to me."

Trying in vain to remain unaffected as I slide her body down the length of mine, I gently lower her to stand and tell my dick to chill the hell out because fucking her should be the furthest thing from my mind right now.

My hands go to her hips to steady her when she teeters, and I hear the sharp gasp my light touch elicits.

"Hurt?" I ask, undoing the button of her pants so I can get a closer look.

Cillian's personal physician, Cotton, checked her out while she was unconscious, but she should get a full work-up, maybe a CT scan just to be sure, now that she's awake.

"No."

The water beats down over her head, plastering her long hair to her body, but I can see the blush of arousal in her cheeks. It's the same silent thrum that ignites every time I look at her.

She raises her arms above her head for me to take off her shirt, then she unhooks her bra herself. Her creamy, pale breasts bounce enticingly when she tosses the garments behind her, and they land with an audible *plop* on the tile shower floor. The bruises and bite marks marring her chest aren't from today, and I trace the first one Hendrix gave her because he smelled me on her. He can be a jealous, territorial ass.

She holds on to my shoulders when I go to my knees and ease the wet denim down her long legs. My lips gravitate to the scars on her left side, and she sighs when I brush kisses across the roughened, reddish skin. Who did this to her is still a mystery, and I'm conflicted about finding out the answer. Part of me hopes she never remembers. But if she does, God have mercy on their souls because they will receive none from me when I find them.

"Constantine."

My eyes lift to hers as I help her step out of her jeans and panties. The picture she creates is stunning, like a Botticelli Venus rising from the waters, nude, wet, and utterly captivating.

"I need to tell you something," she says softly.

I run my hands up her thighs and around to her lower back. Not to entice, but to let her know I'm here. I'm hers. And I'm not going anywhere.

She touches my face, her fingers tracing the curve from my forehead to my cheek. Thick emotion clogs her throat when she chokes out, "I love you, too. I should have said it when you told me, but... and then... and then when Aleksei... I was so afraid that I'd never get to... I just thought you should know."

Tristan, Hendrix, and I are not good men. We're surely bound for hell as penance for the things we've done. By some miracle, Aoife came back. Her heart found us just like she promised. How in the fuck do we deserve such a precious gift?

With our gazes locked, I rise to my full height and take the small bottle of liquid soap from the shelf, lathering some between my hands.

"I never doubted it for a second. *Você é meu coração.*"

Her smile is shy and small, but I see it, and damn, is it a wonderful sight.

Playfully, I brush a dollop of sudsy foam on her button nose, and the water raining down on us rinses the rest from my hands when I slip them around her, desperate for that physical connection to help ease the fear that I almost lost her again. But she's alive. She's here. With us. Where she fucking belongs.

"May I?" she asks, her hands already at the button of my jeans.

I stand motionless as she concentrates on undoing the zipper, then slides her hands up to remove my shirt. After she's done, I kick off my pants and push them with my foot to join her pile of clothes. Her shaking palms immediately go to my bare chest, covering where my heart beats only for her.

She stays just like that for long minutes, hands and eyes fixed on me, as tears fall like raindrops down her face. Eventually, her chest heaves when she breathes deeply, and she tips her head back, those cornflower blue eyes filled with such sadness.

"I don't know who I am anymore."

I cup the back of her neck and press a tender kiss to her sweet mouth. "No matter who you choose to be, you'll always be ours."

"I have so many questions, but I don't want to think about any of them right now. Can you just hold me for a little while?"

I pull her to me with a gentle tug. Her slick skin and warm body feel like heaven when she cuddles against me.

I hold my girl tight as my thoughts turn to Aleksander, wondering when he'll come for her—

because he will. We just need to be ready when he does.

"How could I forget you and Tristan and Hendrix?"

Her sudden question breaks the quiet of the white noise generated by the curtain of water cascading over us.

"You didn't. Not really."

She pulls out of my arms and reaches for the pump bottle of shampoo sitting on the inset shelf, and I lower my head when she goes up on tiptoe, intending to wash my hair.

"When did you get so freaking tall?"

I hook one arm under her ass and heft her up off her feet so she can reach me more easily.

"Sixteen."

That's when I shot up five inches practically overnight. Hen did as well around the same time.

"I missed out on so much." The grief in her voice pierces me like a serrated dagger.

After lathering my hair, she plays with it, alternating between flattening the strands with her palm and spiking them up to create a mohawk. When she's done, I turn around and back up into the spray so she can rinse the shampoo out.

Her legs lift and circle my waist, placing my achingly hard cock I've been trying to ignore right at her pussy. I stifle the groan that wants to come when her wet heat beckons me to fuck her against the shower wall.

Eyes on me, she licks her lips and rotates her hips, and the tip of my shaft notches at her entrance.

"Aoife," I warn. There's only so much willpower I can muster with her naked in my arms.

She braces her hands on either side of my face, her fingertips digging into the back of my neck.

"I don't want to be her yet. I want to be your Syn for a little while longer."

What she says holds more meaning than she realizes.

"Please, Constantine. I just need to feel something good. I need you."

There are so many reasons why this is a bad idea. She's a mess—mentally, emotionally, physically—and needs time to heal. But just like she needs me, I need her, too, and I don't care if my ribs or the rest of me hurts like hell where Aleksei's guys kicked the crap out of me.

"I'm yours," I tell her, and that's all the permission she needs.

Using the grip her thighs have around my waist, she impales herself on my cock, and we both moan at how fucking good it feels. Life-affirming and real.

We're both battered and bruised, and I should stop this, but the bliss that comes over her face has me backing her up against the white tile wall.

Holding her up with one arm, I let my other hand wander her body, caressing her curves and tracing patterns on her soft skin. She shudders, her body becoming increasingly responsive to every movement of my fingers. My thumb brushes against her rosy nipple, making it flush a deeper shade of pink and harden under the attention. The temptation is too much, and I lean forward to take the puckered bud in my mouth.

"God, yes." Her spine bows and a low moan leaves her lips as I languidly stroke my tongue over her skin.

I'm a man on a mission, wanting to steep her in pleasure so she feels nothing but me and my touch. My mouth. My body.

She maps my face, exploring my lips, my eyebrows,

the creases of my eyes, like she's discovering them for the first time. The energy that sparks between us is palpable, always there and ever-present.

My hand roams the concave of her hip which gives way to the valley of her waist before it comes to rest on the swell of her stomach. She jerks at the sensation of my finger running circles around her belly button stud.

"When did you get this?" I ask, giving the sexy diamond a light tug.

"A year ago when I dyed my hair blue."

Blue? She said she missed out on so much, but so did we. Years of her life that we will never know or get to experience.

She gasps when I ease out of her, then gently thrust back in, and she angles her chin to look down between us where we're connected.

"When did you get pierced?"

"On Hen's seventeenth birthday. Tristan chickened out at the last minute."

Her mouth breaks out in a smile that sends my heart rate soaring.

"It feels really good," she says, intently watching the slow glide of my cock as I fuck her. "Did it hurt?"

I don't reply that I felt nothing because I'd been conditioned to block out pain since I was a boy. She doesn't need that reminder of our childhood or the shit all of us went through to make us worthy to lead the Society once we came of age.

"A little."

Her needy whimper delights my ears as my middle finger teases its way down her taut stomach to her clit. A wave of blissful sensations passes through us simultaneously when I press against the tiny bundle of nerves and her pussy clamps down, practically choking my cock. I'm not going to last long, and I need her there with me.

Syn writhes and moans as I swirl faster and faster circles that send shockwaves reverberating through her entire body. Each stroke of my cock, each press of my thumb on her clit, ignites an explosion within us both that seems to feed on itself until neither one of us can hold back any longer. Gentleness turns to punishing as we chase our orgasms. Her moans become louder and more desperate, and she cries out my name as frenzied currents carry us higher and deeper into each other until we catapult off that cliff together and fall into euphoria.

As we ride the aftershocks, our mouths meet, our kiss languorous. My tongue flicks her lower lip, and she hums when I take it between my teeth and pull.

"I've never felt anything as incredible as the way you feel inside me," she whispers against my mouth.

"Love you, sweet girl."

I have ten years of those words stored up, and I plan to say them every fucking day for the rest of our lives.

She holds my hand to her chest. "*Mo chroí.*"

The water starts to cool, and we both groan when I reluctantly slip out of her. I crank the shower handle as far as it will go, hoping to get a few more minutes of warm water, then quickly soap her body and hair.

When I get to her scars, she quietly says, "He had a constellation tattoo on the right side of his neck."

She doesn't notice that I've gone rigid as she turns around under the spray to rinse her hair.

She doesn't see how those eight words cause my world to fall apart until my humanity is stripped bare, and there is nothing left but betrayal and revenge.

I saw her drawings in her journal. The cluster of graphite stars I thought I'd seen before but couldn't place.

But now I know.

I thought things couldn't get any worse. I was so fucking wrong.

CHAPTER 4

I can tell something is weighing on Constantine's mind as he towels me dry, but I don't pry because I'm too overwhelmed with my own tangled thoughts. My memories are a fucked-up jumble of puzzle pieces. It's like the hard drive in my brain was corrupted, and I'm only able to recover small bits of data at a time. The guys, my parents, what happened that horrible night. But there's something else there. Something important that won't come out of the shadows and into the light for me to see. It's frustrating to feel this split within me where I want to remember but also wish I never do.

Constantine wraps the towel around me and tucks the end piece to secure it above my breast. He unfolds another towel and does the same around his waist.

Want me to dry your hair? he signs, and I can't help but swoon a little at the offer.

"Thank you, but I can just braid it. It'll be easier."

He takes a lock of my hair and examines it.

I like the red.

I smile up at him. "Me, too."

His throat must be hurting again, and I try to recall what I used to do to help him. It hits me at that moment that my interest in taking ASL classes in high school wasn't because of the kind elderly woman at the grocery store. It was because of him. Constantine was right. I hadn't really forgotten them at all. Small remnants of each of them stayed with me.

I take a good, long look at the boy who would serenade me with his guitar. A boy who has grown into a man even more beautiful than the memory of him allows. A decade's worth of time has changed him. Hardened him. His face is colder and more distant, his gaze filled with sadness and pain, his aura tainted by a haunting darkness. They're what frightened me the most when we first met.

But I didn't just meet them. God, everything is so fucking confusing.

Stepping into him, I hug his warm body. Once I walk out of this bathroom, a new reality will be waiting for me. But so will Tristan and Hendrix, which is why I let Constantine go and open the door.

I'm overcome with joy when I see them sitting on the bed. My lost boys. My childhood friends who have become my lovers. Dangerous men I was inexplicably drawn to from the second we met.

My anxious heartbeat counts off every second when nobody says anything. I honestly don't know what I would say or how to act. The stuff that's happened between Hendrix and me, the fact that Tristan went down on me, what I willingly let them do, what happened between us last night, what happened with Constantine just now—it all coalesces into a giant ball of uncertainty.

"Hi."

Tristan is the first to move.

"Fuck that. Come here," he says, opening his arms wide.

But before I can go to him for the hug I so desperately want, Constantine yanks me back.

I frown in confusion when he signs, *Stay here with Hendrix.*

"Why? What's going on?"

Constantine snatches a pair of sweatpants from a pile at the end of the bed that wasn't there before and looks at Tristan. "Talk. Now."

Tristan and I share a baffled look.

"*Now*," Constantine gruffs out when Tristan doesn't move.

"What the fuck for?" Tristan asks, but Constantine is already walking out of the bedroom. Tristan turns and asks, "Did something happen?"

I'm about to say no when Hendrix says, "Other than them fucking?"

My eyes snap to him, embarrassed heat creeping up from my neck to my cheeks because clearly, he and Tristan heard us.

Tristan kisses the side of my head. "Let me go see what's up. Stay here, okay?"

It's not like I have any other choice. I still don't know where *here* is.

"Okay."

He quietly closes the bedroom door behind him, leaving me in awkward silence with Hendrix.

I glance at the pile of clothes, hoping there's something I can wear. "Do you mind if I get dressed?"

With a devious grin, he leans forward on the bed, slams his hand down on the stack of folded clothes, and slides it out of my reach. "What you're wearing is fine."

My eyebrows shoot up because I don't know whether he's joking or being serious.

"I'm wearing a towel."

His gorgeous blond head cocks to one side, and those exquisite blue eyes sear me with a stare that sends goose bumps marching in formation down my body.

"And which *you* would that be? My best friend or the other one?"

The sharpness in his voice causes uneasiness to prickle the hairs on my arms. Gone is the kind friend from my past, and in his place is someone harder. Meaner. But beneath his veneer of coldness and hostility, I can see the vulnerability, and what he said the other morning has new meaning now. The malevolent forces that ripped us apart broke each of us in unimaginable ways.

"There was this girl. It didn't matter that we were just kids. I loved her as much as a young heart could. She was my sunshine. My little golden-haired angel. My soulmate. Everything in me died the day she was taken. The only light I had to guide me was extinguished, and I've been living in the dark ever since."

I close my eyes and focus on that part of my life, flinching when I compel the unpleasant memory forward. As children of the Council, we were brought up with violence and cruelty in order to make us stronger. To prepare us for the roles we would take on as adults. Power. Money. Control. Manipulation. All in the name of the fucking Society. The one thing they couldn't control was our hearts. We loved each other deeply and fiercely.

"I don't know yet," I reply, opening my eyes to see the hope on his face crumble, but I don't let the heartbreaking sight stop me from speaking the truth.

In a morbid way, I gained my freedom by pushing who I used to be into a dark grave. But that freedom came with great sacrifice, one of those sacrifices sitting before me now.

Holding the towel together in one hand, I slip onto the bed and into his lap. His muscles stiffen and pull tight when I straddle his lap and cup his morning-stubbled cheeks.

"I'm so fucking happy to see you," I tell him.

It's a bizarre thing to say, but it's how I feel. The way Syn sees them is different from the way Aoife did. Jesus, I sound like I'm two different people. A psychiatrist would have a field day inside my mind right now.

He traces a fingertip across the faint bruising on my neck. "And I'm so fucking sorry for how I treated you."

I touch our foreheads together, something I used to do to help center him when his internal demons would try to surface.

"Never apologize to me. If you hadn't noticed, I kind of like you being a cocky, irritating, possessive asshole. I've got the bite marks to prove it."

A rush of pent-up air explodes from his lips in a relieved chuckle. "You always were trouble."

He had called me that in the gym when we were sparring, and it had sounded so familiar. It was Hendrix's nickname for me.

"I like firefly, too."

A myriad of emotions dance over his face before his arms draw me closer. The tears well up and threaten to fall, but I swallow them back. There is a special kind of solace here in this moment, and I don't want to ruin it by crying. We exchange a glance that says everything that neither of us can bring ourselves to speak out loud —how much we've missed each other, how much pain our absence has caused, and how profound it feels to be together again.

He sweeps flyaway strands of wet hair away from my face, and his gaze drops to my mouth, its effect as visceral as if he were kissing me.

"*A chuisle mo chroí.*" I recite the Gaelic words of my Irish heritage that translate to "the beat of my heart" but vernacularly mean "my beloved."

"I missed you so much. Losing you broke us."

A soft moan escapes as warmth spreads through me when his tongue slips inside my mouth. His kiss is soft yet desperate. His hands fist the towel at my back as if he's somehow scared that I'll vanish into thin air the second he releases me.

"I'm not going anywhere." And no one will ever keep us apart again.

His body relaxes against mine, and I feel his racing heart slow its frantic beat. The guys and I have been gifted a second chance, one where we get to choose the outcome this time around.

With that singularity in mind, I make a difficult decision. One born from the fire and the knife that scarred my body. One of vengeance. For them and me and my parents. Our enemies want Aoife Fitzpatrick? They fucking got her. And they will regret ever bringing her back.

Grabbing what I can from the pile of clothes before Hendrix can move them again, I hop off his lap. There is no modesty left between us anymore. That ship has long since sailed.

His eyes turn to cold steel when I unwrap the towel and let it fall to the floor.

"I want to kill whoever did that to you."

I touch my side, allowing my fingers to trail over the rough, raised crisscross pattern, no longer ashamed of the horrors that mar my pale skin. It's who I am. *I am the phoenix.*

Wait.

It suddenly dawns on me that Constantine called me Aoife in the hallway. He called me 'his heart' in Portuguese when Aleksei was about to kill him and said it again in the shower.

"How long have you known?"

As I hurriedly don the clothes that are way too big because they're men's sizes, Hendrix gets off the bed and takes over rolling the waistband of the sweats down low on my hips, so they won't fall off.

"A few days. Con figured it out before that, but the fucker didn't say anything."

If they've known that long, then…

The note. *He knows. Trust no one.*

Oh, my god.

Alana.

I run out of the room at a dead sprint as if the hounds of hell are nipping at my heels.

CHAPTER 5

Cillian McCarthy's compound is a maze of corridors and rooms, the place more securely guarded than Fort Knox. I'd heard of him but had never met the man before. The Society keeps tabs on all the big global players. People of power. People with wealth. People of influence.

As one of the heads of the Irish mafia, Cillian spends most of his time in Ireland, and after what happened this morning, I don't think it's a coincidence that he's here in the States. But for what purpose? I'm grateful he saved our asses, but until I know his true agenda, I don't exactly trust him, and I absolutely don't fucking trust Evan. He goes to Darlington Founders and is in Aoife's biology lab. Con had mentioned him the other day. Said he got weird vibes off him when he went to pick Aoife up from class.

But Evan will have to wait at the back of the line because finding out exactly what happened this morning takes precedence. Eva is dead, and we don't know anything about Patrick or my dad and mom. Malin didn't answer the one time I tried to call him before my phone up and died, and there's been no word from Con's father, Gabriel, which makes me think the Stepanoffs took out the entire fucking Council.

I catch up to Con as he's descending the grand staircase. Something transpired between him and Aoife in the bathroom, and the fact that he wouldn't say anything in front of her has me worried.

"Will you slow down and tell me what's going on? Is Aoife okay?"

He doesn't stop. "Syn."

"What?"

"She doesn't want to be called Aoife." His voice cracks at the end, butchering her name.

I'll see if they have any chamomile or peppermint tea for his throat. Other than some minor scrapes and contusions, Hen and I didn't sustain any injuries when the side of the house blew, but Con is another story. Aleksei and his men beat the shit out of him. He wouldn't let Cotton look at him, but I can tell by his movements that he might have a cracked rib or two.

The stairs curve to the foyer, and I jump the final four steps in order to grab Con's arm to make him stop. I'm taken by surprise when he turns around, fists my shirt, and shoves me back against the stair balusters with a snarl.

"Did you know?"

My hand circles his wrist and pulls, but his grip is too tight, his anger too substantial. Even injured, he'd kick my ass without blinking.

"If I knew what you were talking about," I calmly reply.

His dark eyes assess me for a few seconds before he lets go of my shirt with a not-so-gentle shove. "I need a computer with a secure line."

Not letting him storm off again, I grab the back of his neck and hold him in place as chaos emanates from every pore of his body. My best friend and my woman almost died today. And it would've been my fault. This damn rivalry between me and Aleksander needs to end, one way or the other. I can't lose someone else I love... and losing Aoife again right after we found her would end me.

"What the fuck is going on inside your head? Talk to me."

His teeth grind together, his muscles so tight, his entire body quakes with barely restrained rage.

"Your father!" he bellows in my face, his accusation drawing me back.

My brows push together in confusion. Not quite understanding, all I can manage is, "I tried to get hold of Malin. I don't—"

"It was your fucking father!"

Everything stops for a fraction of a second as I look at him, trying to comprehend what he's implying. I barely have a chance to process any of it before he slams his fist against the baluster beside my head. The vibrations from the impact of flesh on wrought iron create a ringing sound near my ear much like tuning forks.

I meet Con's enraged gaze with an unwavering one of my own as something ugly and ominous slithers up my spine.

Stupidly, I reply, "I don't know what you're talking about." But god help me, I think I do.

Con's voice splinters when he barks, "The drawings in

her journal. Do you remember the ones of the stars? The pattern? She said the man who attacked her had them inked on his neck. Right side."

I can only shake my head. I refuse to believe it. I won't. There must be another explanation. Another person with that specific tattoo in that specific place.

No. He wouldn't. He knew what she meant to me.

In an instant, I finally understand the true depth of my father's deception. The decade of lies he fed me that I so willingly and naïvely believed. Aoife and her family weren't run off the road by a drunk driver. My father sent his right-hand man to kill the girl who was my everything because James Fitzpatrick was at the head of the Council, making Aoife next in line to the throne.

A gaping chasm rends my chest in two, ripped apart by a father's betrayal.

I try to move, to take a step forward, but my limbs feel as though they've been submerged in a glacial pond, the frigid chill numbing my body. Forcing a deep breath into my lungs, I slap on a guise of composure I absolutely do not fucking feel as I fight to keep what little control I have left.

"I did this."

"No, you didn't," Con replies through tight lips.

Fast footsteps approach as two guards come around the corner, Evan following close behind them. Great. We have an audience.

Con looks over his shoulder before turning back to me. Lowering his voice to just above a whisper, he says, "We have to tell her."

How do I tell the girl who is my world that I'm responsible for destroying hers?

Evan looks at the damage Con's fist caused. "Cillian

isn't going to be happy when he sees the bent metal railing."

What a pompous ass.

"Can we have a minute?"

Of fucking course, he doesn't give us one.

"He wants to see Syn."

"I don't give a shit what Cillian wants."

"The man saved your lives," he counters as if I'm indebted to Cillian for a service I never asked him to provide in the first place.

Feeling helpless and despondent over the girl who has suffered so damn much and whose heart I will soon break once again, I channel my frustrated anger his way.

"We don't owe Cillian McCarthy or you anything but a thank you."

Evan sighs and shoves his hands into his front pockets. "I'm a friend, Tristan. I always have been even when you didn't notice I was there."

"Bullshit," Con says before I can.

I know Evan is a sophomore because Con mentioned that he accessed his student record, yet I can't recall a single time last year I saw him on campus until he suddenly popped up in Syn's orbit.

I thrust my finger at Evan. "I don't trust you. I don't trust Cillian. And unless you plan on killing us, we're leaving. With Syn. Right fucking now."

We need to get her out of here and somewhere safe. Regroup. Make a plan, gather our alliances, then make our move. Scorched earth style.

"I'd rethink that if I were ye."

Cillian's thick Irish brogue draws my attention to the far end of the foyer. Leaning a shoulder to the wall, he's the quintessential Irishman with stark red hair, matching beard, and clover-green eyes. But there's a lethality there that brokers no argument that this man is not to be trifled with.

The guards' hands go to their shoulder holsters as I slowly approach their boss, Con at my heels because he will always have my back.

"I'd like some answers."

One bushy eyebrow arches, and I can't tell if he's being condescending when he replies, "Ye havenae asked me a question yet, wee Amato."

With his mossy gaze stationed on me, his chin lifts ever so slightly, but it's a signal that tells his men to stand down.

"We're leaving."

His mouth curves under his short beard. "I heard ye the first time, lad. Still not a question."

"Your men saved us."

"Aye."

"They destroyed my friend's house."

He smirks. "Aye."

"Why?"

"Now we're getting somewhere, wee Amato," he cheekily replies.

His amusement at the situation *and* his juvenile nickname for me piss me off.

Cillian pushes away from the wall and sweeps a hand out for Con and me to follow him into a side room that connects to the foyer.

"I don't think so."

With an exasperated huff, Cillian chuckles. "Bloody hell, you're as fecking pigheaded as she is."

Con's hand lands on my biceps, fingers digging in. A reminder not to do anything dumb. Like punch Cillian's smug face.

"Leave Syn out of this."

"I'm not talking about the bonnie lass."

There's a commotion above us on the stairs, followed by Syn's frantic voice calling my name. Her red hair flies wildly behind her as she barrels into me and practically climbs me like a frigging tree.

Throwing her arms around my neck with a strangling hold, she sobs, "I swear I didn't know. I didn't remember. Please forgive me. *I didn't remember!*"

She rambles frantically, not seeming to notice the stocky Irishman and the men with guns standing nearby.

Gasping like she's fighting for air, I band an arm under her to hold her to me and gently cup the side of her ravaged face.

"Breathe, Red."

She's freaking out and not making any sense.

Tears leak from her beautiful, devastated blue eyes. "You don't understand. Oh god, Tristan. I'm so sorry. I didn't remember." She takes a shallow, stuttered breath. "Dierdre…"

At the mention of my sister, Syn's gaze falters when our eyes meet, her expression brimming with sorrow and regret. Her lips part as if to speak, but the words get trapped.

"Syn." I shake her, needing her to finish but scared to death of what she wants to tell me.

"…is my mother," tumbles out of her mouth.

But Alana is her adoptive mother.

"The fuck?" Con mumbles.

Syn's tears turn into rivers as she watches what she said sink in and rip me apart.

Dierdre... *is Alana?*

My sister is alive?

What.

The.

Fuck?

I should be happy. I should feel any other joyous emotion other than the knife that twists inside my gut, killing me a thousand times over.

Because at that moment, I realize with a jolting clarity—it's not just my father who betrayed me.

Dierdre is Alana. Syn's mom. The woman who has spent the last ten years taking care of Syn in Dilli-*fucking*-wyll, Virginia on a farm raising chickens. She had Syn. And she never tried to contact me. She let me believe she was dead. She kept Aoife from us. The sister I loved, and adored, and *grieved* is nothing more than a duplicitous liar. Just like our father.

"Tristan, I haven't been able to contact her. I think something happened to her."

I slice an accusatory look Cillian's way. Is that who he was referring to a minute ago?

Not smug anymore, and without me having to ask, he nods.

What the hell is going on?

Not able to bear being touched right now, I push Syn off me as the ground underneath my feet shifts when the weight of the truth pounds inside my skull. Every memory, every tear I shed, every goddamn word I spoke to the heavenly stars, hoping Dierdre would hear them, rushes forward like a torrent and crashes into me. Like with Aoife, I'd spent the last ten years believing Dierdre was dead, mourning her loss, hating our father, and plotting revenge. The grief that has been my burden for a decade because I thought I failed her morphs into a volatile blend of anguish and fury.

My entire life has been crafted by lies. I mourned and grieved for nothing.

"Tristan."

No. I shut everyone out. I'm suffocating. I need air. I need to be alone. I need to hurt something.

"Tristan, wait!" Syn pleads.

Crashing through the foyer in my attempts to get to the front door, I pass a shocked Hendrix at the bottom of the stairs and shove a guard out of my way when he tries to block my path. I practically shred the hinges from the door when I throw it wide open and disappear into the night.

CHAPTER 6

Self-loathing hurls a red-hot poker through my chest as I helplessly watch Tristan walk out the front door.

What is wrong with me? How could I look at Alana for ten years and not see who she really was? *Ten years.* Shame coats my skin like a thick, sticky tar. Papa would be so ashamed of me. For burying who I was. I hid like a coward, shoving my life so far down the rabbit hole of my subconscious that I became a different person who was happy to live a lie as long as I could forget my past. And I hate myself for being so weak.

When I go to follow Tristan, ready to throw myself at his feet and beg his forgiveness, Hendrix snatches my wrist and wraps me in his arms. I don't deserve his comfort. I don't deserve their devotion. I have brought nothing but chaos and destruction. I'm the cause of all the awful shit in their lives.

"Just give him a minute to fall apart," Hendrix says as he holds me.

My fingernails embed in the hard muscles of his back

as I cling to him. I know I just said that I didn't deserve his comfort; I take it anyway.

Con appears over Hendrix's shoulder, but I struggle to look directly at him, so I stare at his chin, not able to meet his dark irises that have the ability to see everything.

"Are you sure it's her?"

I wish I wasn't. I wish that part of my memory stayed forever locked away from me. But that would be cruel, too. Tristan deserves to know his sister is still alive. That she's a beautiful grown woman with a beautiful soul who loved me unconditionally and treated me wonderfully for unknown reasons. I barely knew her when I was little since she was so much older than me. Which makes me frown as question upon question builds a mountain inside my mind. How did she know who I was? How did she find me at the hospital? My first recollection after *that night* was waking up in a white-washed room in so much pain, and she was there, holding my hand, telling me everything was going to be okay.

But why would Alana lie? Why would she pretend to be someone else? Why would she hurt Tristan like that?

You did, you stupid bitch. Hypocrite much?

"I'm sure."

"Jesus fucking Christ," Hendrix mumbles, rubbing soothing circles on my back that don't lessen my self-hate one bit.

"I think she's in trouble. We need to find her."

Regardless of what she's done, she's still my mother in every way that matters. I love her.

A masculine throat clears from ten feet away, and it's then I notice a massive, bearded, Jolly Green Giant staring at me.

"If yer wonderin' 'bout Alana, she's not in danger."

I expel a pent-up breath I didn't know I was holding, hoping that what he said is the truth but not trusting it.

"How do you know?"

In answer, he just smiles with straight, white teeth that gleam against the fire red of his short-cropped beard.

"It's good to see you again, lassie."

Not in the mood for small talk, my reply comes out clipped and harsh. "I don't know who the fuck you are."

His lips purse in a pout-slash-fake-grimace that I don't find amusing at all, and he claps a hand over his heart in mock affront.

"Me ego cannae take such a hard blow. It's a tender one."

He's joking while I'm free-falling, and that makes me livid. There is nothing humorous about any of this.

With a lethal step forward, my hands curl into tight claws, ready to take on every single person unlucky enough to breathe the same air as me. Cillian's men react.

"No!" Hendrix shouts, grabbing the back of my shirt to keep me stationary, and one of those guns switches from me to him.

"Put your fecking guns away, *eejits*," the man says, and the two men comply like well-trained dogs. The red-bearded giant strokes his chin with his forefinger. "You are so much like yer da."

"What?"

"Yer da. James. Ye looked more like yer ma when yer were wee, but now yer look just yer da." He moves his hand across his chest in the symbol of the holy cross, much like a Catholic priest does, then casts his eyes up to the ceiling.

"What?" I ask on repeat because I think he broke my brain.

Evan motions for the armed men to leave, and I wonder what role he plays in this crazy-as-hell situation. He's still a mystery I've yet to solve, but one thing is crystal clear—he must have known who I was the entire time.

Removing my wary attention from Evan, I ask the giant, "You knew my father?"

"Aye."

Con and Hendrix, who have been quiet during the entire exchange, come to either side of me, and I instinctively grab both of their hands, needing them to anchor me to this reality because it feels like every part of me is wanting to scatter into the wind like dandelion fluff.

"How?"

"James was me kin. Fourth cousin. Ma's side of the family."

My jaw drops open. He's family? Papa's cousin? He's my relative? To a normal person, this would be great news, but it only makes me angry.

"Then where the fuck have you been my whole life?"

As far as I recall, we had no one. No grandparents. No aunts or uncles. There were no framed pictures or photo albums that I can recollect ever looking at. No one ever visited. Nothing. My family consisted of my parents and my guys.

That toothy grin appears again, and Constantine yanks on my hand when I lunge forward with a snarl.

At my threatening display, the man's mirth-filled

expression falls away. "Careful, *cailín*. I'm not yer enemy... unless you make me one."

Not my enemy? I'm not dumb enough to take his word at face value.

I look up at Constantine. "I want to see Tristan."

He's been out of my sight long enough, and I'm getting antsy with the need to go to him—something the Irish giant picks up on. I should ask him his name, so I stop referring to him as giant. I think Evan mentioned it upstairs... Cotton? Cillian?

"Go tend to yer mate. When yer ready, a hot meal will be waiting as will answers to whatever questions ye want to ask me."

With the world around me spinning in dizzying circles, I can only deal with one thing at a time, and Tristan is my primary priority.

The giant briskly walks off with the two men, and they disappear through a side doorway, but Evan loiters for a hesitant second.

Hendrix bristles, becoming overly territorial the longer Evan stares at me.

"Fuck. Off."

I can't see Evan anymore because Hendrix purposefully steps in front of me, but I hear Evan's loud sigh, then his footsteps as they grow fainter and fainter.

With my hand still firmly gripped in Constantine's, Hendrix turns back around and rolls his eyes.

"That guy is a twat."

"Tristan," I state and am pulled back once again, this time by Constantine, when I try to leave.

"Give him more time."

I gently wiggle my hand out from his. "He needs us."

We need each other, now more than ever.

"He doesn't want you to see him weak."

Why do strong men think that feeling any type of emotion equates to weakness? It doesn't make you less of a man. It just means you're human.

Using Hendrix's turn of phrase, I reply, "Then he can tell me to fuck off."

Hendrix muffles his chuckle that comes out more like a snort.

"That fucking sassy mouth," he mumbles, lovingly patting my ass, and I promptly swat his hand away.

"Who was that?" I ask, peering toward the empty space the giant had been occupying.

"Cillian McCarthy. Irish mafia, and someone you do not want to piss off," Hendrix replies.

An ironic, startled laugh almost erupts from my throat. Mafia? I had accused Tristan of being the son of a don. If what Cillian said is true, then I'm the one related to the mob. Good god.

I compartmentalize that revelation into a tiny box to open later. There is already a stack of them, one sitting precariously on top of another, a tower of instability as high as my mind can see. Too many questions to find answers to. Too much to deal with all at once.

So, I follow my broken compass.

There's an internal compass inside every person, the one that guides you and keeps you on the path that you were meant to travel. Your true north. Clearly, my compass is broken. Tristan says I have no choice, but he's wrong. I do have a choice. My broken compass led me to them for a reason.

"I'm going to him. Please don't get in my way."

CHAPTER 7

The tepid night air does little to help the constriction in my chest when I step out onto the front portico and see Tristan on his knees in the grass, head bowed low, shoulders hunched forward in defeat. The front lawn is so expansive it gets swallowed up by the darkness. Cillian's house is bigger than Hendrix's family estate but not as ostentatious or grandiose. There are no million-dollar pieces of artwork, or gold-framed portraits of stuffy-looking old men, or Rodins perched atop marble pedestals. From what I've seen, the interior of the mansion is simple and homey, like the inside of a fire-warmed cottage. Its dark, distressed wood floors and antique furnishings transport me back in time to what I imagine a traditional Irish home would look like two hundred years ago. I'm sure once the sun comes up and I'm able to see the property better, the outside will be just as gorgeous.

A swish of noise to my left has me twisting around to find guards quietly patrolling. Makes sense that Cillian would require protection since he's allegedly mafia. But after what happened this morning, I'm wary of men with guns, so I watch the two nearby to make sure they don't get too close to Tristan. They only give him a furtive glance as they stroll the perimeter of the house, and I wait for them to move far enough away before I leave Constantine and Hendrix standing in the open doorway and walk barefoot down the steps and onto the wet grass. Droplets of dew squish between my toes and slick my heels, muffling my approaching footsteps, but Tristan must hear them or sense me because he looks over his shoulder. So much hurt reflects in his golden gaze that it almost breaks me. There is no memory I can conjure where I've ever seen Tristan cry, not even after his father would strike him with a whip until his skin flayed from his back. I search for the circular burn on the back of his hand, and the hate I used to carry for Francesco Amato comes back a thousand-fold. As awful as it might sound to some, I hope Francesco becomes a casualty in whatever war Aleksander started today. And if not, then I'll make sure he is.

Tristan straightens up when I lower down and crawl into his lap, but he gathers me close, his strong arms clutching me to him. I hold him as tightly as I can until his breath shudders out and he burrows his head between my breasts.

I run my fingers through his hair and kiss any part of him my lips can touch.

"What can I do? How can I fix this?"

The songs of cicadas fill the air with ear-splitting intensity, their noisy racket drowning everything else out.

My eyelashes get caught in soft wisps of Tristan's hair when they flutter up. Constantine and Hendrix have taken a seat on the top portico step, mirror images of one another with their elbows resting atop splayed knees. Even though they don't show it outwardly, I can feel their distress from here as they look on.

"Please forgive me."

Tristan's head whips up so fast I flinch back to avoid getting knocked in the chin.

"You did nothing wrong, Aoife... Syn... *fuck!*" He lowers his forehead to my collarbone. "Sorry."

"It's okay if you want to call me Aoife. I just don't like her very much right now. And, yes, I know how crazy that sounds since I'm her. It's going to take a little time for me to get used to hearing it again. I kind of liked Syn."

His mouth presses to the skin exposed by the collar of my shirt. "I liked Syn, too. I fell in love with her."

He trails off, and I forget to breathe. *He loves me?*

The sudden influx of exhilarated happiness that fills me to bursting makes my chest hurt. Happiness is the last thing I should be feeling. I killed people today. It doesn't matter if they would have done the same without a second thought, their blood still stains my hands. I'm a murderer who took the lives of men who had family and friends and someone out there who cared about them. And it scares me to realize how... *detached* I feel about it. It's fucked up. I should be sitting in a ten-by-ten concrete prison cell, not feeling ecstatic that both Constantine and Tristan have told me that they love me. Maybe I should be grateful for that part of Aoife that remains inside me, otherwise I'd still be curled in a fetal position on the floor upstairs.

But the woman I am now isn't Aoife anymore. The ugly lessons that were ingrained into me as a child of the Society hold no power over the love, compassion, and kindness that Alana showed me every day for ten years.

I know the power I hold now. I was groomed to step into my father's role in the Council. Maybe I can make a difference. Enact change.

Or maybe, I need to burn the entire organization to the ground. The roots of evil grow thick under the soil that the Society was built upon. Too many wealthy men in positions of power who abuse that power and everyone else around them.

"Syn?"

Tristan pulls me back from where my thoughts had led me, and I kiss his downturned lips. "Yeah?"

"How is she? Was she happy living on the farm?"

I soften at his questions. Tristan may be cocky and full of himself a lot of the time, but his heart is a good one. After everything he's been through, he never lost his capacity to love.

I lean back a little in his arms, so I can touch the scar that slices through his eyebrow, then the small bump on the bridge of his nose where it was broken. The bump is familiar, a gift from his asshole father when he was nine, but the eyebrow scar is new, and I want to ask him how he got it.

"There was never a day where she didn't smile. We would dance in the kitchen to the most horrible country music when we cooked. We laughed a lot. She beat me every time we played Trivial Pursuit." I chuckle when I think about how she kisses Cocky Bastard's beak every morning, thanking him for waking her up to enjoy another day. "She raises chickens and feeds the stray cats that wander onto our property. The small barn on the property is now a cat hotel. She likes sitting out on the back porch to watch the sunrise."

A lone tear slips out, and I catch it with my thumb. Tristan may hate showing any weakness of any kind, but he lets me see his vulnerability.

"She was happy, Tristan. I don't know why she never tried to contact you or why she told me that my name was Synthia and kept who I really was a secret."

Or why she would encourage me to attend Darlington Founders when she must have known the guys were already there. It makes no sense.

The risks she took were enormous. The fabrications she wove and had me believe, fragile and on borrowed time. The psychiatrist, Dr. Westmore, who Alana made sure I saw every week for three years had said that I was repressing traumatic memories as a survival mechanism. During my regular office visits, Dr. Westmore threw words at me that I didn't understand, like dissociative amnesia, state-dependent remembering, motivated forgetting, and retrieval inhibition. I had to Google that shit up. She said that when my mind was ready to deal with whatever happened to me, the memories would resurface.

Joke's on her. I absolutely *was not* ready, but I'd walk through hell and make deals with the devil if it meant stopping Aleksei from shooting Constantine right in front of me.

"I think I know why," he says so quietly that I almost don't catch it.

"You do?"

"Do what?"

"Know why," I reply.

"Huh?"

Is he purposely being obtuse, or did I mishear what I thought he said?

"Never mind," I say when Constantine and Hendrix walk over, apparently done with waiting on the steps.

"Hold on," is the only warning I get before Tristan braces his arms around me and stands up.

How is he able to do that? I'm not light by any means, but he just lifted me from a sitting position like I weighed nothing. The amount of strength that must take has my belly swooping.

With his back turned to his friends, Tristan sets me on my feet and shrugs a shoulder to dry the wetness on his cheek, erasing any evidence that he'd been crying. I help him straighten his T-shirt by smoothing down the stretched fabric, but there's nothing I can do about the dark patches dotting down his sweatpants from his knees to his ankles where the damp ground soaked through.

Finally composed, he pulls me in front of him and holds me back-to-chest with one arm across my waist. Hendrix averts his gaze from where Tristan's hand splays possessively across my stomach, but he's not quick enough to hide the flicker of jealousy I notice before he schools his features, and it disappears like it was never there to begin with.

"Did she tell you?"

Lines furrow deep grooves above my eyebrows. Was I supposed to tell Tristan something?

"Cillian made a vague comment alluding that he knows where Dierdre is."

A fire ignites in Tristan's whiskey-brown eyes. In a

way, I'd rather see it than the desolation that was there minutes ago. But just as quickly, it burns itself out. He digs the heel of his palm across his brow bone and sighs heavily.

"I swear to fucking god. I can't handle anything else right now."

Hendrix shocks the hell out of me when he coldly replies, "Too *fucking* bad, so suck it up."

"Hendrix," I hiss, and that iciness gets transferred to me.

"He's not the one who just had his house blown to bits or watched his mother die right in front of him."

"And you're not the one whose sister faked her death and hid Aoife from us for ten goddamn years!" Tristan roars.

Taken aback by Hendrix's remark, I dumbly ask, "Eva's gone?"

I'm horrified when he makes a two-fingered gun with his hand and points it at his head.

I don't remember Eva well because she wasn't a big presence in my childhood, and I definitely didn't recognize her when we met last night. However, that's beside the point. Hendrix lost his mother in almost the same brutal manner as I lost mine. Wanting to give him whatever solace I can, I reach for his hand, but he moves it away. The rejection stings.

"What about your dad?"

He shrugs a disdainful shoulder. "Don't care."

Jackass Hendrix has reemerged, and I want to smack it out of him. I understand that he's hurting and he's angry, even if he doesn't want to admit it, but it's counterproductive.

"Will you stop?"

One perfectly formed blond eyebrow hikes up, and I mimic him by doing the same.

"We think Aleksander and Aleksei took out the Council. I haven't been able to get hold of anyone."

The juvenile stare-off between Hendrix and me abruptly ends. Everyone is dead? It's as if history is repeating itself where I'm back in Ireland helplessly watching the carnage of my family unfold and not able to stop it.

"Don't," Constantine gruffly snaps when my eyes get glassy. "They don't deserve them."

He's right. Francesco Amato, Patrick Knight, and Gabriel Ferreira were cruel, sadistic men who enjoyed inflicting pain on their sons.

I tap a closed fist to my head, trying to knock the reluctant memories loose. "The twins' father. I can't rem—"

"Nikolai Stepanoff."

Once Tristan says his name, it all comes back. I met Nikolai and the twins once at a Society gala in New York a few months before Papa sequestered me away in Ireland. Aleksander asked me to dance. I never got the opportunity because he and Tristan got into a fight.

"He died five years ago, Red. Aleksander took over as the head of the family. Whatever happened today is all on that stupid fuck."

"So, how does Cillian McCarthy fit into all this?"

"That's what we need to find out," Constantine gravely answers.

CHAPTER 8

Cillian and Evan stand from their chairs at the end of the table as soon as we enter the formal dining room. There are no guards, just them—or if there are, they've hidden themselves well. Six place settings are spaced out along one end of the long table that could easily sit twelve people. Covered platters of food line up like ants down the center, and a delicious smell of whatever is hidden underneath the silver cloches perfumes the air.

With the lights turned low, shadows created by the cracking fire in the stone hearth playfully dance across the walls. The room is so cavernous, the fire doesn't offer much warmth—which is good because it's the end of summer—and does little more than provide ambient light, but its effects are calming. Tranquil. Something I'm sure Cillian planned on. I doubt much gets past his attention.

"Welcome, lass," Cillian says and pulls out the chair at the head of the table for me to sit. A seat usually reserved for the head of the family, and one that symbolizes importance, honor, and respect. I'll add clever to Cillian's list of characteristics that already include astute, Irish, mobster, and gigantic Jolly Green Giant.

"We're good here," Tristan says.

He and Constantine choose seats at the opposite end of the table, as far away from Cillian as they can get. Hendrix drops down in a chair next to them and pulls me into his lap, using his muscled arm like a seat belt to keep me there. I decide to pick my battles and let it go because I don't want to argue in front of Cillian and Evan. It would be a whole other story if they weren't here.

I casually inspect the red stag on the crest inlaid into the wood. The design is delicate yet beautiful. A family crest, perhaps.

"*Forti et fideli nihil difficile* which loosely translates into '*Nothing is difficult for the strong and faithful.*' The McCarthy family motto. The McCarthys are one of the oldest families in Ireland. The name derives from *carthach* which means loving."

"You can skip the history lesson." Eyes hard, Tristan leans forward with his elbows on the table. "Do you know where my sister is?"

With an exasperated huff, Cillian sits back down, this time in the head chair that he had pulled out for me.

"You lot are a prickly bunch. I'm glad ye were never like that," he says to Evan, who, once again, is staring at me. I'm beginning to feel like a zoo exhibit.

"If you don't stop fucking staring at her, I'm going to take that knife and cut your eyes out." To emphasize the threat he made, Hendrix reaches an arm across the table as far as it can go with me sitting in his lap and grabs a carving knife resting beside one of the covered platters.

Cillian's jovial Irish brogue disappears, and he says in a perfect, deadly American accent, "You even try that, boy, and Cian behind you will put a bullet in your head."

Like a family of meerkats, we simultaneously turn our heads to look behind us and see no one there, but I don't doubt what Cillian said. I'm sure we've got several eyes on us.

Not finished, Cillian continues his tirade. "You are still drawing breath because I fucking *allow* it. I have no obligation to you. Only to her," Cillian says, pointing at me, and I tense up for being singled out. "So watch what you fucking say to me and show some fucking respect while you're in my fucking house. You get one pass with me, and your broody friend next to you already used that good grace up when he killed one of my men." Cillian whips the cloth napkin out angrily and stuffs it into his lap while mumbling, "Bloody stupid English and your goddamn superiority complexes."

I lean forward until I can see Constantine. "You killed someone?"

Suddenly, Constantine pushes up from his seat only to be shoved back down by Tristan.

"Your man shot at me, and Aoife was the casualty. Con had every right to retaliate," Tristan says, sliding into the leadership role he's used to playing. "With that being said, we mean no disrespect. A lot has happened in the last twenty-four hours, so I'm sure you understand why we don't trust you. Or him," he finishes with a scathing glance at Evan.

I dig my fingernails into Hendrix's thigh in warning when he shifts under me. Just to make sure he doesn't try to leap up and lunge across the table at Evan, I lean back and press as much weight as I can into him, knowing full well he could just toss me off him like a pillow if he wanted to.

Needing to stop things from escalating beyond the hot testosterone-filled tempers that are already boiling over, I ask Cillian, "You said you would answer any of my questions."

Cillian drags a basket of rolls toward him and rips one in half, then dips it in what looks like a gravy bowl and takes a bite.

"Aye," he replies with his mouth full.

"You're Papa's cousin, which means you're mine as well."

He nods.

I ask Evan, "What is your role in all this?"

Cillian quickly steps in before Evan can open his mouth. "He's mine, lass. Me *mac*."

He gets four perplexed looks.

"My son."

The irony isn't lost on me. I actually do know the son of a don, or whatever the hell Cillian calls himself in Ireland. Don sounds too Italian. I'll have to look it up.

Hoping to be subtle, I compare Evan and his father. Evan looks nothing like Cillian. Evan's hair is jet black not red. In a way, if I squint a little, Evan kind of resembles Constantine.

"Congratulations," Tristan replies dryly. "Now, where's my sister?"

Serving himself slices of roast beef from a serving plate, Cillian glances up. "Who said I know where Alana is? I only said she was safe."

"Her name is *Dierdre*, and don't play me for stupid."

He waves his fork in my direction. "You gonna eat,

lass?"

What the hell. He seems to want to draw out this bizarre conversation, and I'm starving.

"Can you pass me whatever that is?" I tell Constantine. I don't care what it is. Food is food right now to my empty stomach.

He takes over and dishes out what looks like corned beef hash, a non-traditional dish that isn't really Irish. It's a bastardized Irish American dish, but something Alana and I would make every St. Patrick's Day. As soon as the steam wafts up from my plate and hits my nose, I voraciously dig in—and groan like a food whore when the flavor hits my palette. Holy shit, this is good.

My fork stops midway to my mouth with my next bite when Hendrix's cock hardens under my ass, and he teases a hand down between my legs.

He's not seriously going to—

I suck in air and almost aspirate my food when he presses a finger into me through the cotton of the sweatpants. I catch the moan that almost—*embarrassingly*—comes out that has nothing to do with how good the food tastes. Fighting the urge to open my legs wider, I clench my thighs together as hard as I can, trapping his hand from wandering any farther, and feel his warm breath on my shoulder when he quietly chuckles.

"Safe and sound, just like I said. She's with friends in Texas."

It takes me a second to get that Cillian is replying to Tristan's earlier comment.

"Who?" Tristan demands, not touching the plate Constantine pushes in front of him.

Cillian's green eyes sparkle with some inside joke

only he gets. "Declan Levine. He owed me a favor."

As if the name Declan Levine was a physical blow to the chest, Tristan crashes back into his chair. It rocks precariously on its two hind legs before righting, and Tristan erupts.

"You put my sister in the middle of a mob war, and you claim she's safe!"

Evan finally speaks up. "There is no war. Keane Agosti runs things now with his wife, Alexan—"

He cuts Evan off. "I fucking know who they are. I also know how they came into power, and how much blood was shed to do it."

Cillian wipes his mouth with the cloth napkin. "Like I said. She's safe."

Something dawns on me and sours the food I'd just eaten. "*How* do you know Alana? And how did you know what was going to happen at Hendrix's house?"

A brash grin slowly grows and spreads across Cillian's face. "I know a lot of things, lass."

"This is bullshit!" Done with diplomacy, Tristan angrily shoves back from the table, hauls me off Hendrix's lap, and takes my hand in an iron grip. "We're leaving."

"Ye are correct, young Amato. Ye are leaving. A private plane is waiting to take ye to yer sister. Now, sit yer ass down, shut the feck up, and eat the food my cook worked hours to prepare. Your last name carries no weight here, so don't think for one second yer blustering will do anything other than make you look like a child throwing a temper tantrum." Cillian's shrewd verdant eyes land on me, and he switches accents again. "And I know Alana because I've been protecting her for the last ten years. Just like I've been protecting you… *Aoife*."

A bolt of jagged white lightning strikes me from out of the blue when what he doesn't come right out and say rings loudly in my ears.

"It was *you*?" I whisper.

The way his steady gaze bores into me tells me I'm right.

"Red?" Tristan asks when my hand convulses in his, my breaths labored.

Beads of sweat track across my brow and down my neck as my left side tingles with licks of phantom fire, burning chemicals, and the ease of the knife as it sunk into me, cutting through layers of epidermis and muscle until the pointed steel tip hit bone; the man with the constellations smiling down at me, his face quickly blotted out by a bright, comforting light. Just as I was reaching for that beautiful light that promised me peace, I was brought crashing back down to earth in a fireball of pain and agony.

"You're safe now. You're safe. I've got you."

He should have left me to die with them.

CHAPTER 9

"Syn," Tristan calls after me.

I keep walking who knows where because I'm already lost. I hate mansions.

Turning a sharp right, I find myself in a room with a wall of windows and a grand piano much like the one I saw at Hendrix's house.

Constantine is the first to get to me. He presses his chest to my back, nothing more, just to let me know he's there.

"Do you think it survived?" I ask Hendrix when he and Tristan crowd around us on either side. "The Steinway in the room with the stained-glass dome ceiling," I clarify.

Hendrix pinches his lips together. Another shrug.

"Do you still play?"

He and Tristan used to play so beautifully, their talents advanced for their age. They would be compelled to perform at Society functions, and I would sit on the floor at the foot of the piano bench to listen—something my mother would chastise me for. Apparently, it was unseemly for the only child of the head of the Council to be seen sitting cross-legged on the floor with her dress hiked up to her thighs.

"I haven't in a while. Not since…"

Not since I disappeared.

Tristan's arm brushes up against mine. "Why did you bolt?"

I didn't stick around to hear anything else Cillian had to say. I'd heard enough. Everyone I have ever met has manipulated or lied to me. I'm so sick and tired of all the secrets.

"Cillian is who saved me from the fire," I reply emotionlessly. The compulsion to shut down and make myself forget is tempting. I did it before.

There's a sharp intake of breath. "How is that possible?"

"James," Constantine says.

That's what I had thought as well. Papa hid me away in Ireland for a reason.

Walking over to the moonlit-bathed ebony piano, I lightly glide my fingers over the white and black keys before taking a seat on the leather-cushioned bench. I loosen my fingers by tinkling out a C-major arpeggio.

"Join me?" I ask no one in particular and scoot over when Hendrix slides the bench out another foot to make room for his long legs. He grunts in annoyance when his knees bump under the key bed.

I begin softly playing Pachelbel's *Canon*. I discovered a couple of years ago that Pachelbel wrote lyrics for that piece of music; the words those of longing, devotion, and forever love that last through time and separation. It hits a little too close to home.

When Hendrix joins in, playing the background accompaniment, I sink into the serenity of the music and just exist in that moment. This song was the first one I taught myself to play on my portable keyboard. I don't know what it is about this specific song, but the melody is like injecting GABA—the chemical in the brain that produces a calming effect when the body is under stress—directly into the bloodstream.

When we finish, Hendrix immediately launches into a fast rendition of Scott Joplin's "Maple Leaf Rag." I watch on in awe, captivated by his skill, as his hands move smoothly back and forth along the keys. Whenever I tried to learn how to do a syncopated rhythm, my fingers would twist into pretzels, and it would sound more like goats jumping across the piano keys.

I bump into his side. "Show off."

He looks at me and winks. I don't know why I find his ability to *not* look at his hands while he's playing hot as hell.

When Hendrix finishes, I let my fingers randomly press keys with no song in mind. "Why did Aleksander do it?"

When I spoke to him at the tower, he didn't seem like a person who'd do anything on a whim, which means he'd been planning what happened this morning for a while.

With barely enough room to fit, Tristan sits down opposite Hendrix on the bench. "Because he's an egotistical asshole who wants something that doesn't belong to him."

"What does he want?"

Tristan's thigh knocks mine when he shifts on the

bench, and he takes my chin, turning my face toward him, the expression on his face serious and deadly.

"He wants what's mine."

There seems to be a double meaning hidden somewhere in that, but I reply to the most obvious one. "It's not really yours, though, is it?"

His grasp on my jaw tightens, and he closes the distance between us until our faces almost touch. His show of dominance sends pulsing tingles directly between my legs. Before last week, I had never known sexual desire and want, and since the night on the patio, I can't shut it off around them. We're having a serious conversation, but all I can think about is Tristan laying me out across the back of the grand piano and fucking me.

"Care to test that, Red?" he challenges, and my clit throbs from his deep timbre at the same time his arrogant reply brings out my stubborn streak. I really am screwed up.

"And if I did?"

My father was the head of the Council before he was murdered. Betrayed by one of his own. The seat Tristan will soon occupy rightfully belongs to me. I don't want it, but I do see the value of such a position. It would provide me with the resources to find my parents' killers and wipe them off the face of the earth with no repercussions.

Tristan grins, and Hendrix reaches around me to shove him off the bench. "No, she doesn't. Cut it out."

With a glower, Tristan picks himself up off the floor. "Bylaws dictate—"

"Will you bloody fucking stop? Our plan was to take out our fathers and take over the Council so we could destroy the Society from within, not perpetuate it and make it stronger. Aleksander did half the work for us. Let's finish it and get the fuck out."

I share a quick side glance at Constantine to see his reaction. He's been very quiet since our shower.

"Plans change," Tristan says.

With obstinate arms crossed over his chest, Hendrix replies, "Not for me. Once it's done, I'm out. I want a chance at a normal life and some fucking peace. That was *my* plan. And I'll be damned if I let you drag her back in."

"If that's what she wants."

Hendrix groans and looks to the vaulted ceiling before settling his blue gaze on me. "But it's not what she wants, and you'd know that if you'd listened to anything she has said this past week."

I really hate that they're talking about me like I'm not sitting right there sandwiched between them, but Hendrix is right. Old Aoife might have been content with following the path Papa set out for me. But Syn isn't. She wants to finish college and go to medical school... *and* I really need to stop talking about myself as if I'm two different people.

I'm also impressed, in a bemused sort of way, that Hendrix actually listened. It feels good to know that through all our recent nasty bickering and arguments, he *heard* me, much like how Constantine *sees* me. Two separate validations that are equally important.

Tristan squats, grabs my hips, and turns me ninety degrees so we're facing one another.

"What do you want, Syn?"

I want them. I want love. I want a family. I want a chance at happiness. A life. An education. I want my body to be whole and not scarred. I want every person who has ever hurt or betrayed me to suffer as much as I've suffered.

"I want revenge."

"With fucking pleasure," Tristan replies and presses a hard kiss to my mouth.

Hendrix slams his hands down on the piano keys, creating a discordant boom of sound.

"Fuck this," he says and slides off the bench, knocking Constantine's shoulder as he walks off.

I'm already up and in pursuit. When he gets to the end of the hallway, he stops and looks both ways, unsure of which direction to go.

I dash to his side before he takes off again. "Hendrix."

"He's going to get you killed because of his stupid, inflated ego."

I twine our fingers together. "I need this. I need the nightmares to stop. Please help me find who killed my parents. I need you."

"Do you?" he snaps.

"Yes, I do. And stop being a jealous asshat. You know how I feel about you."

Using his grip on my hand, he yanks me forward, knocking the breath right out of me when I slam into his chest.

"I used to know how Aoife felt about me, but you're not her."

"The voice in my head says I am."

His head jerks back, perplexed. "I'm going to pretend I didn't hear that."

"I think that's best." Going up on my toes, I kiss the underside of his chin. "I will always be your Aoife, and you will always be my knight in tarnished armor."

He huffs, but it's filled with self-deprecating humor. "Don't remind me," he says at the nickname I used to call him. He caresses my tender, swollen cheek. "And you know damn well that I'd follow you into hell if you asked."

"I'm asking. I can't do this without you. Let's go get Alana, and then we can figure out everything else afterward."

He tucks my head under his chin when I hug him. Constantine is my sanctuary, but Hendrix is my strength.

"I hate fucking Texas," he grumbles.

CHAPTER 10

I grip my armrest when the plane violently shudders. "It's just turbulence. And you're crushing my hand."

Relaxing the white-knuckle grip I have on Hendrix's hand, I mumble, "Sorry."

The past hour has been spent in stilted silence. No one has spoken a word. Not after we left Cillian's house. Not in the SUV as we were driven to a private airfield. And not when we boarded Cillian's luxury Gulfstream G700.

As soon as the plane was airborne, Constantine disappeared into the back room where there's a bed. Tristan has been brooding and staring out the window, and Hendrix has been quietly sitting beside me, eyes closed but not asleep, whereas I have been trying not to freak the hell out. I never liked flying.

Needing to do something to distract myself from my nauseous stomach, I unclip the seat belt and stand up.

"I'm going to stretch my legs," I tell Hendrix.

I practically climb over him to get out from my

window seat because his long legs are blocking my way.

One of the staff, a pretty, dark-haired woman, approaches me. "Can I get you anything, Miss Fitzpatrick?"

It's on the tip of my tongue to tell her my last name is Carmichael, not Fitzpatrick. It feels weird to be called my real name again after a decade of being called Synthia Carmichael, just like it's weird to think of Alana as Deirdre and not Mom.

"Is there a way I can send a text message to someone without, you know…" I make a descending motion with my hand to indicate a plane going down and crashing.

The woman's ruby-red lips spread in a smile. "Of course. The plane has Wi-Fi, so feel free to use your phone to text or access the internet."

Uh… I look down at my borrowed men's clothes that have no pockets in the sweatpants.

"I lost my phone."

I assume I lost everything I brought with me to Hendrix's family estate, including my laptop and backpack that contained my journal. I couldn't care less about most of it, but the journal is a completely different story. Ten years of my life, my dreams, my fractured memories, exist on those pages. Losing it is like losing a part of myself again.

"There's a laptop you can use, or you can borrow my phone."

So freaking nice. "A laptop would be perfect, thank you."

"Right this way. May I offer you a drink or something to eat while you work? It'll be another two hours before we land."

"Ginger ale?" I don't think my stomach could hold

down anything solid right now.

The inside of the plane is a lot bigger than I would've expected—plush, leather executive seats that have extendable footrests, a galley that looks like a Michelin-star kitchen, a full bedroom suite at the back with a king bed and en suite that includes a shower.

I'm escorted to a small, partitioned room on the right side of the plane near the front, and I stop short when I see Evan sitting at a round table with a laptop opened in front of him. Cillian insisted Evan come with us, something the guys were not at all happy about.

The woman immediately blushes when he looks up. "Pardon the intrusion, Mr. McCarthy. Miss Fitzpatrick would like to use the Wi-Fi."

He slides the laptop over to where the unoccupied seat is next to him. "Be my guest."

I'm already slowly backing away. "I can wait until you're done."

He stands and waves me over with a curl of his fingers. "I'm done."

The woman touches my arm. "I'll be right back with your drink."

"Thank you," I reply and walk over to the empty seat next to Evan. "Is it okay for me to email Raquelle? She was expecting me back already, and I haven't sent proof of life, so I know she's worried."

His mouth turns up in a smirk. "Proof of life?"

"It's a thing with her," I reply.

He smiles, and it's such a nice, friendly smile. I don't know how to reconcile him being the son of a mafia kingpin with the nice guy I met in class. But if Cillian is a distant cousin, that makes Evan my cousin, too. I went from losing all my family to gaining another one unexpectedly.

Evan waits for me to sit, then returns to his chair. Neither of us says anything for a good two minutes. So fucking awkward.

"So," he says, relaxing back like we have all day.

"So," I reply, then, "Cousins, huh?"

"*Distant* cousins," he emphasizes and pushes his glasses up the bridge of his nose.

"Do you wear those all the time?" I ask.

"I have contacts, but I don't like them."

More awkward silence.

Evan glances at my exposed arm, seeing the scars. "We met before, but you probably don't remember me."

"I don't. I'm sorry," I reply and want to pull down the sleeve of my shirt but don't.

"It's okay. I didn't think you would." I freeze up when he reaches across the table and covers my hand. "Dad brought me to the private clinic where they treated you. He said they had to put you in a medically induced coma but that your subconscious would be able to hear me if I talked to you." He chuckles. "I read to you every day. *Hatchet. Where the Red Fern Grows. The Island of the Blue Dolphins.* When you were stable enough, you and Dierdre were sent to the States, and I never saw you again. Dad said I wasn't allowed to contact you, but I asked about you often. If you were okay. If you were happy." His eyes rove over me in an appreciative way. "You look so different from the little blonde girl I read to every day at the hospital."

I gape at Evan, completely at a loss for words. Holy shit. I didn't know any of this.

I remove my hand from under his and wrap my arms around my waist as a few of the puzzle pieces begin to click into place.

"The scholarship to DF was just a way to get me there, wasn't it?"

He pulls his bottom lip between his teeth and nods.

I thought I had been accepted to the prestigious university and awarded the Knight Foundation scholarship based on my merits and grades. I worked so hard in high school to catch up and excel because I was behind due to my year in hospital and follow-up treatments. But like everything else, it was all a fabrication.

"Why?"

Drumming his fingers on the tabletop, he replies, "It was time."

"Time for what?" I demand to know.

We're interrupted when the woman comes back, carrying two drinks, one ginger ale and one sparkling water that she sets down in front of Evan.

"Thank you, Candace."

Her face blushes a deeper shade of pink as she leaves with a quiet, "You're welcome."

"She likes you."

The ice clinks against the glass as he takes a sip of his drink, his eyes never straying from me. "Trust me, I've noticed."

"Not interested?"

"Not in her, no."

I down my ginger ale, needing it to help soothe my suddenly parched throat, and immediately regret it when my stomach protests.

"You okay? You look a little green."

I place my empty glass down on the table. "Hate flying," I manage to mutter.

Evan starts to say something else, but I talk right over him.

"I feel like I'm a pawn being used in some game I didn't know I was playing, and if I don't start getting some answers soon, you and Cillian are not going to like what happens next."

His entire demeanor changes at my threat. Evan is a man who wears two masks, and the sweet, kind guy I met in biology lab vanishes.

"Don't threaten me."

I don't back down at his severe reproach. "Then stop talking in riddles."

His sudden bark of laughter startles me and makes me jump. "It's scary how much you and Andie are alike."

I'm so confused with the change of subject. "Who is Andie?"

"Another cousin. You'll meet her and more of our Irish brood when we get to Texas."

How many cousins do I have?

Getting annoyed that he hasn't given me any straightforward answers, I swivel my chair around, intending to leave. I'll go find Candace and see if I can still use her phone, but Evan stops me before my butt leaves my seat.

"James called in a marker, and my father is bound by blood oath to fulfill it."

I spin my chair back toward him. "That sounds very draconian and John Wick-*ish*."

His face alights. "I love those movies. Have you seen the last one? Not as good as the others, but that roundabout scene and the one at the stairs was—"

"*Evan.*"

He sighs and rests his elbows on the table, hands

clasped together. "If you're wanting me to tell you what promise James made my father swear to, I can't because I honestly don't know. Dad wouldn't tell me where he took you or where you were, only that you were 'safely hidden in plain sight,'" he says with finger quotes. "Then, all of a sudden, Dad sent me to DF last year, somehow knowing you would be coming. I had no plans to attend university at all, to be honest, but like you, my life is shaped by what my father wants, and I get little say in the matter."

"You sound like Tristan," I remark, reflecting on how both men feel trapped by their fathers' aspirations and wants.

He quirks his mouth to the side, and a small dimple pops in his left cheek. "The Society and the mob aren't so very different. We're just not as polished or pretentious."

I groan and scrub my hands over my face. "God, I hate that stupid name."

Whoever thought to call it the Society wasn't very imaginative.

Evan's hazel eyes go smoky, and he becomes enigmatic again. "He's not going to give it up for you."

Great. We're back at riddles.

"Give what up?" I ask, but I'm pretty sure I know what he's implying.

I don't want to lead the Council. I never did. But that's not going to stop me from using it to find who murdered my parents and hunt down the man who left me with horrific scars.

Evan sits up straighter when Tristan suddenly walks into the small, partitioned room, amping up the tension with his larger-than-life presence. He has purple crescents of fatigue under his eyes, and his hair is sticking up in all directions as if he's been constantly running his fingers through it. He looks tired, yet still so damn gorgeous.

"Hey," I say, happy to see him.

Tristan makes his way over to me, a dark scowl marring his face when he notices Evan. I tilt my head back on the chair to look up at an upside-down Tristan.

"You good?" He bends over and softly kisses me.

"Better now," I reply with a smile, reaching up to cup his stubbled cheek.

Evan breaks the moment with, "I've got to ask. I get that all of you knew each other as kids, but when did—"

"It's none of your fucking business," Tristan tells him.

Evan replies with all seriousness, "It will be if you hurt her."

I slide my hand to cover Tristan's mouth before he has a chance to retort with something I'm sure will be offensive.

"Would using my school account be okay to send a message to Raquelle?"

Evan taps the space bar on the laptop, and the home screen lights up. "The connection is secure. No one can trace it or find your location," he assures me.

I suddenly realized something. "I want someone on her, watching over her. I need to know she's safe. Can you or Cillian make that happen?"

"I'll handle it," Tristan butts in.

"It's already been taken care of," Evan replies, and the pressure that had been crushing my chest releases in a whoosh.

Not able to express the sheer gratitude I'm feeling, I

say a simple, "Thanks, Evan."

"No problem. I'll give you some privacy. Just holler if you need help," he says as he leaves.

Tristan watches him go, then hops up on the table. "I don't trust him."

He may not, but I do.

"The feeling appears to be mutual."

Tristan gently closes the laptop just as I swipe the touchpad and move the cursor. "I wouldn't risk directly contacting Raquelle. I'm pretty sure Aleksander will have eyes on her."

He's probably right.

"I just want to let her know I'm okay and won't be coming back today."

He scoots across the table a few inches to the left until he can bracket my chair with his legs. He pats his thigh, and I immediately climb up onto his lap, bracing my knees on the table to straddle him. One of his hands goes around me to support my lower lumbar so I don't slip off, while the other sinks into my hair at the nape of my neck.

"We need to stay out of sight for a while until we figure out our next move. Aleksander is smart. We need to be smarter."

Being told to hide and give up my dreams is unacceptable. It's my life, and it should be my choice with how to live it. A choice that has been continuously taken from me by other people's agendas. I will never give another person that kind of power over me again. Not even the guys with their best intentions.

"After we see Alana, I'm going back to Darlington, with or without you, but I'd prefer with you."

Tristan's grasp is punishing when he tugs my hair by

the roots. At any other time, I would get turned on by his show of dominance.

"You are not going back to Darlington."

I flatten my palms on his shoulders and not-so-gently slam him backward on the table and sit on his chest.

"You only get to boss me around in the bedroom."

I run the tip of my nose up the thick column of his neck. I don't know if it's a type of scent memory, but I love the way the guys smell. There's a strange kind of comfort in their different scents that I want to bury my nose in and breathe in, like they're my air.

The light brown of his irises gets eclipsed when his pupils dilate. "Aoife," he growls.

"Yes?" I snake a hand behind me and cup his already impressive erection that I remember all too well from the blow job I gave him in the shower the other morning. The way I want him, Constantine, and Hendrix all the time now is ridiculous—and in this case, inappropriate, since Tristan and I are having a serious discussion—but my hormones and my body don't give a damn.

"I'm being serious," he says through gritted teeth when I rub him through his sweatpants.

His normal attire is usually dress pants and a nice shirt, but Tristan in a pair of casual sweats and tee that mold to every bump and swell of muscle is pure eye candy.

"So am I," I whisper against his ear.

I grapple onto his shirt when he jackknives into a sitting position and takes my mouth in a deep, toe-curling kiss that leaves me a panting, needy mess in his arms.

"As much as I'd love to fuck you on this table, I'm not

going to give Evan the pleasure of seeing you come."

That thought is as sobering as a cold bucket of water dumped over my head. It also reminds me that we're on a plane full of other people who work for Cillian.

"I'm going back to DF."

"No, you're not."

Knowing I'm not going to get anywhere with him about the matter while he's still worrying about his sister and Aleksander and thousands of other things, I dismount from his lap and place a quick kiss to his cheek.

"Yes, I am."

"Aoife, for fuck's sake."

I swipe the laptop from the table and rush out before he can stop me. I head to the front lavatory. Not the most ideal place to hide out, but it's the only place on the plane that has a lock on the door other than the cockpit where the pilots sit.

Once inside and the door latch secured, I sit down on the closed toilet lid and prop the laptop on my bent legs. The cloying stench of the blue disinfectant water competes with the apple and cinnamon air freshener sitting on the lower shelf and unsettles my stomach even more.

Not wanting to be in here for longer than necessary, I hastily log on to my student account and type out a quick email to Raquelle.

Hey. It's Syn. Something's come up, and I won't be back today. I'm okay but I don't have a phone anymore, which is why I'm emailing. I promise that I'll explain everything as soon as I get back. I don't know when, but I'm hoping by Wednesday. Take good notes for me in class.

I delete the next sentence I write and tap my foot while thinking about the best way to tell her to stay away from Aleksander that won't freak her out, then decide against it. Evan said they had someone on her. I have to put my faith in him and Cillian to keep her safe until I return.

Just one more thing to do.

I unlock the door and poke my head out just as Candace walks by.

"Hey! I'll take you up on that offer to use your phone."

I hope Keith doesn't fire me when I call out sick for the rest of the week.

CHAPTER 11

My gaze clashes with Evan's when I enter the main cabin. He smirks, and I sneer. There's something needling me about him that I can't exactly pinpoint. Then again, it could be because of his very blatant interest in Aoife that doesn't seem so… cousin-*ly*.

"Why does she have to be so fucking stubborn?" I grumble and throw myself in the seat across from Hendrix.

When my eardrum pops, I yawn and vigorously massage the outside of my ear to equalize the pressure. When that doesn't work, I pinch my nose and mouth closed and blow, and that does the job.

Hendrix cracks an eye open.

"She wants to go back to Darlington," I inform him.

He lolls his head to the side to face me, the set of his jaw like stone. "The fuck she is."

"Why don't you go tell her that because she's not listening to me."

I sweep an arm out to where she has barricaded

herself in the restroom. I could easily get in if I wanted to, but I know if I did, it would lead to a fight I would lose. Regardless of what I said, I would give in to what she wanted. I'm pathetically clutched by the balls when it comes to her. Because she owns my ass. I'm so screwed.

Hendrix scoffs. "When has she ever listened to me?"

He has a point.

"She seems to be handling things well, considering everything that's happened," I comment.

He glances toward the front of the plane where she's holed up in the lavatory. "I'm no doctor, so I don't know what kind of psychological shit she's dealing with right now. But what happened this morning, what she did. And then her breakdown. And now? She acts like everything is normal." He drags a weary hand down his face. "Fuck, I don't know."

I reach across the aisle and grasp his arm. "I'm worried about her, too."

I'm at as much of a loss as Hen is on what to do. We'll need to watch her closely and support her in any way she needs. Make her see a doctor if it comes down to it. Dierdre should have done more to help her, not feed her lies and pretend to be her fucking adoptive mother. My sister has a lot of explaining to do.

"How are you dealing?" he asks.

How am I dealing? Not good. I don't know up from down right now. And I'm so damn angry.

"I'm going to kill Aleksander."

"Hate to say I told you so, but we should have done that years ago. And now that he knows she's alive—"

"*I know!*" I practically hiss, trying to keep my voice down.

Hendrix sits up, throws his legs into the aisle, and leans over my way. "Then why did you open your big fucking mouth and tell him who she really is?"

I thought it was impossible to get angrier. Hen heard her screams. He knew what Aleksei would do to her. Aleksander was the only person who could stop his brother. I didn't know she would take everyone out and kill the doppelgänger bastard.

"You would have done the exact same thing, so don't you dare throw that in my face."

Con walks out from the back room, scratching his head which makes sections of his hair stand up at odd angles. The swelling on his face has gone down, but the deep purple and blue bruising is more vivid.

He looks around, and I know he's searching for Aoife. I thumb over my shoulder.

"Need coffee," he mumbles, but he makes a beeline to the bathroom and parks himself right outside the door, waiting for Aoife to emerge. Even though Con had my back with Cillian, he's been acting colder than usual with me since we left the estate.

While I was on my knees and cursing the heavens, a startling epiphany smacked me in the face. Dierdre faked her death around the same time my father sent Malin to kill Aoife and her parents. The contemporaneousness of past events is piling up like an overflowing mound of putrid dog shit.

"I need to tell you something."

My pulse jumps erratically just thinking about how I'm going to make Malin suffer in the most horrific ways imaginable. For every inch of burned skin that mars Aoife's body and for every slice of the knife that marks her pale skin, Malin will experience them tenfold by my hand.

Hendrix grunts out a complaint of irritation. "Can it wait until after we've landed?"

I know the longer I stall, the more enraged he's going to be at Con and me.

"Fine."

I easily acquiesce because the discussion about my father's involvement in what happened to Aoife isn't something I'm too thrilled to have with him. I don't even know if my father is alive or where the hell Malin is. Or Mom. I don't share a lot of love for my mother because she was cold and loved my father more than she ever loved me, but I hope she wasn't one of Aleksander's casualties. She also suffered under Francesco's controlling fist.

Turning his earlier question back onto him, I ask, "How are you doing?"

He knows I'm talking about what happened with his mother.

The corner of his eye twitches. I haven't seen that 'tell' in a long time.

He blows out a breath. "Relieved."

Eva Knight was a cunt for the perverted things she forced on her son. Hen hasn't ever told me or Con the full extent of what happened when he was thirteen, but it fucked him up mentally and is why he's never been able to have a normal relationship with a woman. I picture all the bite marks on Aoife's body. We'll need to come up with a safe word or something for her to use when she's with him. I know he doesn't want to hurt her, but I also know that when his beast comes out to play, it's hard for him to stop.

"I don't care what else is going on or how messed up

things are right now, but Con and I are here for you. Whatever you need. Brothers to the end."

"Brothers to the end," he repeats.

"I'm sorry to bother you," a soft feminine voice says.

Hen and I look up at the woman who offered us drinks as soon as we stepped onto the plane. Blonde hair secured in a sleek ponytail, ruby-red lips, kohl-lined brown eyes, and an hourglass shape accentuated by the tight-fitting skirt suit she's wearing. She's the type of woman we would've happily taken to a hotel for a night of debauchery.

Her cheeks blush when she asks, "You're Hendrix Knight?"

Hen tends to attract a lot of attention wherever we go. It's amazing how many people recognize him just from his Instagram. I used to give him a lot of shit over it. Con and I have stayed away from social media as much as possible, whereas Hendrix thrives on it like the attention whore he is. He's tall, blond, blue-eyed, and loves to play up his posh British accent. Attributes that make women instantly fall to their knees, eager to suck his dick. He treats them like shit, using them for his own needs, but they keep coming back, begging for more—like Serena.

"I am."

Hen doesn't eye-fuck her with a lascivious rake of his gaze like he normally would when a pretty woman approaches him. His eyes don't wander from her face. Hers do. She looks him over appreciatively and teethes her bottom lip, smiling demurely.

"I'm Melissa."

"Don't care," he replies, and her smile drops a little.

"I, um…" She looks over at me, then back at him. "I

follow you on Insta. I'm a huge fan."

Bingo.

Hendrix sends her a blank look.

I take the small bag of yogurt-dipped pretzels sitting on the attached tray table beside me, rip into it, and pop one into my mouth.

"Can I get you anything?" She breathes out "*anything*" seductively, making her silent offer of something more than food or beverage clear as day.

"I'm good," Hendrix tells her.

Melissa doesn't take the hint. "I'm free for the next hour if you want to talk... or do other things."

She makes the mistake of touching him by teasingly tip-toeing her fingers across his shoulder and down his arm. Before Hen can shrug it off, Melissa's hand is yanked away by a fuming Aoife.

"You touch him again, and I will break your fucking hand."

Melissa's face contorts with pain as Aoife bends her wrist at an unnatural angle, and then her eyes go wide with fear as Aoife increases the pressure.

"I won't. I'm sorry. You're hurting me," she pleads on a sob.

"Syn, let her go," Evan says from where he's sitting.

No one in the cabin seems too eager to jump in and pull Melissa away from Aoife. Con could easily do it since he's standing right behind her.

Almost a minute goes by before Aoife finally releases her. Cradling her arm to her chest, tears track down Melissa's face, running her mascara. She hurriedly bolts toward the front of the plane with her head tucked down.

The biggest smile spreads across Hendrix's face. "You

jealous, firefly?"

The look Aoife aims at him would wither a lesser man's balls into raisins.

"Fuck you. You're an asshole," Aoife seethes and stomps her fine, infuriated ass into the back bedroom.

CHAPTER 12

The plane hits another pocket of turbulence, and I almost drop the laptop and Candace's phone. I was lucky that I was able to catch Keith at closing since he stays late to oversee the cleaning and prep work for the next day.

"...says she'll take your shifts."

I miss most of what Keith says, but the important thing is he isn't going to fire me. He was actually very understanding about me blowing off a week of work because of a family emergency. That's the excuse I gave.

"You are hands-down the best boss I've ever had."

Keith chuckles, which is a rarity. "I'm the only boss you've ever had. Hold on, Shelby wants to talk to you."

There's a staticky shuffling sound before Shelby's cheerful voice comes over the line.

"Hey, country girl. I don't want you to worry. Becs and I will cover your shifts. Everything okay?"

I hate lying to one of the only truly nice people in my life.

"It will be. And thank you so much for covering my ass. I owe you big time."

"I'll hold you to that. I hope you like babysitting rambunctious toddlers."

I smile. I don't know if I do or not since I've never been around young kids.

"Deal. Thanks again. Give Keith a big bear hug from me."

"Will do. Sending good thoughts and virtual hugs your way."

We hang up, and I open the bathroom door, ready to get out of the confined space and away from the godawful stench of disinfectant.

"Thanks for letting me borrow your phone," I say to the person standing next to the door before I realize it's Constantine and not Candace.

Half of his face looks like he got hit with a gender-reveal powder cannon. I set down the laptop and phone on the nearby jump seat before gently touching the bruises on his cheek.

"The swelling has gone down. Were you able to get some sleep?"

No, he mouths. *Missed you.*

My heart does a somersault inside my chest that has nothing to do with the jostling of the plane.

"Want to come lie down with me?"

I'm not tired and wouldn't be able to fall asleep anyway, but I can help him relax, rub his head, give him whatever he needs so he can get a few minutes peace.

He nods yes.

I take his hand and turn around, ready to lead him to the back room, only to stop when I see one of the female crew members talking to Hendrix. No, not talking—

flirting.

Jealousy rises swiftly. She's blonde, busty, and looks too much like Serena. And until that very second, I hadn't thought about all the women Hendrix has slept with over the years. I remember vividly the sounds coming from his bedroom when he was screwing Serena. How he told her before taking her upstairs that I was nobody. The way she stumbled into the kitchen the next morning, barely dressed and all sexed-up, looking thoroughly ravished and completely satisfied. And then the way she taunted me and made fun of my scars.

Those old insecurities well up like a summer thunderstorm. So does the red-hot rage when the woman touches Hendrix, the tease of her fingers down his arm telegraphing the message in big neon letters that she wants him. Something dark slithers up from that broken place inside me that whispers I will never be good enough or pretty enough or desirable enough for any man to want me. I tell it to go fuck itself because Hendrix is *mine*, just as Tristan and Constantine are mine. We were ripped apart from each other for ten years, and I'll be damned if I allow anyone else to come between us.

I'm snatching her wrist and yanking her hand off him before I realize I've even moved.

"You touch him again, and I will break your fucking hand."

I'm ashamed of the thrill I get at the fear I see in her eyes when I snap her wrist back, and she starts crying.

"I won't. I'm sorry. You're hurting me," she wails.

Her plea only makes me increase the pressure.

"Syn, let her go," Evan says, but I don't take my eyes off the blonde.

I don't want to hurt her, but I can't seem to stop. Jealousy is in control of me right now, and I get mad at Hendrix for making me feel this way. I know where Constantine and Tristan stand when it comes to how they feel about me. They said they loved me. But Hendrix hasn't said anything at all. Am I just another one of the 'toys' he likes to play with, and once he's done with me, he'll walk away? Have the years apart stolen away the boy who was my best friend and irreparably broken us completely?

I don't know how much time goes by before I finally release the woman. I can feel the weight of everyone's eyes on us. Remorse and shame batter my conscience as I watch huge crocodile tears stream down her face. I want to be a doctor, for God's sake. Do no harm. It's the main tenet of the Hippocratic oath.

When the woman rushes off with her arm clutched to her chest, I look down at my hand. At the blood I can still see that's not really there.

"You jealous, firefly?" Hendrix says, grinning widely and sounding very pleased.

I glare down at him as my anger transfers from myself to him.

"Fuck you. You're an asshole."

I don't want to be like this. Like Aoife used to be. Violent and unhinged when my anger gets out of control. I thought I was a monster because of how I looked, but there's another monster lurking inside me. One I was forced to become as a child.

Hendrix is out of his seat and following me as I storm off.

"Admit it. You *are* jealous."

"Shut up."

The back bedroom in the aft of the plane is small with little room for me to pace out my irritation and calm down. The king bed takes up most of the space, and a perfect Constantine indentation rumples the bedcovers where he'd been lying.

Hendrix blocks the doorway, so I can't escape.

"Why are you mad at me? I didn't do anything."

I hurl the contempt I feel at him. "You didn't tell her to stop. I'm not a complete idiot, Hendrix. I may have been a virgin until recently, but I know when a woman is offering something more than an in-flight beverage."

The grin on his stupidly gorgeous face turns Cheshire. "Come here, Trouble."

Even though hearing his childhood nickname for me makes me ridiculously happy, I balk at his audacity and have the urge to childishly stomp my foot.

"No. And stop smiling. This isn't funny."

"From where I'm standing, it kind of is."

Sexy smirk cemented in place, he strides forward; I take a step back.

"I'm not them. I can never be them."

My voice chokes up. I will never be beautiful. My scars will never fade, and no amount of skin grafts or plastic surgery will make them go away. The man with the constellations on his neck ruined me.

Hendrix stalks closer until my back bumps up against the curved cabin wall, and he towers over me.

"Who will you never be?"

Our gazes meet, the magnetic pull of him too strong for me to resist, but all I see are unwanted images of him with...

"Serena." I can't hold his intense blue stare, so I lower my eyes to his chest. "Or every other woman you've been with."

I saw enough on his IG feed to know he has a type. Blonde. Skinny. Gorgeous. Huge boobs.

Lean but powerfully muscled arms cage me in, and then Hendrix is right there in front of me. The curve of his ribcage cuts into my torso. Every exhale of his warm breath tickles my forehead and cheeks, stirring the small hairs that have curled around my face. I soak in his body heat. His smell. *Him*.

"Drop to your knees, baby, and I'll show you exactly who my cock belongs to because it sure as shit isn't the woman out there."

Sinking to the floor, my body is already obeying before my brain catches up, and I snap out of it.

"I'm not going to suck your dick."

But god help me, I want his cock in my mouth, fucking me deep until my throat is raw and I'm gagging on him. I want every filthy, depraved thing that he, Tristan, and Constantine want to do to me.

"Look at me."

Another command that I'm hungry to obey, but I force myself to shake my head no.

He takes his hand from the wall and circles my neck, gripping tightly. I'm embarrassed at the moan I make and how moisture gathers between my legs at his indelicate touch. Why do I like it so much when he does that?

Keeping the pressure steady, Hendrix dips his head.

His deep voice rumbles when he tells me, "You have it all wrong, firefly. All those women were not *you*. Don't you see that it's always been you? I've been chasing your ghost for ten fucking years, trying to feel *something*. But I never did because the only time I ever felt anything real was when I was with you. My fucking soul was ripped out when we lost you."

My anger swiftly abates as desire and longing flood in to replace it. This damaged man who used to be the boy I adored has suffered so much. They all have. But we never lost the core of who we were to each other. Childhood soulmates and best friends and everything that was ever good in the cruel world we lived in.

My chest heaves with the exertion to pull in air, and I fist his shirt. "*So. Was. Mine.*"

I don't know how he does it, but I'm suddenly flung onto the bed with Hendrix on top of me. The mattress sinks beneath his weight as heat and need spill over into a want so deep, I burn from it. It grows into a flashfire when his mouth crashes over mine, and he takes and takes and takes. Hendrix wrecked me the first time he kissed me. This kiss is no different. Every stroke of his tongue is brutal and possessive and claiming.

"You don't think I'm jealous, too? I see how easy you are with them. How you seek them out first. You sleep in Con's bed every fucking night with Tristan while I lie alone, wanting you so damn badly."

He yanks at my T-shirt until his hand touches my bare stomach, then roams the soft, fluid lines of my abdomen, skimming his hand along the curve of my hip where the skin is roughly textured.

"I... I didn't know."

From the moment 'they' met, Hendrix and Syn had been fire and ice. It confused the hell out of me how I could want him so much when he acted like an asshole most of the time. I know why now. My heart never forgot who he was, even when I forced my mind to.

Hendrix wrangles the roll of the sweatpants away

from my hip bone and shoves his hand beneath the material, seeking out my most intimate area. My pelvis bucks up, and I moan loudly when he doesn't waste any time and sinks two fingers inside me. Pleasure mixes with pain. I'm still tender from last night, but Hendrix helps soothe the sting by strumming his thumb over my clit. Sparks of light dance along my vision as pleasure coils tightly in my belly.

"This is mine," he declares as he quickly builds me up. Hendrix can make me come so effortlessly with just one touch or a spoken word, like the night on the back patio. "You're mine, Syn."

He keeps calling me Syn, whereas Tristan calls me Aoife. My past and my present. There has to be meaning to that.

"*Hendrix,*" I cry out when he does some incredible, wonderful thing with his fingers that causes every nerve synapse from my head to my toes to light up.

"I don't want anyone else. Not Serena or any other woman. Only you."

My pussy clamps down as his words send me soaring just as my orgasm sends me flying, and before I've even had a chance to catch my breath, he says, "I fucking love watching you come. Again."

Again?

"Hendrix," I whimper, sinking my fingers into his hair when he seizes my lips with another decadent kiss.

A whole-body shudder shakes me as he continues to caress my inner walls with his fingertips, drawing out every last drop of pleasure he can wring from me.

"Hendrix."

As much as I'm desperate for him to make me come again, I want it to be while he's inside me. I need to feel that intimacy, that connection, with him.

"Hendrix," I say for a fourth time and cup the sides of his face. His cobalt eyes are fraught with mania when they look down at me.

I understand better than anyone that there are no guarantees in this life. There are no promises of a tomorrow that may never come. My childhood was stolen from me, just like the past ten years were stolen from me, and I don't want to live with one more regret.

Not caring that Hendrix may never feel the same way, I give him the piece of my heart that has always belonged to him. I loved Hendrix, Tristan, and Constantine as a girl, but I fell in love with them as a woman.

"*Tá mé i ngrá leat.*" I love you.

I know he doesn't understand what I said, but I hope he feels it in the frenetic beating of my heart.

Hendrix stills. "What?"

With shaking hands framing his face, I touch our lips together in the barest of kisses.

"Can you hold me?"

His kiss-swollen lips open, then close. I can't decipher the thousands of emotions that cross his face because they change swiftly. Any form of tenderness wasn't something we were given growing up. Even Papa, as much as he loved me, was never tender or affectionate.

"Of course," he says, rolling to his side.

His arms close around me at the same time mine wrap around him, and he buries his face in my neck. My fingers dive into his soft blond hair, gently massaging, and he sighs contentedly as every ounce of tension seeps away with each stroke of my hand.

I'm facing the door and glance over at Constantine

and Tristan, who have been barricading the doorway with their bodies. I knew they were standing there the entire time. We share a look that speaks volumes.

"There's enough room," I tell them.

Constantine pulls the door closed when he and Tristan step inside, and they join us on the bed.

CHAPTER 13

I feel a hand squeeze my calf and blink my eyes open to see Evan at the foot of the bed.

"We've landed."

"We have?" I sleepily ask on a yawn but can't move because I'm wrapped around Hendrix, half-lying on top of him, with Tristan at my back, and have Constantine's arm thrown across our middles from the other side.

With as much as I detest flying, I'm surprised I slept through the bumpy descent and touchdown on the tarmac.

Tristan grumbles and starts to stir, which creates a domino effect and rouses Constantine and Hendrix.

"Car's waiting outside to take us to Falcon Tower. Candace left you some of her clothes to change into. She put them in the bathroom."

Clean clothes that aren't sweatpants in men's sizes would be fantastic.

"Tell her thank you."

Evan's thumb brushes across my ankle bone. "Will

do." He seems nonplussed when he gets three male scowls aimed at him. "I'll meet you outside at the car."

Constantine rolls off the side of the bed to give Tristan room to sit up.

"Your *cousin* needs to watch it."

I don't reply to Tristan's remark and focus my attention on Hendrix. His startling eyes are slightly bloodshot from sleep.

"Hey." I kiss the hollow of his throat.

"Hey back."

Constantine returns from the bathroom, holding the clothes Candace left for me, and I crawl over Tristan, planting a kiss on his lips along the way.

I take the bundle from Constantine's hands, raise high in a stretch so I can plant a swift kiss to his lips in thanks, and trundle into the adjoining bathroom to change clothes. The mirror reflects the horrible state of my hair. It's naturally wavy which means it frizzes at the slightest amount of humidity. I take the rubber band I found at Cillian's from my wrist and quickly pull my thick tresses up into a ponytail.

"Can we make a stop somewhere for food?"

With the plane safely on the ground, my stomach has settled and is happily reminding me that I didn't eat much of the food Cillian fixed for us.

"I'll grab some bags of pretzels."

I wiggle into the white bohemian button pullover blouse and poke my head out so Tristan can see my grimace. "No airplane food. I want a cheeseburger. Very well done," I add, just to mess with Hendrix.

Constantine takes over buttoning the first two buttons on the blouse, making sure my boobs aren't on public display since I'm not wearing a bra. I grip his forearm to hold myself steady and step into a pair of black stretch designer leggings that cut off above the ankle.

"Will you ever go back to being blonde?" Tristan asks from the doorway, his heated gaze set upon my bare sex as I struggle to fit into the tight Lycra.

There's a saying about the carpet matching the drapes, which mine clearly do not. I stifle a giggle when I think about how ridiculous *down there* would've looked if I colored it the same as my rainbow-streaked hair last year.

"Do you want me to go back to being a blonde? Constantine said he liked the red."

I honestly don't care what my hair color is. The only reason I started dying it different colors was to distract people from staring at my left arm. I'd rather have people notice my hair color than the burns.

Tristan rubs his thumb over his lower lip in serious contemplation. "I wouldn't mind seeing you as a blonde again. Just saying."

"If anyone cares to know my opinion, I'm with Con," Hendrix states, finally getting up from the bed.

Con clears his throat, and I caress the backs of my fingers over his Adam's apple. "How's your voice feeling?"

He grabs my wrist and brings my hand up to his lips. "I'm good."

My freaking heartbeat stutters and trips over itself every time I hear him talk. It also reminds me how he lost his voice in the first place. If there is one man who deserves to be wiped off the face of the planet, it's his father, Gabriel Ferreira.

Papa never subjected me to the cruelty and abuse that

the guys suffered regularly at the hands of their fathers. Papa showed me that love, kindness, and compassion were just as powerful as hatred, fear, and brutality. It was an odd dichotomy given the fact that he also taught me how to harness my anger and kill without remorse.

"Where's Gabriel?"

The guys haven't said anything about him. Tristan recently saw his father, and Patrick Knight was at the house last night, but not a word has been said about Gabriel.

Tristan slides by me and rummages around the bathroom vanity until he locates a toothbrush and a small tube of toothpaste.

"We don't know where anyone is, which could mean that Aleksander had them killed. I'll try to reach out to some contacts once we get to Levine's."

He finishes brushing his teeth and rinses the toothbrush off, then applies more toothpaste and hands it to me.

"You could've used Evan's laptop."

"Hell, no."

Hendrix's deep tenor carries from another part of the plane. "Can we please get off this fucking plane now?"

Tristan tips my face up with a fingertip. "When we get to Falcon Tower, you stay close and don't leave our side."

Jesus, not that again, but I keep my mouth closed. Some battles just aren't worth it. I look at Tristan and Constantine. *But some are worth everything.*

Sitting in the cramped back row of the eight-passenger Escalade, I watch the lights of skyscrapers and tall office buildings blur past my window. Whenever I think of Texas, I think of cowboys and the Wild West, not thriving metropolises that are all chrome, steel, and glass. Then again, Texas does boast three of the top ten largest cities in the States: Houston, San Antonio, and Dallas.

I peek over at Tristan's stoic profile. Similar to the drive from Cillian's estate to the private airfield, no one has spoken a word. The car ride has been done in deafening silence, and the closer we get to our destination, the broodier Tristan becomes. I don't have to be a mind reader to know that he's anxious about seeing his sister. I am, too. I don't know how to feel about her or what she did because in every way that has mattered over the last ten years, Alana... Dierdre... has been my mother.

Leaning sideways, I rest my head on Tristan's shoulder. His arm snakes behind me, and he pulls me as close to him as my seat belt allows.

"We'll be there in about five minutes," Evan says from the driver's seat.

"Tell me about Andie. What's she like?" I'm curious about this other cousin I never knew existed.

Evan taps a button on the steering wheel and turns off the soft music that had been playing.

"She's pretty cool, if a bit intense," he replies, hitting the blinker and making a right turn at a stoplight. We pass by a large police precinct with several officers milling about outside on the sidewalk.

"She was at the same school as us in Switzerland," Hendrix pipes in from the seat in front of me.

Only the male children of the Council were allowed to attend the exclusive Swiss boarding school. Daughters were expected to attend an all-girls school in Connecticut.

"Oh?" I reply, hoping to sound casual as that familiar green-eyed flicker of jealousy tries to worm its way out into the open.

Hendrix winks at me over his shoulder. "I know what you're thinking, and the answer is no."

"Andie's birth mother was a McCarthy, but they disowned her when she married Maximillian Rossi," Evan says and slows the vehicle to turn into what looks like a parking garage.

I hold my hands in a T for time out. "Thank you but I'll forgo the genealogy lesson for now. You can fill me in later once my brain doesn't feel like it's been tossed in a blender."

It's almost four in the morning, and I'm dead tired, sore, and in need of a gallon of coffee.

The SUV stops at an understory guard station, and we're greeted by several men who are clearly packing weapons under their shirts.

If Cillian is Irish mafia and Andie is also a McCarthy, then... good grief. Are all my relations in the mob?

Evan's window lowers with a quiet whir as two guys approach the Escalade carrying upside-down mirrors on long poles.

"They're checking for bombs and tracking devices. We may be asked to step outside for a pat down."

I meet Evan's eyes in the rearview mirror. "Seriously?"

Tristan tenses beside me when a terrifying-looking brickhouse of a man leans down and braces his tree trunk arms on the driver's side door. His face is slashed with scars, and tattoos run up his neck and swirl around the back of his shaved head. His stone-cold gaze briefly flicks to me.

"She's waiting for you," the man says with a thick Russian accent.

"Thanks, Pearson."

What an odd name for such a menacing brute.

"Holy shit," Hendrix says as we drive forward and pull into a parking space near the elevators.

"Pearson is ex-bratva and Declan's right-hand man. And FYI, he and Declan are together."

Together? *Oh.* They're lovers. Got it.

A light somewhere above us flickers and creates a strobe effect inside the car. The flashes also bring to attention two more men standing guard outside the elevator.

I peel myself from Tristan's side and look out the window. Nothing but concrete and empty parking spaces.

"A skyscraper in the middle of the city isn't where I would expect a mafia kingpin to live."

Evan shuts the engine off, twists in his seat, and peers back at me. "Declan isn't mafia. He's an arms dealer. Andie is a bit of both. Her husbands used to work for Maximillian Rossi... you know what? It would be easier for her to explain things."

Husbands? As in plural? Surely, I misheard him, but apparently not because Tristan says, "I thought she just got married to Keane Agosti."

"She did, but she's also married to Jaxson West, Liam Connelly, and Rafael Ortiz. Open ceremony. Not exactly legal, but—" Evan blows out a breath. "I'm shutting up now."

I gawk at him, then raise eyebrows at Hendrix when a wicked smile glimmers to life on his gorgeous face.

"No," I preempt whatever crazy thought he's having.

Marriage is something I've never allowed myself to think about. And from the examples I saw growing up, not something I ever wanted. The wives in the Society were expected to look pretty, spread their legs when summoned, pop out a legitimate heir along the way, and turn a blind eye to the copious affairs their husbands were having. My parents were the exception. Or so I thought until *that night*. The fight they had in front of me right before the bullets started flying, the things they said without coming right out and saying them, makes me wonder what secrets they were keeping from me. Papa had hidden me away in Ireland. He'd accused Mama of betraying him. He insinuated that she was willing to trade my life for... what, I have no idea.

Evan opens the car door and gets out.

"Ready?" I ask Tristan.

I can see the 'no' forming, but he jerks his chin and doesn't let go of my hand when he slides across the seat and follows me out.

Evan takes the lead as we walk over to the elevator bay. One of the guards presses the up button, while the other holds a finger to his right ear and speaks quietly into what I assume is a wireless mic.

Within seconds, the elevator doors slide open, and— *holy shit*. The guy standing in the center of the elevator is jaw-droppingly gorgeous. Rich caramel skin and jet-black hair surrounding an exotic face. But it's his light blue eyes that stand out the most. I amend that thought when the man's full lips part in a smile, and he greets us with a friendly hello in an accent similar to Constantine's when he speaks Portuguese.

"Andie apologizes for not being the one to meet you when you arrived, but Sarah woke up from a bad dream, so she's getting her settled back down."

He steps aside, and we take that as our cue to cram inside the lift. It's spacious enough that I don't feel claustrophobic with five large men crowding me.

"Andie has a daughter?" I ask.

The man presses his thumbprint to a biometrics panel, and the lift whirs to life as we start to ascend.

"Niece. Sort of. But yeah, our daughter, too."

I don't know how to respond to that. I slide closer to Tristan's side and readjust the grip of our hands by accordioning our fingers together.

"I'm Rafe, by the way," he adds.

A long pause of silence follows, made more uncomfortable by the fact there is no tinny elevator music playing softly in the background.

"Rafael Ortiz?" Tristan cautiously queries, and Rafe nods.

As if Rafe is a potential threat, Tristan clutches me tightly to him just as Constantine hems me in from the other side. I love how the guys immediately jump in to protect me, but it irks me at the same time because I don't need men to ride to my rescue.

Rafe notices their reaction to his name, and his stunning blue eyes roll skyward as he sighs.

"I'm not my father. Or my brother. And they're dead, so chill the fuck out. Pardon my language," he says to me.

"I've heard worse," I reply but don't get to say more because the elevator jolts to a stop, and the doors slowly gape apart...

...to reveal Alana waiting for us on the other side.

CHAPTER 14

My hand unintentionally crushes Aoife's, and a strangled noise vibrates my throat when I see my sister standing there. Older but the same as I remember. Her dark hair is shorter, angled at her chin, and her skin carries the deeper bronzed hue of someone who enjoys being outdoors. There are laugh lines etched into the creases of her brown eyes and in the corners of her mouth. She looks good. Healthy. Happy. And seeing it makes me furious.

While Deirdre was off playing mom and living a peaceful, contented existence, I was having the shit beat out of me on a daily basis by our father and being forced to live a life I never wanted. I loved my sister, but she apparently didn't feel the same way. She could've taken me with her. She could've reached out at any time over the last ten damn years and let me know she was alive. That Aoife was alive and with her. Instead, she left me in hell and never looked back.

My sister stares at me, and I despise the concern I see

as she takes in the state of my bruised face and swollen lip.

"Are you okay?" she asks like she has every right.

"Don't," I snap. She doesn't get to pretend like everything is normal.

Dierdre's gaze briefly falls to where Aoife's hand is joined with mine before rising to look directly at her. She holds her arms apart as if she's expecting Aoife to come to her; however, Aoife doesn't rush forward and embrace her like I expect her to. Aoife's message to Deirdre is loud and fucking clear. My girl just chose sides. She chose me.

Dierdre's arms listlessly fall to her sides. "Hey, sweetheart. It's so good to see you."

Is she for real?

"You don't get to call her that."

My sister's eyes flash with hurt. "She's my daughter."

The anger I had been struggling to hold in erupts. "She's not your fucking daughter!"

Aoife lays her free hand against my chest. "Tristan, don't."

The tension that suddenly spikes the air around us could choke a person to death. It significantly skyrockets when I catch sight of the man notoriously known as the Grim Reaper stalking down the hall toward us.

Jaxson West's reputation is well-established in our world. The blood, death, and body count left in his wake speak for themselves. Not to mention, the guy is certifiably crazy.

"This her?" he asks Rafe, his pale green eyes behind his wire-framed glasses completely focused on Aoife while he ignores the rest of us like we don't exist.

He doesn't see Con, Hen, or me as a threat. He should. Mr. West isn't the only Grim Reaper in the room. Con's moniker in the Society is Death for a reason.

"I'm standing right here. Ask me yourself," Aoife sasses, and I want to pick her up and throw her back into the elevator and get the hell out of there.

Jaxson's lips twitch. "Your rooms are ready. Down the hall. Pick whichever. The entire floor is yours. Andie fell asleep with Sarah, and I'm not going to wake her just to come down and say hi. Give me your hand."

His long, inked fingers wiggle for her to place her hand in his, which she does. He turns her index finger over onto a tablet I didn't see him holding.

"What are you doing?" she asks as a black line moves down the screen.

"You can now access the elevator and doors using your fingerprint. Anything above level fifty is off limits, so your biometrics won't work for those floors."

Con observes with interest. He loves techie shit.

"What about us?" Hendrix says when Jaxson starts to walk off.

"What about you?" Jaxson coldly replies and disappears around a corner, the sound of a door opening and clanging shut soon following.

Aoife bends forward and peeks around me. "Who was that?"

"Jax." Rafe backs up until he's inside the elevator. "I'll leave you to yell at one another. Just try not to break the furniture or dent the drywall. Fridge and pantry are stocked if you're hungry. If you need anything, just pick up any phone and hit the star, or ask one of the men. Sleep in as late as you'd like. We'll see you whenever you're up and about. Expect chaos."

What the hell does that mean? And what men?

When the elevator doors close, we're plummeted once again into uneasy silence. Dierdre fidgets in place as she looks expectantly between Aoife and me.

"Why are you still here?" Hendrix throws at Evan when he continues to loiter like an asshole.

"Fuck you, Knight."

Evan is an interesting conundrum. By all general appearances, he looks soft. Non-threatening. His good-boy, clean-cut persona would fool anyone, but you can't grow up the son of an Irish mafia don and not be tainted by it. I see the stain on his soul and the steel underneath his exterior. And if he thinks for one second that he's going to weasel his way into Aoife's life, using the pretense of being related... *distantly*... he's going to learn real fucking fast that ain't ever happening.

Dierdre shifts side to side on the balls of her feet. It's something she used to do when agitated.

"Can we please sit down and talk?"

"No," I automatically say at the same time Aoife yanks my hand and says, "Yes."

For fuck's sake. I don't want to talk. I don't want to sit and be forced to listen to whatever false excuses my sister wants to spew to rationalize what she did.

Aoife turns to Evan, and without her having to say anything, he pivots on his heels and leaves in the direction Jax vanished. There must be exit doors that way that lead to a stairwell or something. It also irritates the crap out of me that he can come and go as he pleases. The guys and I will have to rely on Aoife to go anywhere inside Falcon Tower. We're mice trapped in a lion's den—albeit a very nice lion's den.

In the span of a few seconds, I soak in my

surroundings. The floor space is open-concept with modern decor in muted colors of gray and slate blue. Floor-to-ceiling windows that stretch along the entirety of one wall offer an incredible view of the city's breathtaking nighttime skyline, and the back wall adjacent to the hallway has a dark wood bookcase—tall enough to require a rolling ladder—running along it from end-to-end.

"Can we talk *privately*?" Dierdre presses, but she directs it to Aoife, not to me.

In response, Con ambles into the living area and drops down onto a U-shaped leather sectional.

"This is as private as you're going to get," I tell her.

Hendrix keeps side-eyeing the modern chef's kitchen to our left. Not able to stop himself, he saunters over and rifles through the contents of the refrigerator. Taking out a carton of eggs and a block of cheese, he sets them down on the expansive granite counter island.

"Omelets," is all he says as he bangs the lower cabinet doors open and closed looking for a frying pan.

Aoife voices quietly, "How could you not tell me?"

Dierdre appears momentarily stricken before she's able to compose her features.

"Shit," she mumbles, rubbing her forehead. "I knew the day would come. The doctors always said you'd remember when you were ready. I just didn't expect..."

Aoife balks. *"Didn't expect?* Surely you knew something would happen, otherwise, why send me to the same college you knew damn well Tristan, Hendrix, and Constantine were attending?"

Dierdre runs a hand through her short hair. "It's complicated."

I can feel Aoife's muscles lock up. "It's not that

complicated. Every day from the second I woke up in that hospital, you *lied* to me."

"I protected you! I kept you safe!"

Dierdre's shout has everyone's eyebrows raising.

Like a coil that suddenly springs to life, Aoife flies forward, but I pull her back.

"You claim to have kept me safe, yet you manipulated me into going to the one town in the world where I would be in the most danger! Do you have any idea what I've been through this past week? What I've done?"

"Synthia, sweetie, please let me—"

Aoife lets go of my hand and juts it out in front of her, palm facing out. "Do you see the blood of the men I killed yesterday because I sure as hell do? It won't wash off no matter how hard I scrub."

Hearing her say that punches me in the gut and makes me realize that Hendrix is right. Aoife was too good for this life, her heart too pure. In the Society, those qualities are a curse because nothing innocent and beautiful stays that way for long—which makes me a selfish bastard because I won't give her up. Ever.

Hoping to be the voice of reason for once, I say, "Look. We're all dead tired. Whatever needs to be said can be done tomorrow."

Dierdre lets out a dejected puff of breath but nods in agreement. "Synthia, please know this. No matter what you think, I love you with my whole heart. I hope you'll give me a chance to explain everything."

Something akin to panic breaks through my anger when she starts to walk away. My hand races out to catch her, and I pull her to me, crushing her in my arms. I allow a moment of profound gratitude to settle between us. Regardless of the hurt I feel, I'm also thankful as fuck my sister is alive.

"She doesn't belong with you," Dierdre hushes next to my ear before she slips free and vanishes from sight.

CHAPTER 15

"Well, that was…" Painful. Surreal. Soul-crippling. I don't know what to feel.

Turning around, I snuggle into Tristan's chest. I think we both need a hug right now. He buries his face in my hair and strokes a hand up and down my spine that does wonders to ease the tightness that has taken root in my shoulders.

"Awkward as fuck?" Hendrix finishes for me.

I don't agree or disagree. Tristan and I will talk with Alana tomorrow and, fingers crossed, get some much-needed answers.

Hendrix cracks three eggs at once into a bowl. I'm riveted as I watch him do it three more times. He has to teach me how to do that. I'm lucky if I don't run half the egg down the side of the bowl when I try to crack only one open.

"When did you learn to cook? Everything you've made has been amazing."

Hendrix's head lifts as he washes his hands under the

faucet. His self-satisfied smile lets me know how much he likes my compliment.

"Self-taught. When I couldn't sleep, I'd sneak down to the servants' kitchen. Cooking helps relax me."

"Want some help?"

"I've got it." Constantine brushes a kiss to the back of my head on his way to join Hendrix behind the counter island.

After washing up, he pulls a knife from a butcher's block behind him and begins dicing the onion Hendrix left out next to a small wooden cutting board.

The lulling sway of my body with Tristan's puts me in a trance, and I think I may nod off for a few minutes as well, because the next thing I know, Hendrix announces that the omelets are ready.

"Did I really just fall asleep standing up?"

Still holding me, Tristan hobbles us over to the bar stools, then lifts me and sets me down on one of the seats.

"Your snore is adorable."

I smack him in his pectoral. "I *do not* snore."

One side of his mouth lifts, and a dimple appears. "Keep telling yourself that, Red."

Noticing that I'm the only one who sits to eat, per usual, I decide that I'm going to make it a priority once we get back to Darlington to eat regular family dinners together at the dining room table.

Hendrix places the most delicious omelet I've ever seen in front of me. "Eat before you crash, baby. You look about ready to drop."

I feel like I could sleep a month, and it wouldn't be enough. Funny how emotional exhaustion taxes your body worse than physical exertion.

Taking the fork Hendrix presents, I dig in like I haven't had food in a week.

"We need to secure a couple of burner phones," Constantine rasps.

Biting the prongs of the fork between my teeth to free up my hands, I sign, *No more talking. Let your voice rest.*

"Any tea around?" Tristan asks Hendrix.

"I didn't see any. Only coffee."

I perk up at that. "I'd love some coffee."

"No caffeine. It'll keep you up," Hendrix replies.

"Coffee," I insist.

He hands me a chilled bottle of sparkling water from the fridge instead, and I look at it with disgust.

"You are so damn dramatic about the stuff you put in your mouth."

I twist the cap off and take a swallow, liking how the bubbles fizzle their way down my throat.

"Seeing as I've had your dick in my mouth, I disagree."

He snorts, amused, then blatantly makes a show of adjusting himself.

"Problem?" I tease.

"You make my dick hard."

He says it with such serious gravitas, I almost choke on my bite of egg. I guess I'm not the only one with a kink. Then again, based on the stuff I've heard the guys say about Hendrix's sex life and from what I heard Serena scream from his bedroom, Hendrix has way more than one. And as much as I'd love to be angry about all the women he's been with, I know it wouldn't be fair to hold that particular grudge. The guys thought I was dead. Besides, Hendrix and I hashed out what we needed to on the plane. I only hope that with my sexual inexperience, I don't disappoint him and can give him what he needs. I'm sure as hell going to try.

As an afterthought, I tell him, "I want you to get tested."

A little late considering the things we've done.

Not offended in the least, Hendrix replies, "Already did. Results came in the other day. I'm clean."

He did? When?

"I don't know whether to be offended by your presumptiveness that you thought I was a sure thing, or grateful that you took the initiative before I ever asked."

"Once I get my cock inside you, firefly, you'll be screaming the walls down with your gratitude."

Warmth singes my cheeks with a hard blush, and I concentrate on eating and not on the throb between my legs his promise elicits.

"Did Dierdre know you were in New York?" Tristan suddenly asks.

I finish off the food and wipe my mouth with the back of my hand. "No. I told her I was staying at Raquelle's dorm for a girl's weekend. Why?"

"Just trying to figure out how Cillian knew what Aleksander had planned."

Huh. How did Cillian know that Aleksander and Aleksei would be there? He clearly had advance warning. Alana disappeared the day before and wouldn't answer my calls or texts. So, why not warn the guys if he knew? Why let us walk right into a trap that could have ended way differently than it did?

Hendrix collects our empty plates and puts them in the sink. "There's a lot of stuff we need to fucking figure out."

Thinking out loud, I relay, "Aleksei said that Aleksander didn't want me harmed."

Why spare me? I'm nobody to him. Just another random girl he presumes the guys are fucking.

I'm met with crickets. That's how deadly quiet the guys get.

"That doesn't make any sense. He didn't know until —fuck," Tristan says to Hendrix as he weaves his hands into his hair, giving the short strands a tug.

I look over at Constantine to see if he knows what Tristan is talking about. He's been quietly listening, but I can see the wheels working in that big, gorgeous brain of his as he maneuvers the different pieces to the crazy puzzle of the last forty-eight hours into place. However, all of it will have to wait.

I hop down from the stool. "Bedtime."

We aren't good for anything until we get some sleep. I'm barely able to string two words together as it is.

Jax said the bedrooms were down the hall, so that's where I go. They must've done some major renovations to convert the large square footage into a livable space. It's four times the size of Aleksander's apartment in the bell tower.

I head inside the first room I come to with an open door. Typical bedroom. I don't snoop around because the large California king is too enticing, and I happily fall face-forward onto the covers. Every muscle in my body weeps with joy when I sink into the softest pillowtop mattress imaginable.

"Who's sleeping where?" Tristan asks from the doorway.

I roll over. "I want you in here with me. All of you," I clarify when Hendrix's mouth turns grim. "And leave the lights on."

"Any particular reason why?" Tristan asks.

I curl my finger in a come-hither, and when they get close enough, I stand and approach Hendrix first. I'm too sore and too tired for sex, but I've been dying to get a better look at their bodies. At the changes that are evident, the muscles and tattoos.

I take the three of them in, each so handsome in different ways, and I have to lick my lips because my throat goes dry at the magnificent sight.

"Do you think there are any cameras watching?"

I saw several on our way up from the parking garage.

"It's almost a guarantee."

Hendrix breathes deeply when I press my lips to the place above his heart.

"I know this is going to sound weird, but can I take your shirts off?"

"Baby, you can do whatever you damn well please if it means I get to feel your hands on me," Tristan replies.

"Do we get to reciprocate?" Hendrix asks, cupping my breast in his hand and letting his thumb play with my nipple until it hardens under his touch.

Liquid heat pulses to life and settles low in my belly.

I think about the cameras and who may be watching, then decide I don't care.

"Yes, but only if you're good." I smile up into his blue eyes.

"So much damn trouble," he mutters, but he's also smiling.

"Be patient. I want to take my time," I tell them and glide fingertips under Hendrix's shirt to explore the muscled ridges that make up his six-pack.

I let my hands feast on how smooth his skin feels, his abdominals and chest warm and solid. Hendrix doesn't have any chest hair, and I find that I like it as much as I like the soft hair that covers Constantine's chest.

As I move my hands higher up Hendrix's body, the fabric of his shirt bunches. Once I get to his shoulders, he places his arms above his head so I can take his shirt off.

I giggle when I can't get his shirt farther than his elbows, and it becomes stuck over his face.

"A little help. You're too tall."

He does that sexy thing only guys know how to do where he reaches behind him and pulls his shirt off by the collar. My heart rate accelerates when his bare chest is finally exposed. I've had the pleasure of watching him walk around the house without a shirt on, but this time is different. More intimate. Because he's mine now. I can touch, taste, and look to my heart's content.

"Stay right where you are," I tell him and go to Tristan. "Hi."

Tristan tips my face up and kisses me sweetly. "Be kind. I'm not as sexy as Hen with his god-like blond good looks."

I dissolve into suppressed laughter at his playfulness. "I think you're incredibly sexy, Mister Amato."

Midnight falls over his whiskey irises, and I make a mental note that he likes it when I call him mister.

I give Tristan the same slow ministrations as I did Hendrix before stepping in front of Constantine.

"May I?" I ask.

I melt under his black gaze filled with so much need as he intently watches me carefully undress him. His torso is a collage of colors from the beating he took... for me. He let them hurt him because Aleksei held a gun to my head. I kiss each and every bruise as I work his shirt up and off.

The melancholy of my question can be heard when I ask the 'what if' that's been bothering me all day. "Do you ever wonder what could have been if Papa never took me away?"

"Every second of every fucking day for the past ten years, Red."

We were robbed of so much, and I don't ever want to take another second I have with them for granted.

Once I'm done, I admire the three stunning men before me. Constantine is broad in the chest and big everywhere. Hendrix is leaner, his muscles more delineated, while Tristan has a streamlined swimmer's body of strong, wide shoulders that taper to a trim waist.

"God, the three of you take my damn breath away."

Tristan's hands compress into tight fists. "You know it's becoming almost impossible for me not to fuck you right now."

I slowly drag my eyes up his long, thick legs, over his hard cock straining to break free from his pants, and across his torso until I stop on his pouty, full lips. "But you won't because you promised to be good."

My core pulsates at the guttural sound he makes, similar to a low growl.

"Hen promised. I didn't."

"Doesn't matter. He implied the 'royal we' when he agreed."

I relish Tristan's laugh when it breaks free. Over the last week, I've stored away into memory every laugh and smile they've given me, each one treasured.

Needing to touch them, I begin with Constantine, tracing the outline of the red and black inked images that start at his fingers and decorate his entire body up to his neck. Upon closer inspection, I recognize the words interwoven into the tattoos as a mix of languages, some written in Portuguese and some in Latin like *Omnis Magna Potestas Ex Sanguine Et Morte Nascitur.* All great power is born of blood and death. It's the dictum of the Society.

Sliding my hand over his shoulder to his spine, his tanned skin breaks out in goose flesh as I circle to his back.

"You and Hendrix have angels."

"You're our angel," Constantine says.

At first, it doesn't click, but when I see the detail of the angel that spans his entire back, I realize he's being literal. The angel *is* me.

I rush behind Hendrix to look at his. I love how her wings are outstretched like she's about to take flight. "The timepiece," I say, remembering the clock on his left side I got a glimpse of when we were sparring at the gym. "*Counting down the minutes until I see you again,*" I mumble as I read the words that slam into me like a bolt from the blue. It's about me as well, just like the clover on the underside of his wrist.

I go back and forth between Constantine and Hendrix, finding more and more images that represent me. They're covered in them. Covered in *me*. Holy shit.

I briskly wipe away the tears that wet my face when I come to stand behind Tristan. Other than the tattoo of his sister's favorite flower on his upper left chest, the only marks crisscrossing his skin are the ugly scars of abuse his father left.

With my arms wrapped around him, I press my lips to every single line that scores his back. His chest shudders as he inhales a shaky breath.

"I couldn't put you on me," he quietly states. "Doing so would mean that I accepted that you were really gone, and I wasn't ready to let you go."

Goddamn these men and the tumult of emotions they wrest out of me so easily. Not many people are lucky enough to find their soulmate. Somehow, for some incomprehensible reason, I was given three. The Society has it all wrong. Great power isn't born of blood and death. Everlasting love is.

Reaching between them, I grip Constantine and Tristan's forefingers in one hand while taking Hendrix's in the other.

"I have another odd request."

I get three varying degrees of arched eyebrows and curious, cocked heads.

"I want to hold you while we sleep," I say, pulling them with me as I step backward to the side of the bed.

"You want to hold us?" Hendrix asks.

I nod, nibbling my lower lip. It's dumb, but yeah.

When the backs of my knees hit the high mattress, I let go and get situated in the middle, then gesture for them to join me. Without another word spoken, Constantine and Tristan lie down on either side of me. Tristan's hand threads its way into my hair, his head on my breast. Constantine pushes his large body flush with my side and snugly nuzzles his face in the crook of my neck. Hendrix crawls between my legs, using my stomach as a pillow. It's a bizarre tangram of bodies that should be uncomfortable as hell with the way I'm splayed, but it's not. I've got my guys. I'm at peace. I'm whole.

With the lights still on because no one makes a move to get up and turn them off, I close my eyes and begin to softly sing "Too-Ra-Loo-Ra-Loo-Ral" until my voice fades away, and I fall asleep.

CHAPTER 16

Air that smells like powdered donuts puffs across my forehead and drags me out of a deep slumber that I don't want to leave. It takes effort, but I'm able to force my eyelids to spread apart and...

"Jesus!" I yelp when the biggest doe-like chocolate brown eyes stare upside down at me.

"What?" Hendrix exclaims from somewhere in the room.

Did he get out of bed last night and sleep on the floor?

Constantine and Tristan raise their heads from where they had been mashed into the sides of my neck.

"What the fuck?"

A tiny girl with the cutest chestnut-brown corkscrew curls scowls down at a still half-asleep Tristan. "You said a bad word."

Hendrix's blond head pops up over the footboard. "What the hell is a kid doing in here?"

The girl points her little cherubic finger at him. "Dat's a bad word, too. Give me five dollars," she says, but her l's sound like w's. It's the most adorable thing I've ever heard.

"What the fuck for?" Hendrix grumbles and pulls himself off the floor.

"Ten dollars." But she holds up six fingers.

"Bite me, kid."

"Hendrix!" I admonish.

Tristan jackknives into a sitting position, but I can't move because my hair is pinned under the girl, who has decided to stand on my pillow while leaning against the headboard.

"Don't mind him. He's allergic to children," Tristan tells her and lifts her up so I can move.

Fuck you, Hendrix signs instead of saying it, and I burst out laughing.

The girl wiggles out of Tristan's grip and plops right down onto Constantine's chest. She gives him the biggest, dimpled smile.

"You have pwetty pictures, too, like my Unkie Jax," she happily says as she touches each tattoo along his collarbone, one by one.

Hendrix's brows are practically at his hairline. *Who the fuck is this?* he mouths. Picking up a shirt from the floor, he quickly dons it.

I shrug, but I can only assume the girl is Sarah.

Kids, in general, are curious and love to ask a million questions, but she doesn't seem bothered by, or even notice, the bruises and swelling on our faces. It makes me wonder how much ugliness she's seen in her short life.

Constantine grunts when Sarah starts bouncing in place, using him as her own inflatable jumping pillow. Rescuing him, I drag her off his chest and sit her in front of me. Thank God, I'm still in the clothes I was wearing yesterday and the guys are wearing pants, otherwise this entire situation would be very, *very* embarrassing, to say the least.

I clap my hands on my knees, then together, before holding them out for her to give me a double high-five. Sarah eagerly mimics me, repeating the pattern. Alana used to play hand-clapping games like Miss Mary Mack with me. Anything to beat the boredom of being stuck in a hospital bed.

"My name is Aoife. What's yours?"

"Sarah," she replies, the tip of her tongue sticking out as she concentrates on keeping up with the pace of my movements, so our hands touch together at the same time.

Tristan gets up and beats Hendrix to the bathroom.

"Asshole."

I distract Sarah from demanding more money for his bad word by speeding up our hand claps.

"Nice to meet you, Sarah. Where's your Mom?"

Not missing a beat, she chirps like it's no big thing, "She's dead—"

Oh, fuck me. Foot meet mouth.

"—but my Auntie Andie is my mommy now. My daddy is dead, too. My unkies are my new daddies. I have four of them." She stops and holds up six fingers again.

I think I just lost my heart.

Like most children who don't understand personal boundaries, Sarah crawls into my lap and grabs fistfuls of my hair.

"Your hair is pwetty."

I'm pretty sure my hair looks like a bird nest after a wild rave. Bed hair does not look good on me.

I brush a curl off her forehead. "Thank you. So is yours."

"Sarah!" a woman's voice rings from somewhere outside the bedroom. And she does not sound happy.

"Uh oh," Sarah whispers, but she's grinning impishly.

The "expect chaos" Rafe mentioned last night is making sense now.

I edge to the side of the bed and pat my back. "Hop on and I'll give you a piggyback ride."

With a squeal, Sarah crashes into me and wraps her arms and legs around me like a koala.

"I'll start coffee," I tell the guys as I carry an exuberant, wiggly, giggling girl out of the room.

As soon as we get to the end of the hallway, we're met by a gorgeous, exasperated woman. Light brown hair that looks blonde at the roots frames a heart-shaped face. Her arms are crossed over her chest, and her bare foot taps a fast beat on the hardwood floor. Seeing her, Sarah ducks her head behind mine and almost strangles me doing it.

"You're not fooling anyone. I see you, young lady. I told you to leave them alone and not wake them."

Sarah lets go, and I about have a heart attack, thinking she's falling, but she lands like a cat and scurries over to the woman, careening into her legs and knocking her off balance.

With the largest puppy dog eyes rife with emotional blackmail, Sarah looks up and puckers her mouth in a pout.

"I'm sowry."

The woman laughs and musses Sarah's curls. "No, you're not." Then to me, "I am so sorry if she bothered you. She has a knack for sneaking away from adult supervision. Thank God we can track her using the security system. Jax saw she accessed the elevator and came to your floor."

Sarah scrambles up the woman's leg and climbs her like a freaking jungle gym, then throws her arms around the woman's neck and gives her a messy kiss on the cheek.

Chuckling, I reply, "No worries. She's beautiful."

The woman smiles, making her eyes crinkle, which draws my attention to them. They're violet. I've never seen anyone with eyes the color of hers. Maybe she's wearing contacts.

"Thanks. I'm Andie. You must be Aoife."

"And I'm Sarah!" Sarah loudly pipes in, and Andie covers her mouth.

"Inside voice, baby girl."

So, this is the infamous lady mobster with four husbands who's my cousin. She's gorgeous, friendly, adores Sarah, and is probably one of the most intimidating people I have ever met. The darkness inside of me recognizes the same in her.

Untangling the rubber band from what's left of my braid, I smooth the wavy tresses down as much as I can and re-tie them into a ponytail. "Aoife or Syn. I'll respond to either."

Jostling Sarah on her hip, Andie looks me over, not concealing her critical perusal at all.

I freeze mid-step on my way to the kitchen when she says, "I hope whoever did that got what's coming to them."

She's referring to the bruise on the side of my face where Aleksei hit me near the temple with the butt of his gun.

Not wanting to go there, I reply, "Yeah, he did."

Speedwalking into the pantry, I scan the shelves for flour because I'm craving pancakes. It's one of my comfort foods. Spying a yellow box of Bisquick, I grab it as well as a jar of molasses. When I come back out, Andie has Sarah settled on one of the bar stools with a box of crayons and paper.

"You and I are definitely related," she says when she sees the jar of molasses I'm holding. "I can eat my weight in that delicious shit."

"Bad word," Sarah says as she draws but doesn't demand that Andie pay her.

"It's not bad if it's used in a good way."

Sarah takes full advantage of that and begins singing the ABC song, but instead of singing the letters, she gleefully replaces them with the word 'shit.'

With a flamboyant eye roll, Andie hushes her.

"Give a precocious child an inch, and they will steamroll over you."

"How old is she?" I ask as I start a cup of coffee brewing in the Keurig.

She sighs dramatically. "Four going on forty."

It's evident the love Andie has for Sarah, and vice versa. It reminds me a lot of Alana and me.

"You're very good with her."

"Thanks."

I follow where Andie is looking up at the ceiling. There's a blacked-out dome camera mounted in the corner. She makes hand signals behind Sarah, then blows a kiss. Weird.

Looking around, I don't see any sweetener or sugar handy, so I resign to drink my coffee without it even though it'll taste bitter.

I lounge my butt against the counter, mug held securely between both hands. "Have you seen Alana this morning?" I ask, taking a sip and immediately scalding the inside of my mouth.

Andie gets situated on the stool next to Sarah and props her chin in her hand. "It's actually five in the afternoon. Can I ask you a question?"

"Okay," I say slowly, drawing it out.

I don't really know her, which means I don't know if I can trust her, cousin or not.

Before she can ask, the elevator doors open. It's a clear line of sight from the kitchen, and I do a double take when Tristan's doppelgänger steps out. There are obvious differences between Tristan and this man—the new guy is bulkier, and his eyes are hazel, not light brown, but their skin tone is similar, and the new guy carries the same air of authority that Tristan so effortlessly exudes.

This must be who she was gesturing at in the security camera.

The man approaches Andie, grabs her face, and kisses her in a way that curls my damn toes, and I'm not even the one being kissed. Andie notices me gawking.

"Keane, this is Aoife."

Keane. One of her husbands. The new mob boss Tristan and Cillian were arguing about at the dinner table. I wiggle my fingers hello like a dumbass.

"Hey," he says, then places a large hand on Sarah's shoulder and asks, "Whatcha drawing?"

"Picture for Aoife."

"For me?" I lean over the counter island to see what she's doodling. "I love it," I tell her at what looks like flowers. I'm not sure. She's four, not Georgia O'Keefe.

Footsteps sound down the hallway, signaling the arrival of the guys. All three look freshly showered. Which reminds me...

"Do you have any clothes I can borrow?" I ask Andie.

"I'll ask Pearson to get you some. He has an eye for women's clothing."

Thinking of the big, scary Russian I met last night, I stifle my snort of disbelief by taking a big swallow of coffee.

Hendrix ignores Andie and Keane and hip-bumps me out of the way, so he can take over because he's a food diva who can't ever let anyone else even make a sandwich by themselves.

Snatching up the box of Bisquick, he grimaces. "Hell no."

"But—" I shut up, knowing it's an argument I'll lose.

Andie groans when Sarah begins quietly singing the ABC song using "hell" this time. Keane does a bad job of hiding his smile and gets flicked in the ear by Andie.

"Don't encourage the behavior."

I get a little mushy when Constantine sits down on Sarah's other side. She passes him a sheet of paper and a red crayon and instructs him on what to draw.

Tristan curves a possessive arm around me, and I can actually feel the tension that takes over his body when he and Keane eye each other up.

"Nice to see you again, Alexsandria."

"It's just Andie." She studies him for a second. "Tessa said we went to the same school, but I honestly don't remember you."

As brush-offs go, that one felt deliberate.

"We ran in different circles," Tritan easily replies. "And you're Keane Agosti."

Keane's eyes narrow. "Yeah."

"Tristan Amato."

Keane makes a grunt of recognition; however, Andie's entire disposition changes, and she blisters Tristan with a look that could melt iron.

"FYI. Tessa is not going to do your dirty work for you. Don't call her again or ask her for any favors. I don't want her dragged back into this life. She's off limits. Understood?"

Nonplussed, Tristan says, "Understood."

Well, I don't understand. What *dirty work* did Tristan ask this girl Tessa to do for him?

Keane jerks his chin at Tristan. "Since you're here, let's get that meeting over with. Come with me. You, too." He aims a finger at Constantine.

My gaze pings between the guys. "What's going on?"

Tristan kisses me lightly on the lips. "We'll be back soon. Stay here with Hen."

"Now wait a damn minute," I protest, which only gets Sarah going again.

"Damn, damn, damn," she sings as she draws.

Keane tickles Sarah around her ribs until she's a bundle of shrieking giggles and drops her crayon. "Time to go squirt. Declan's going to take you to the park before it gets too late."

Artwork forgotten in lieu of a promise to the park, she swiftly pecks a kiss to Andie's cheek and hurriedly jumps down off the stool, running her little legs as fast as they can toward the elevator.

I hold my hands out in front me in a what-the-fuck gesture. Hendrix shrugs as he mixes ingredients in a large glass bowl, but he won't meet my eyes.

CHAPTER 17

CONSTANTINE

Almost as soon as we get into the elevator, the doors open again to what looks like a gym. There are distinctive grunts of exertion and fists slamming against flesh. Jax and another man are sparring in a boxing square in the center of the room while Rafe leans against the ropes, giving them feedback on their technique.

Keane lifts Sarah onto his shoulders when she tries to make a break for it. "I'll be right back after I drop her off."

So, basically, get the fuck off the elevator.

"But I want to play with..." Sarah's high-pitched whine of protestation is cut off when the doors close.

"I don't want to be here longer than necessary. Once I talk with Keane and see my sister, I propose we get the hell out of Dodge."

See my sister, not get my sister. But I don't question him about it. I don't trust Dierdre. Not after all the shit that has gone down. Everybody is the enemy as far as

I'm concerned.

"Ask him if he can spare a few burner phones and a laptop," I tell him.

And I need to figure out where we can go and lay low for a while until we plan out our next move. Somewhere off grid that Aleksander doesn't know exists.

Tristan and I slowly make our way over to the square. The moves Jax and the other guy are doing look like a mix of fighting techniques—Krav Maga, jiu jitsu, boxing —much like an MMA fighter.

"You just get up?" Rafe asks.

"Woken up by a hyperactive four-year-old is more like it," Tristan replies.

From his side profile, Rafe's cheek creases with a grin. "*Mariposa* can be a handful. Jax! Stop dropping your damn shoulder," he shouts when the other guy gets in a left hook to the face.

A sweaty Jax holds up a middle finger, then promptly lifts his shoulder and blocks the guy's next punch. They're not wearing gloves, only hand wraps that cover the bottom knuckles and wrists. This isn't just two men play-fighting. This is street fighting. Raw, aggressive, underhanded, and dirty.

"Fuck me. That's Liam Connelly," Tristan side-whispers.

Liam's reputation is as bad as Jaxson West's. He's Declan Levine's enforcer. I study the gray-eyed behemoth, looking for weaknesses in the way he fights and finding none.

Liam fakes an uppercut and drops down, sweeping Jax's feet out from under him. The floor vibrates at the impact of Jax's big body hitting the mat. Liam takes advantage and grapples him in a chokehold.

"Get off me, fucker."

"Then tap out, asshole."

Jax goes limp, signaling he's done. Liam springs to his feet, and an exhausted Jax rolls over onto his back, arms flung over his face as his chest rises and falls.

"Why don't you go beat up on the new guys?" Jax suggests.

Liam looks directly at me, smirk firmly in place. Challenge accepted, motherfucker.

I take off my shirt, and Rafe clicks his tongue when he sees the beat-up state of my body.

"Looks like someone already did."

Tristan slides in front of me. "Con, man, don't. Your ribs are broken."

I have a lot of anger that needs an outlet. Anger at Aleksander and Aleksei. Hating myself because I couldn't protect Syn. She almost died because I wasn't strong enough to stop Aleksei. All my training, every life I was forced to take for the Society, meant nothing when Aleksei held a gun to her head. I'd never been so scared in my life.

I need this, I sign.

"Fuck. Fine. But you know she'll lose her shit if you get hurt."

Then I'll have to make sure I don't get hurt.

I'm already barefoot, so I don't have to kick off any shoes before I duck under the ropes and step into the ring. Liam picks something off the mat and comes over with a roll of tape, but I shake my head no. I don't want to wrap my hands. I want to feel every hit and every slice of pain that travels up my arm with each blow.

"You sure?"

I nod yes.

"Not much of a talker?" Liam jokes.

"He doesn't talk," Tristan says from the corner.

"Like, at all?"

I fucking hate when people talk about me and not to me. I should be used to it. Still pisses me off, though.

Jax moves to the other corner where bottles of water are set out on top of a metal stool. He takes one and guzzles the entire thing, but his awareness stays cemented directly on me.

"Will the two of you get on with it so I can go fuck my wife."

"Our wife."

Rafe and Liam break out in matching shit-eating grins just as I throw a forward jab that connects with Liam's face.

He wipes a trickle of blood from his mouth. "So, it's like that, huh?"

Yep.

We circle each other in the ring, deciding who will hold the dominant position. Liam stops; takes a step back. His gaze flicks over me in contemplation, trying to suss my weaknesses through my injuries. The angle of his jaw hardens with determination, and he explodes forward with a roundhouse kick aimed directly at my head. I barely manage to tuck and roll in time.

"Looks like you may have met your match, Liam."

"Shut it, Rafael."

Using the distraction to my benefit, I execute a punch-kick combo which completely knocks Liam off balance. He counters with a flurry of kidney punches that hurt like hell because of my ribs. I'm able to get him to back off with hard knee thrusts to his stomach.

"What the fuck? I was only gone for five minutes,"

Keane barks, but my focus never strays from my opponent.

We spend the next five minutes trying to beat the shit out of one another. Our sparring becomes more desperate as we duck and weave away from each other only to clash moments later, neither of us wanting to relent. I'm most definitely going to feel every one of Liam's punches later, but the fight itself does wonders to help release some of the chaos that has been boiling over inside of me.

In my peripheral, I see Rafe hold up a Benjamin. "Hundred bucks says Liam takes him down in the next two minutes."

"You're on," Tristan agrees.

"Are they seriously betting on us?" Liam's breaths are coming hard and fast.

I grunt in answer and jump out of the way when the slight dip of his right arm signals that he's about to strike. Twisting under and around, I use the heel of my foot to kick out his knee.

Fingers pinched together and held between his teeth, Keane shrills an ear-splitting whistle.

"That's enough."

"Aww, come on! I had a hundred on the line," Rafe complains.

Liam holds out a fist, and I bump it. It's that simple. Fight's done and no hard feelings.

Jax walks over with two hand towels. He tosses one at Liam's head but holds the other out for me.

"Good to see the rumors aren't just bullshit—Death."

I want to roll my damn eyes. Can't stand that godforsaken name, but coming from him, it's a compliment. A show of respect.

I take the towel he offers and mop the sweat from my face. Tristan and Keane are deep in discussion when I exit the boxing square and grab my shirt. The T-shirt sticks uncomfortably to the sweat on my back when I slip it over my head and take a seat on the elevated platform of the ring next to Rafe.

"Your business is with Declan, so I don't know why you wanted to meet with me."

"My father wants access to the ports you control here."

We don't even know if Francesco is alive. If not, Tristan just inherited the entire Amato empire.

Keane crosses his arms over his chest. "The answer is no."

Tristan bristles. No isn't a word he's used to hearing. "Shouldn't this be something you want to discuss with Andie and Declan first?"

Keane cocks his brow at Jax as if saying, *"Did you hear what this asshole just said to me?"*

"There's something else we need to clear up. I can't let your woman's problems be a distraction for Andie. We've got our own shit to deal with and Sarah to look after."

"Not asking for your help, Agosti. And that woman's name is Aoife. You have no fucking clue what she's been through. I don't give a fuck about your problems or your mob war. I only care about her, and if Aoife wants to try and build a relationship with Andie, you *will not* get in her way."

Keane shoves into Tristan's personal space, thumping chests and getting up in his face. "That so?"

I prepare to jump in, but Rafe beats me to it and shoves Keane away from Tristan.

"Aoife's family now. She deserves a chance to get to know Andie and Declan. And you damn well know that Andie wants the same thing."

Keane drags a hand across the dark stubble of his jaw. "We can't get involved in their civil war. So goddamn stupid. A bunch of rich assholes with nothing better to do than fight over who is top dog of a secret society that doesn't mean shit."

Tristan's spine goes ramrod straight at Keane's slight. "Like you're any better. The mob is nothing more than thugs with guns. At least we're discriminating about who we kill. I heard about what you did in New York, all the families you slaughtered."

Keane jabs a threatening finger at Tristan. "You don't know a damn thing."

"Whatever, jackass. I'd like to see my sister now."

There's a bell-like ding, and Jax reaches down to snatch a phone off the floor. His blond brows scrunch behind his glasses as he looks at the screen.

"That may not be possible since Andie, Aoife, and your sister just left the building."

CHAPTER 18

I'm stuck in a baffled disposition as I watch Tristan and Constantine leave with Keane.

"They'll be okay," Andie assures me. "And it gives us some time to get to know one another better. I'm Andie, by the way," she says to Hendrix's back.

He lifts a casual hand hello, not quite being welcoming and not quite being outright rude.

"That's Hendrix."

Needing to do something to help ease the pent-up nervous energy I'm suddenly feeling, I go to the fridge and grab whatever fruit is available: Honeycrisp apples, navel oranges, and red seedless grapes. Perfect for a simple fruit salad. Not wanting to waste time searching the kitchen for a cutting board, I lay out multiple sheets of paper towel across the countertop. As Hendrix spoons circles of batter onto a hot griddle, he reaches behind him with his free hand and casually cups my ass when I try to grab a cutting knife from the block next to the gas hob.

I never liked being touched, but I've come to crave all the casual touches from the guys—the way Tristan constantly plays with my hair, or the possessive way Constantine holds me, or the deliberate sexual come-ons from Hendrix. It feels good to have someone touch me because they want to, not because they're curious about what my scars feel like.

I kiss Hendrix's shoulder blade and turn back around to Andie.

"I didn't know I had any other relatives until Cillian told me."

The string of falsehoods I've been force-fed since I was born turns my stomach. It also makes me wary of the woman sitting in front of me. How can I trust what she, Cillian, and Evan say when my own damn parents and the woman I loved as a mother all lied to me?

She chuckles like she's recalling an inside joke. "I hope he didn't mess things up too badly. He's a good man, just rough around the edges."

I wash my hands, then rinse the apple with tap water before cutting off the outer skin and dicing it into cubes.

"He was the one who saved me." I'm still reeling over that revelation.

Her lilac gaze drops to my scarred arm. "I didn't want to pry."

I temper my reply with a fake smile. "That's good because I don't want to talk about it."

Hendrix twists slightly to look over his shoulder at me before returning to flipping the pancakes.

"Cillian kind of saved me, too. Not in the same way, but it's a long story that will require bottles of tequila. When he called and asked if Dierdre could stay for a while, I didn't ask any questions. He protected Declan after—" She pauses. Taps a nail to the granite counter. Shakes her head. "Rafe told me what happened last night with Dierdre, and I feel like I can't *not* ask now. Are the two of you in danger?"

Her worry sounds sincere, and I'm not sure how to answer her question because Aleksander is the one who should be worried. The things he set in motion won't end well for him. I'll make sure of it.

"Not if I can help it," I eventually reply.

I lift the orange up to my nose for a sniff, then start peeling it. Vibrant pops of citrus fragrance the air and mix with the buttery aroma of pancakes.

"Is there anything I can do to help?" she asks.

I find her offer both sweet and suspicious. Would it come with strings attached or future favors owed to the mob? That seems to be the way of things with her and Cillian.

Setting the orange down, I brace my hands on the lip of the cool granite. "Actually, there is. You can tell me how Cillian knew what Aleksander and his brother had planned and why he didn't warn us."

I hear the barely audible whoosh of the gas turning off, then Hendrix is at my back. He's a good half foot taller than me, which puts the top of my head at his clavicle. I get distracted when his long fingers curl into my hip, sending tingles scurrying across my skin.

Andie summons a placid poker face, much like the one Constantine wears when he doesn't want you to see that he knows something you don't.

"Answer her."

Andie's shrewd, violet eyes darken ominously at Hendrix's gruff command.

"I'm going to let that slide… this time. Next time, I'll

kick your ass if you ever talk to me in that tone of voice again."

Hearing her threaten Hendrix triggers old, buried wounds. There was nothing I could do when I was a kid to protect him from the horrors his father inflicted upon him. But I'm no longer a kid.

"You won't ever get that chance, *cousin*," I enunciate with a deadly calm.

Hendrix hardens his grip on my hip while another, lower, part of him hardens against my backside.

Andie's brown-blonde hair sweeps her shoulders when she sits back, tilts her head. "I apologize. I tend to react badly to male authority." Something vibrates, and she stands up and takes a cell phone out of the back pocket of her jean shorts. "Sorry. I need to take this."

As soon as she spins around, phone to ear, and paces to the windows, Hendrix runs his hand across my stomach and yanks me backward.

"I want to fuck you so bad right now."

I gasp when he takes my earlobe between his teeth and moan when he does something wicked with his tongue that has my eyes rolling back.

"Hearing you talk shit like a badass makes me crazy."

A throat clears, and I blush scarlet at Andie's knowing grin.

"After the park, Declan is going to take Sarah to dinner and keep her with him and Pearson until morning. It's been for-*fucking*-ever since I had a girls' night out."

The only thing close to girls' night out I had were the stargazing picnics Alana and I would take whenever the mood struck, and the night sky was clear and cloudless.

"And you're coming with me." Andie walks over,

hooks her arm through mine, and drags me away from Hendrix.

"Wait—" I try to protest, but she's already whisking me away and unceremoniously shoving me into the elevator.

A furious Hendrix charges after us. "What the fuck am I supposed to do? I can't leave this bloody floor without—"

The elevator doors close.

"Take me back," I demand and go for the biometrics thingy so I can make the elevator return to my floor. I stop short when I see Andie's pale face and thinned lips.

She waves a dismissive hand at me. "Just hate closed spaces. I'll be fine."

I mash my finger to the pad and hit various buttons. "I can't leave the guys."

And I'm freaking starving. I wanted those pancakes.

"On the contrary," she says when the loud *bing* indicates we're at our destination and I'm being herded once again.

"I need to talk to Alana."

"You can do that, too, since she's coming with us."

"Coming with you?" Alana asks from the couch where she's reading a paperback. Like she's on fucking vacation.

I stutter to a halt and become a deer in headlights. I wasn't prepared to see her yet, and I wanted Tristan with me when I did.

"Uh, hey."

Her smile is soft and very, very guarded. "Hey, sweetheart."

Andie slinks away, trying to be inconspicuous and failing miserably. I could kick her right now for putting me in this awkward confrontation that I was in no way ready for.

Alana sits up and genteelly crosses her legs. I'm used to seeing her in regular clothes. Jeans and a tee. Her makeup, styled hair, and the dressier trousers and crop blouse she's currently wearing are a stark reminder of the posh, wealthy lifestyle she used to enjoy as the daughter of Francesco and Helena Amato.

She sets aside the book and clasps her hands tightly in her lap. "Tristan not with you?"

"I honestly have no idea where he is. Keane snapped his fingers and demanded he and Constantine go with him. Then Andie kidnapped me."

Hendrix is probably losing his mind. He's also trapped and can't go anywhere.

"I did not kidnap you!" Andie yells from one of the back rooms.

"She really did."

Wiping her hands down her slacks, Alana stands and licks her nude-glossed lips. "I know you must be so confused."

Understatement of the year.

Instead of saying, *now why would you think that,* I just ask, "Why?"

One minuscule three-letter word that feels bigger than the universe because I'm not asking her why Tristan and I should be confused. That one interrogative represents all the other millions of whys I want to know.

Andie rushes into the room dressed in a new outfit of black leather skintight pants that fit every curve of her shapely, toned body, and a red halter top that does wonderful things for her chest.

"Nope. All that shit can wait until after I get thoroughly tipsy and maybe do some bad karaoke." She says to Alana, "You look fine." Andie thrusts an outfit at me. "You, however, need to change. Quickly."

I stand there like an idiot, holding the sexiest black lace bustier cami top I have ever seen and a pair of black high-waisted liquid leggings.

"You're out of your goddamn mind."

CHAPTER 19

I am officially Alice at the bottom of the rabbit hole after she scarfed down the "Eat Me" cake and grew nine feet tall, and every creature in Wonderland could see her from a mile away. That's how exposed I feel in this outfit. My disgusting burns are on open display, and I want to both cringe and preen because if it weren't for the scars, I'd think I'd look hot as hell.

The bar Andie whisked Alana and me to isn't that different from the Bierkeller, if you don't count the four gorgeous female employees doing a Coyote Ugly on top of the bar. It's barely past six o'clock, and the place is already packed, mostly with men wearing suits fresh from a long day at the office. It's weird being on the other side of things as a customer and not a waitress. I'm a fish out of water, and my blatant gawking makes that extremely evident.

"You look beautiful!" Alana yells at me over the small high-top table Andie told us to sit down at while she ordered our drinks.

I made sure to sit at an angle, so my left arm faced the wall and was out of direct view. The ambient temperature in the bar borders on stifling from all the body heat being given off. Sweat beads between my breasts and along the dip of my spine.

I shrug a bare shoulder in response to Alana's comment and continue to look around. We've barely spoken to each other since Andie ambushed us with this out-of-the-blue girls' night out to a bar. I hate the wall that has sprung up between us, its reach so high that it seems insurmountable. I used to be able to tell Alana anything, and now I can't even summon a single syllable to say.

Regardless, whatever conversation we're going to have, it's not going to be in a public bar surrounded by strangers. So why am I here again? Oh yeah. My pushy cousin who doesn't understand the word no.

The upbeat country song ends, and the bar erupts with raucous male shouts of appreciation as the women who'd been dancing blow kisses, send winks, and get back to serving drinks.

I jump when four shot glasses get slammed down on the table.

"Drink up because the guys will be crashing our fun soon."

I look expectantly toward the entrance but only see one of Andie's bodyguards who followed us here. There are several others wandering around, ever vigilant and watchful. It's sad that she can't go anywhere without an entourage of armed escorts.

Andie takes one of the drinks, throws her head back, and consumes the entire thing.

I contemplate the clear liquid in front of me. "You

know I'm not legal, right?"

But I'm tempted. Alana didn't keep alcohol at the house, and my party life at school was nonexistent, mostly because I wasn't invited to any of them. I yearn to experience this rite of passage that every other young adult gets to have. Drink, dance, be loud and silly and reckless.

"They won't card you." Andie holds up a second shot glass, waiting for us to lift ours.

"It's alright if you want to," Alana tells me.

"I don't need your permission."

I feel like shit as soon as I say it. I don't mean to be a bitch, but I can't get past that she lied to me and hurt Tristan in the cruelest of ways.

Lifting the small drink, I mumble, "what the hell," then proceed to choke as it burns its way down my esophagus.

"Oh my god," I cough. "Is this tequila? My throat is on fire."

Because I'm not twenty-one, I'm not allowed to make drinks or work the bar at the Bierkeller, but I can deliver them to the tables.

"Yes, and you need at least three more of them."

Alana daintily sips hers like a fine wine, whereas I'm about to spontaneously combust. That was awful. How do people drink this crap?

Shaking my head, I push the shot glass across the smooth wood of the small table. "Nope. One is enough."

Of course, Andie doesn't listen to me and signals one of her bodyguards, who promptly goes over to the bar and flags down a bartender.

"I thought tequila shots involved lime slices and salt."

Andie makes a sour, disgusted face. "This shit is pure

deliciousness on its own."

"At three-thousand dollars a bottle, I hope so," Alana says.

"What?" I exclaim a little too loudly and garner a few head turns from the table next to us.

The bodyguard, a man who looks like he could be Raquelle's bigger, taller brother, comes back over with a tray laden with drinks.

"Thanks, Z," Andie says as she removes them one by one and lines them up in the middle of the table. There are a dozen total. She really is out of her mind.

Rubbing her hands together excitedly, Andie makes eye contact with me, then Alana.

"Here's the game. Truth or dare. You fail to answer a question or do a dare, you have to drink."

"No."

"Yes."

"No," I say more sternly.

"I'll start," Andie replies.

Jesus fucking Christ.

Andie aims her unnerving violet gaze at me. "Truth or dare?"

Stubbornly, I cross my arms over my chest, refusing to play. Unfortunately, one of the guys sitting at the adjacent table to my left goes slack-jawed when he sees the burns on my arm. He elbows his friend beside him.

Every second they stare, the tighter my skin constricts until its confines strangle me. There's an idiom where someone says they feel uncomfortable in their own skin. For me, that figure of speech is a physical manifestation. The longer these assholes stare, the more painful my skin squeezes around me until it feels like I can't breathe.

But before I can say the very unkind thing that's on the tip of my tongue, Alana beats me to it.

"Fuck. Off."

I've never heard her utter even a mild cuss word before.

At being called out, both guys' eyes widen, and their heads whip back around to the people sitting at their table.

"Want Z to take them out back and remind them it's not polite to stare?" Andie asks, all serious.

"No. I'm used to it." The rude stares still bother me, though. People need to learn to mind their own damn business.

Alana doesn't try to expound platitudes or tell me to ignore them. I go stock-still when she reaches across the table and brushes her hand down my hair, looping a loose strand behind my ear. Examining my bruise, her finger traces its outline.

"We haven't gotten a chance to talk, but could you at least tell me if you're okay. Did you get hurt?"

I circle a sarcastic hand in front of my face, because obviously I did.

Alana sighs. "Sweetheart—"

"Can I get a basket of fries?"

I'm starving. I'm also not stupid. Hard liquor on an empty stomach equals trouble for someone like me who doesn't drink. But I have a sneaking suspicion that is exactly Andie's intent.

Andie texts someone on her phone. "Done. Z will get it. Okay, truth or dare."

"Truth," Alana replies.

The music coming over the inset ceiling speakers changes from country to an upbeat Top 40 pop song,

179

but I can barely hear it over the din of overlapping conversations taking place around us. The acoustics in the bar are horrible and echo off the walls like a loudspeaker. I'm getting an earful of someone telling his buddy about a coworker he banged during lunch in one of the men's restroom stalls at work. Classy.

"Why did you fake your death?" Andie asks, and her question rams into me like a wrecking ball. Is she really going there just like that?

I eyeball daggers at my cousin, killing her a million times in the most gruesome ways my mind can imagine.

"What is wrong with you?"

She has the nerve to actually fucking shush me.

"My father was going to give me to a man who I despised. A marriage contract had been signed without my knowledge or my consent. I only found out about it right before I… did what I did," Alana says, looking down at her hands to pick at a cuticle. "I was sold like a cheap whore. I didn't know any other way out."

"You too?" Andie says, and I think my jaw hits the table.

I pound my palms on the tabletop. "Wait, wait, wait. Back the hell up. How can you be married to someone without knowing about it?"

I get double incredulous, raised eyebrows.

"You, of all people, know how things work in our world. Women don't get a voice," Alana replies.

That's not true. My mother was an integral, high member of the Society. My father never treated her like secondhand chattel. Not to mention, I was next in line to lead the Council.

Andie points at herself. "And I wasn't officially

married to the sadistic asshole. Only promised to him, but same difference. Alright, your turn," Andie says to me.

The abrupt switch takes me by surprise.

"Not a chance in hell."

She picks up a drink and pushes it at me. "You know the rules."

I could argue. Yell that this game is absurd. Get up and leave. But damn my curiosity. If this is how I get some answers, then I'll play along.

"Whatever." I tip the drink back and get the same fireball sensation scorching a trail of lava down my throat.

After I flip over and place the empty shot glass on the table, I ask Andie, "Truth or dare?"

"Seeing as I just said a truth, it's Alana's turn again."

"That's cheating."

"Truth," Alana quickly says.

Andie sticks her tongue out at me in victory like a five-year-old. The eye roll I give her in return is just as childish.

Turning in my seat in Alana's direction, I consider the woman who I love so much but who I'm also so angry with.

I already know what I want to ask. There must have been some shady stuff done in order to get me a new social security number, a new name, and I'm sure a fake birth certificate. Like witness protection kind of stuff that only the federal government can do. Without those types of identification, I wouldn't have been able to enroll in public school or college.

"Why did you pretend not to know who I was?"

I pick up a drink and offer it to her, expecting her not

to answer, so I'm completely floored when she does.

"Caroline was the only person I trusted. I went to her for help. She told your father, and that's how I met Cillian. I was with him that night." Her glossy eyes bore into me with a deep sadness. "I couldn't let you die. Cillian gave us both a new life. Somewhere safe where no one knew who we were."

My heart gives one gigantic thud.

"But I thought..." I thought Cillian was the one who saved me.

He never actually said he did. Only that he was there.

And so, apparently, was Alana. She brought me back from death. Her arms tenderly held me as I bled all over the living room rug, still smoking from the fire that had charred the left side of my body. So much horrific pain. I wanted to die. I wanted it all to end. But she wouldn't let me go.

Black occludes my vision and circles around me, fading everything away in a fog of gray. I'm back in that room at the mercy of the constellation man who took everything from me.

"So, you and Tristan?"

Like coming out of a trance, I snap to attention. "What?" My head swivels around so fast I get dizzy. Or maybe the effects of the tequila are hitting me faster than I thought.

"You and Tristan," she repeats, but it's the biting way she says it that tells me she doesn't like the idea of me and her brother together.

Regardless, there is no way I'm telling my adoptive mother that I'm in a relationship and sleeping with three men.

"Pass," I reply.

Andie grins devilishly. "Drink up, cuz."

I draw back from the table as far as my chair will let me. "I didn't agree to a truth."

"So, you want a dare?" Andie counters just as my basket of fries gets plunked down in front of me. I take a fry, still hot, and bite into it.

"Yep," I robotically reply before realizing my faux pas and say, "No."

God only knows what dare she'd demand I do.

Andie taps a black-polished fingernail to one of the shot glasses. Dammit.

I drink that one and immediately feel its compounded effects when it mingles with the other two in my stomach. My thoughts go a little fuzzy, and my mood seems to mellow like melted candle wax. The tension in my body eases, and I slump forward, elbow on the table and propping my chin in my hand, as the world around me goes soft and a little fuzzy. Tequila isn't so bad.

Or maybe tequila is the devil because the next thing I know, when Andie asks me truth or dare, my slightly inebriated brain chooses dare.

CHAPTER 20

"Will you calm down?" Tristan says as we follow Rafe and Keane down a busy sidewalk heading to who knows where the hell Andie took Syn.

The five of us bulldoze our way through slow ambling pedestrians who are too busy looking at their phones and not where they're going.

"You fucking calm down."

I couldn't leave our floor because I couldn't access the elevator or stairwell door. I hate feeling trapped, and he damn well knows it.

Con brushes up beside me, a gentle shoulder bump, but it's enough to recenter me. I release an irritated breath that I regret immediately when my lungs fill with the exhaust fumes from idling cars stuck in bumper-to-bumper traffic. The sooty emissions choke the air from a mass exodus of people trying to flee downtown and get back home. The ones who stick around after their nine to five workday stay for the restaurants and bars that litter the city, wanting an extra hour or two before they venture back to their chaotic suburban lives of familial responsibility, a nagging spouse or hyperactive kids they want to avoid. Others, the single ones, stay because being around people is better than returning to an empty apartment alone.

"How do you know where they are?" Tristan asks.

Keane smirks over his shoulder. "Tracking device implanted in her arm. You should get Aoife one."

That actually horrifies me. "No one is chipping Syn like a goddamn dog."

Tristan, however, gets a thoughtful look on his face. "It's not much different than location share on her phone."

"Which she gets the choice to turn on and off," I point out. Having something inserted into your body that you have no control over takes away that choice.

"We're here," Rafe says.

The heavy beat of music thumps out into the street from the nondescript bar whose only obvious accoutrement, other than the name of the establishment, is a giant neon sign that decorates the front window, flashing "Girls, Beer, and a Good Time" in bright, blinding hot pink.

As soon as Keane pulls the heavy solid wood entrance door open, we walk into chaos. The bar is crammed with loud noise, louder shouts and cheers, and more people than should be legally allowed by the city's fire marshal.

A bass-heavy remix of Rihanna's "S&M" blares in surround sound from all directions, but it's what's happening at the bar that has me, Tristan, and Con stopping dead in our tracks.

The recessed lights above the bar act as spotlights,

instantaneously drawing my gaze to Syn's seductively writhing body. She's dancing with three other women on top of the bar, but my eyes are only for the hot redhead dressed in a sexy, form-fitting outfit that showcases every sinful curve of her luscious body, long legs, and toned arms.

Syn usually hides her scars with long sleeves, but the outfit she has on now is far from the rooster tees and shorts she parades around the house in. And fuck me if my dick doesn't go rock hard at the sight. Those sleek black pants she's wearing appear poured on, and her legs look a mile long with the high-heeled ankle boots adorning her feet. All that gorgeous flame-red hair is loose and flowing over her bare shoulders. Her moves are carefree, her face flushed, her smile wide and dreamy. There's zero sweet or innocent in the way Syn dances. The rotation of her hips, her hands in her hair, head back and eyes closed, are all pure seduction and sex. Something the men lasciviously ogling her are very aware of.

She looks so beautiful, and so fucking *mine.*

"Is that?" Tristan starts to say.

"Yeah."

"Fuck me."

Yeah.

Con doesn't wait around. He parks his ass right in front of where she's dancing, but I can't seem to move. That jealous, possessive beast inside of me wakes up and bares its teeth. I want to kill every single man here for looking at her with lust in his eyes. For wanting what doesn't belong to him.

"Should we get her down?" Tristan asks, but he's just as affected by her as I am.

Syn is our Siren, and we would gladly die just for the chance to touch something so breathtaking and magnificent.

"Let her have her fun," Rafe says.

I honestly forgot that he and Keane were there.

Something in the back corner of the bar snags their attention—or should I say two someones. Andie and Dierdre are watching Syn, amusement on their faces.

I haven't been able to process the fact that Dierdre had Syn all these years. Both of them were only a few states away, so close and right under our noses.

"You want to go deal with that?" I ask Tristan.

"Not particularly," he replies.

The sooner he has whatever talk he needs to have with his sister, the sooner we can leave Texas. Each second we're away gives Aleksander more opportunity to solidify his control within the Society and spin what he and Aleksei did. The truth wouldn't matter because we wouldn't be there to tell anyone what really happened.

"We're taking Andie home. Stay as long as you like. Z will drive you back to Falcon Tower," Keane says, indicating who Z is.

"Take my sister with you."

"You sure?"

Seemingly satisfied with Tristan's nod, Keane and Rafe disappear into the crowd.

"You can't avoid her forever, T. Say what you need to say so we can get gone."

My feet finally decide to unroot from the floor. It takes a few shoves and one not-so-accidental elbow to someone's face before I'm able to push a path through the three rows of men blocking me from getting a front-row seat to my girl.

Syn's pale bluebonnet eyes widen, and she falters a step when spots Tristan and me just as we slot in next to Con. I rove my gaze up her long-legged length in clear appreciation and crook my finger for her to come closer. My blood pumps wild, funneling directly to my aching cock when she drops down in front of us. The image she makes on her knees—an enticing position of supplication—fires to life every salacious synapse in my debased brain until all I can think of is how many ways I can ruin her. Syn was virginal and pure as white fucking snow, but her sexual curiosity is the exact opposite.

She leans in, her voice low and soft as she sings the lyrics to the song. Something about how good it feels being bad and pain is pleasure, but it's when she gets to the part about whips and chains that my cock jerks excitedly.

Con's the only one who has gotten to fuck her. I know we need to deal with a lot of shit right now, but I don't know how much longer I'm going to be able to hold back and not take her like a savage animal. Syn has had me twisted up since the moment we met, before I even realized who she really was. I should be ashamed of the thoughts in my head. She was my childhood best friend. My sunshine. But there is nothing friendly about the things I want to do to her.

"You drunk, firefly?" I ask when I detect traces of vanilla and caramel on her breath and see her glassy eyes and dilated pupils.

"Maybe a teeny tiny little bit," she says with a mischievous curl of her decadent lips. "Andie dared me."

A pushy asshole encroaches into my space, his shout obnoxiously loud. "Damn, baby. You are one hot little piece. Come sit on my lap, pretty girl."

Hearing his disrespectful comment, a hot wave of rage curls its tendrils around me.

Tristan tips back on his stool to see who said it. "What the fuck did you just say?"

Con stands up in a single, smooth, intimidating movement, ready to beat some manners into the annoying ass, but it's Syn who puts the wanker in his place.

"Why would I want you when I have them?"

One by one, she pulls Con, and then Tristan by the collar, and kisses them. Every second I wait for her to come to me is torment. When she does, Syn slides gracefully off the bar into my lap, grabs my throat in her delicately strong hand, and strokes her tongue inside my mouth like she fucking owns me—which she does. I taste the tequila she must have been drinking, and I swear I get drunk off her kiss.

The breathy mewl she releases when I fist her hair at the nape and pull is something I'm desperate to hear over and over. With the long line of her neck exposed for the taking, I fucking take, not caring one iota that we're in a bar and have eyes on us.

The lights above us dim, and the music pulses a slower, hypnotic beat. I scoop under her thighs and lift her up, loving the heat of her pussy against my stomach when her legs wrap around me.

I pull back slightly, so I can see her eyes. "How tipsy are you?"

I want her to have a clear enough head for what I have planned.

Draping her arms loosely over my shoulders, Syn wrinkles her nose and squints her eyes. So damn cute.

"Would it matter?"

"No." Brutal, honest truth.

Time stands still when she bursts into melodic laughter. The beauty of her happiness is mesmerizing because *I* did that. I put that smile on her face.

"You going to let me fuck you tonight?"

With her lips at my ear, she pants, "Yes."

"No, she most certainly *is not*. Get your hands off her, Hendrix."

I turn around—Syn still in my arms, her mouth doing dangerous things to my neck—to see Tristan holding back a livid Dierdre.

Well, shit.

CHAPTER 21

Hendrix sets me on my feet, and I don't resist when Alana snatches my arm and pulls me away from the guys.

"We're going to the ladies' room. Do not follow us," she says to Tristan.

Alana navigates through the crowd with me in tow, the short distance to the back hall feeling like a walk of shame. Or worse, like I'm a recalcitrant child who needs to be scolded for being naughty.

As soon as she shoves the restroom door open, she loses her shit.

"What in the hell do you think you're doing?"

The level of her ire hits me like a slap across the face. I was going to tell her about me and the guys when Tristan and I talked to her. I'm not hiding our relationship or what they mean to me, not from Alana or anyone else.

Speaking to her not as my adoptive mother but as Tristan's older sister, I reply, "You remember how close

Tristan, Hendrix, Constantine, and me were as kids."

"That doesn't mean you make out with them in a public bar!" she shouts.

The severe fluorescent strip lights imbue the one-stall restroom with a hideous shade of yellow, causing everything in the small, enclosed space to look jaundiced.

Alana pinches an aggravated line across her forehead. "Are you sleeping with them?"

I'm given a moment of reprieve when the door cracks open.

"Oh, gosh. I'm so sorry. I didn't know it was occupied. It wasn't locked," a woman hastily rambles.

I turn to the sink to wash my hands, needing the extra time to think about how I'm going to broach the subject of being in love with the three men who used to be my childhood best friends.

"You don't understand," is what I wind up saying, which isn't helpful at all.

"I think I understand perfectly. Jesus, Synthia. You're not a kid anymore, and neither are they. And Hendrix —"

I don't like how she sneers his name like he's someone disgusting and beneath her.

Drying my hands with paper towels from the dispenser, I rotate back around to face her.

"What about Hendrix?"

"You don't understand the man he's become. He's not the little boy you once knew. He's twisted and—"

"Stop."

She rants right over me. "Has he told you what Eva—"

"I said stop."

"And Constantine is—"

My temper bubbles to the surface. "Enough, Mom!"

Calling her Mom puts an abrupt halt to whatever secrets she was trying to spill. Those secrets are the guys' to share with me, not her. So much has happened to all of us during the years we were separated, and that amount of baggage takes time, love, and patience to unpack.

A fleeting... *something*... passes over her face. "Hendrix and Constantine don't care about the collateral damage they cause or who they hurt. They're dangerous."

"So is Tristan, or does he get a free pass because he's your brother?"

Tristan's darkness is more subtle, not as visible as mine or Hendrix's or Constantine's. He hides it behind a cocky attitude and smart-ass wit. That doesn't make him less deadly when crossed. The exact opposite. He showed me a brief glimpse of it when we were caught outside in the rainstorm. I remember the fear that skated up my spine when I turned around. His cold, deadly expression when he thought I was about to walk away and leave.

As I toss the balled-up paper towels into the trash receptacle, I experience one of those metaphorical lightbulb moments of clarity. She seems to be aware of a lot of things for someone who faked her death and erased her existence.

"How long has Cillian been spying on them?"

Alana averts her gaze. Her refusal to answer tells me what I need to know.

Blood oaths, manipulations, and secrets. Evan saying he was forced to attend Darlington Founders, and his proclamation that *'it was time'* when I questioned him about my acceptance to the prestigious university. And Alana is neck-deep in all the subterfuge.

A heavy melancholy settles over me. Is there no one I can trust? Has my life been one giant fabrication that benefits everyone else's purposes but my own?

"When we get back to Falcon Tower, you're going to tell Tristan and me *everything*."

With the toe of my borrowed boot, I hook under the foot handle at the bottom of the bathroom door to open it, only to stumble backward when it gets shoved inward from the outside.

"Excuse me," I start to apologize to the person trying to get into the restroom, but it never passes my lips because Aleksander Stepanoff's cold, gray eyes lock directly on me.

Taken by surprise by his sudden appearance, I'm frozen in place as he forces his way inside.

How is he here? In Texas. *Fuckfuckfuck.*

Hatred and fury quickly overtake the shock when I fixate on the man with him whose gun is pointed directly at Alana.

Aleksander makes no move to attack. Just stands there, staring at me. I stare back, but it's not him I see. His face blends with that of his twin brother's, and I'm transported to the garden when Aleksei was going to kill Constantine. My mind goes into sensory overload as my frenetic heartbeat pumps adrenaline into my muscles until I'm vibrating from the potency of it.

"Please don't do anything we'll both regret. I only came to talk," Aleksander says in that oddly soft, cultured voice that is incongruent for a man his size.

His words are laughable because they're pure bullshit. The Angel of Death has come for me, but I won't go down without a fight.

"Just to talk."

He shows me his hands. He's not carrying a weapon. If he's trying to get me to lower my guard, he fails miserably. Aleksander doesn't need a weapon to wreak havoc. He's just as deadly as any gun.

"You have my word," he promises.

This time I do laugh. It's hollow and very fake, and it dies as suddenly as it begins.

"You're delusional if you expect me to put faith in your word after what you and your brother did."

A frown furrows his brow, dipping low and ominous. There are a few fresh scratches on his face and the ridge of his eye is swollen. He apparently walked away from the explosion practically unscathed.

"Aleksei is dead."

Apparently, I have a death wish because I confess, "I killed him."

Nothing. No reaction. His cruelly handsome face is completely blank.

"I know. That's not why I'm here."

That's it? No threats about all the horrible ways he's going to make me suffer for what I did?

He pauses, takes a cautious step closer. "If I'd known you were…" As if he had just become aware of her existence, Aleksander's astonishment shows when he notices Alana. "Well, this is quite unexpected."

Warning bells go off when Alana visibly trembles, and her fingernails dig sharply into my arm, hard enough to break through the skin.

"I wonder what Gabriel will think when he finds out you're alive."

Gabriel Ferreira?

I intentionally position myself in front of Alana, ensuring that I'm the target should the other man decide to shoot.

Aleksander's companion, however, moves strategically around me, pressing the barrel of a Glock against Alana's chest and using the momentum to back her up into the urinal stall, effectively separating us and trapping her.

"You hurt her," I hiss through gritted teeth, "and I'll kill you."

Aleksander gentles his tone. "I promise no harm will come to Ms. Amato. You can trust me, Aoife."

He knows who I am, who Alana is. What the fuck is going on? And how did he find out where we were or get past the guys without them noticing?

"Says the asshole with the goon holding a gun to my mother."

"She's not really your mother, though, is she?" His head quirks in a curious manner. "Do you remember me?"

I remember a boy with a sweet smile and moonlit eyes who nervously asked me to dance. I also remember the fight he and Tristan got into. He wasn't so sweet then.

"No," I prevaricate. Knowing Aleksander's hot button, I say, "I don't know how you got in here, but Tristan will come looking for me soon. Hendrix and Constantine, too."

"I've got eyes on them."

His words hang in the air, and I take them exactly as the threat he intended.

There are too many people in the bar, including three men I love who I wouldn't hesitate to die for. Innocent souls who would become casualties if Aleksander's men opened fire. Playing along seems to be my only option right now.

"Alright. You want to talk. You have my attention."

I flinch when he caresses a finger across my cheek, over my shoulder, and down my scarred arm. It's surprisingly gentle, and it bewilders and infuriates me in equal measure. He has no right to touch me like that.

Acting on instinct, I grasp under his arm, targeting the pressure points of his ulnar and median nerves. But Aleksander responds swiftly, using his imposing body to trap me against the wall next to the sink. His muscles, hard beneath his tailored blue dress shirt, mash against my soft flesh. I try to knee him in the groin, but he forces his thigh between my legs, making our position appear more intimate than it really is. The pressure on my torso from neck to stomach increases as he pushes himself flush to me, trying to hold me in place.

At Alana's startled cry, I cease my struggles. I won't let my impulsiveness be the reason she gets hurt.

"Come back to Darlington."

My head cracks against the wall when I look up at him. "*What?*"

With his head bowed, his blond stubble chafes my cheek as he speaks. "I'd like for you to come back."

Is he for real?

"You really are crazy."

I press my fingers deeper into the muscle, as hard as I can, but still no reaction from him. His entire arm must be completely numb by now with how hard I'm bearing down on the nerves.

"Consider it a truce."

"What about Tristan, Constantine, and Hendrix? You

tried to kill them."

If I can somehow get the man's gun, I'm going to put a bullet straight through Aleksander's head.

He inhales through his nose in frustration. "I promise not to touch them... unless they touch me first." He smiles, all dimples and boyish charm, and it completely changes his appearance.

This entire interaction with him has me reeling.

"Why would I believe you?"

The pressure on my chest dissipates when he slowly edges away. Aleksander's size is substantial, tall and wide-shouldered. It makes me feel small in comparison.

"Because I will never lie to you, *pevchaya ptitsa*."

He called me that before when I went to see him at the bell tower, and I still don't know what it means.

"Everyone lies to me," I mutter. It slips out before I can stop it.

With a touch so tender it feels like the fragile bloom of a flower unfurling, he pries my fingers from his arm.

"*I* won't," he vows with a vicious sincerity that makes my heart rate quicken. "But you'll figure that out soon enough. And when you do—" He grazes his fingertips over my burns, but I don't feel it. "You'll come to me, and I'll give you what you want most."

I meet his storm-cloud stare with a cold one of my own. "And what do you think I want?"

"Revenge."

His declaration seduces my ear like a whispered promise.

Keeping his eyes tethered to my face, Aleksander increases the distance between us. "See you soon, Aoife."

The other man rushes to the door and checks the

hallway. At his nod, Aleksander slips outside of the restroom, leaving me standing there with a million chaotic thoughts, none of them good.

One forever second goes by. Then two, then three.

"Wait!"

"Synthia, no!" Alana calls out as I run after him.

I catch up to Aleksander just as he gets to the back exit door. Hearing me over the booming, pulsating music coming from the bar, he stops and looks over his shoulder.

I don't think about what I'm doing, only that he promised to tell me the truth.

"Is everyone dead?"

He's smart enough to read between the lines and know who I'm referring to.

"Aleksander, we've got to go," his man urges.

Aleksander waves him off like a pesky fly, pivots toward me, and replies, "Of course not."

"But you killed Eva Knight."

"I did," he replies matter-of-factly.

"Why?"

He doesn't blink. He doesn't waver or look away.

"Because her husband asked me to."

Shocked at his bluntness, my hand involuntarily covers my mouth. Hendrix watched his mother die, and it was his father who ordered her death.

"Why would Patrick do that?"

"He said he would give me his vote if I did something for him. It was a business exchange. I didn't question his reasons."

The way he casually talks about killing Eva is cold and detached. *A business exchange*. How can someone's life be worth so little?

Do I tell Hendrix? What if Aleksander is lying? I don't think he is. For some insane, inexplicable reason —because surely, I have lost my fucking mind—I believe him.

"What about everyone else? Tristan's parents? Constantine's father? Where are they?"

Aleksander's smile returns, as do those damnable dimples. "Oh, they're still very much alive. I wouldn't want to spoil your fun," he replies enigmatically and disappears into the dusky evening.

A gust of wind from the alleyway slams the exit door shut, the crack of sound like that of a gunshot.

Something I'm all too familiar with.

CHAPTER 22

A swirling eddy of wind whips my hair all around, obscuring my view of the nighttime skyline. Everything looks so pretty from this perspective of forty stories up, the city like a forest of skyscraper-shaped Christmas trees decorated in a geometric pattern of white window lights. The synchronous flashes of the red aviation obstruction beacons that stick up from the tops of buildings look like fireflies hovering in the air.

"How could you let that motherfucker get near her? I thought you had men covering the bar."

I blow out a weary breath when I hear Tristan's furious voice through the French doors that lead out from the living room onto the balcony.

The guys are understandably upset, but I couldn't take it anymore and came out here.

"You don't get views like this in Ireland," Evan says as he studies the stunning cityscape spanning as far as the eye can see.

My hair whips around my head in a frenzy when the wind picks up.

"It's beautiful in a different way than the country, but I prefer rural life. Fresh air, zero light pollution, the sounds of insects and animals instead of cars and people," I lament.

Unafraid of the height, I brace my hands on the thick metal balcony railing and lean over.

"You're about to give me a heart attack. Could you, maybe, not do that, please?"

I glance over at Alana where she's sitting on an oversized deck chair. She hasn't spoken much, but then again, with Tristan and Hendrix yelling at everyone, no one's had the chance to say much of anything.

Flipping positions, I rest my butt against the railing and contemplate my adoptive mother. She was my larger-than-life hero. The one person I trusted. Someone who I knew would always be there to lift me up when I was at my lowest. But now, Aleksander has me questioning everything and everyone.

"I love you, Dierdre."

Her startled brown eyes fly up at my use of her real name.

"No matter what happens next or what anyone says, I will always love you. I couldn't have asked for a better mother."

A shaky hand flutters to her chest. The dull pearlescent light catches the glimmer of tears that pool in her eyes.

"I love you, too. So very much, Synthia."

"I know."

She gave me ten years filled with that love. Even through the horrendous agony of my injuries, surgeries, and recoveries, I woke up every day fighting to live, if only for her. It was her love that saved me when I felt like I couldn't take another breath or endure another second of the unending pain that tormented me day after day.

Love is the purest of emotions. It can take you to the highest highs, but also drag you down to the lowest of lows. Love can make you blind to the truth. It can be manipulative and used as a weapon. Love can bring life, but it can also kill. History is littered with the atrocities done in the name of love.

"Why did Aleksander say that Gabriel would be interested in knowing you were alive?"

Her tears turn to a wide-eyed fear that she isn't able to hide quickly enough.

Evan moves nearer, his body creating a barrier against the brisk wind. "Tell her."

Alana's wide eyes are contagious because mine gape incredulously at Evan. How does he know?

I don't know whether to feel hurt or royally pissed. Every fucking person seems to be aware of something that I'm not, and the only person who openly said he would tell me the truth is Aleksander. The enemy. How goddamn ironic is that?

I turn my back on her and feign interest in the nighttime urban landscape. I'd retreat inside, but I'm not in the mood to be yelled at. In my current disposition, it would only lead to a physical altercation.

"Gabriel is the man my father sold me to. I was to be his wife. Once Aleksander tells him..."

She doesn't have to finish. I know exactly what Gabriel Ferreira will do. He'll hunt her down and kill her. Just like he did his first wife, Constantine's mother, when she tried to leave him.

Gabriel is a cruel, violent man who gets off on the pain he inflicts on others. Look what he did to Constantine. The thought of being Gabriel's wife terrified Dierdre enough that she asked my mother for help, faked her own death, and changed her name to escape him.

The bleakness of the situation, *of everything*, pulls at me like a lead anchor in a fathomless ocean, dragging me under until I'm drowning. But it's in that moment I remember the power I wield—as a woman and as James Fitzpatrick's daughter. The only way I can truly be free, the only way I can protect those I love, is to take back what's rightfully mine.

It's time for the phoenix to rise.

"Evan, can you get Alana to Cillian tonight?"

"What? Why?" Alana asks.

"Gabriel can't get to you if you're with Cillian in Ireland."

Metal legs scrape against the concrete floor when she bounds out of the chair.

"Absolutely not! I'm not leaving you."

Evan apparently takes my side because he says, "I'll call him now to let him know and get the plane refueled and prepped. Should take about an hour. Is that soon enough?"

I'd rather it be right this second. "Thank you, Evan."

"I am *not* going!" Alana plants her fists at her hips, her obdurate stance conveying her displeasure.

I go over to her and take her face in my hands, needing her to see my resolve. I won't budge on this.

"Yes, you are. And you're not going to fight me on it."

Naturally, she tries, but I expected no less.

"Tristan is going to be furious if I disappear again. I haven't gotten a chance to talk to him or explain what happened."

He will be upset—at first. Once he finds out about Gabriel, I'm confident that what I'm asking her to do is the same thing he would've done. Unfortunately, I don't have the luxury of time to make him understand. Aleksander could have already told Gabriel where Alana is.

I kiss her on the cheek. "I need you to go hug your brother, tell him you're tired and going to bed, then go get your stuff and be ready to leave with Evan as soon as possible without saying a word to anyone, especially Tristan."

I'll tell him after she's gone. He's not going to be happy. It's a fight I don't want, but one I'm prepared to have with him.

Alana scrutinizes me for a long minute, and I use that time to memorize every detail of her face. Her laugh lines and subtle crow's feet that are starting to appear at the corners of her eyes. The way one eyebrow arches just a little higher than the other. The ever-present rosy blush on her cheeks.

"You're planning something."

I am, but I won't confirm it. The reason why unsettles me greatly. I love her and want her safe, but I don't trust her. Not anymore.

As an afterthought, I ask, "Who's taking care of Cocky Bastard and the other animals?"

Perplexed, she answers, "Mike. Why?"

Okay, good. One less thing I have to worry about.

"*Synthia*, talk to me."

I give Evan an exasperated side glance, silently asking

him for a little help to get her moving.

"Go with Evan."

He tries to take her arm, but she pushes his hand away.

"Don't do it. Whatever crazy thing you're thinking about doing—don't. Come with me. We can start over again in Ireland. You loved it there."

The fact that she knows that reminds me of the mountain of duplicity I've been buried under for way too long.

No more running away. No more hiding. No more fucking secrets.

I'm taking back my life.

I'm going back to Darlington.

I'm going to reclaim my family's seat on the Council.

I'm going to find who killed my parents.

And God help anyone who gets in my way.

CHAPTER 23

Slumped against the balcony railing, I hunch my shoulders, bring my elbows together, and curl into myself to conserve body heat, but it doesn't prevent the cold shiver from dancing over my exposed arms. The ambient temperature is muggy and warm, but the wind chill and the higher altitude make it feel much colder than it really is. I should've changed clothes as soon as we got back to Falcon Tower.

The French doors click open, and from the way my pulse suddenly skyrockets, I know it's Constantine who walks out onto the balcony. I'm astonished it took them this long to come looking for me. Constantine may possess a shit-ton of patience, but like Tristan and Hendrix, he has no problem barging into a person's space when he feels like it.

Goose bumps explode like fireworks from the furnace of his body heat when his chest collides with my back. He reaches those defined, muscled arms around me to grab the deck railing, effectively barricading me in, and

I have no choice but to angle my head on his shoulder so I can see his face. Dark, sullen, and so incredibly gorgeous. My haven when everything around me is falling apart.

"You've been out here a while."

My eyes close, and I soak in the cadence of his voice. I love hearing it. Every utterance. Every word spoken. All of them a gift.

"Just needed some space."

In the fifteen minutes of solitude I've gotten since Evan left with Alana, I've been thinking about what Aleksander said. The doubts he planted with his insinuation that the guys are also keeping things from me. Those tiny seeds of doubt have a way of growing into a jungle filled with dangerous creatures that lie in wait, ready to strike you with their sharp, poisonous fangs. I can't give Aleksander that kind of power over me. My weakness, however, is my curiosity. I don't doubt that he knows something. The question I need to answer for myself is: Am I willing to play his game to find out what it is?

Afraid that Constantine will see right through me, I stare off into the blackness of the horizon. "Don't go after Aleksander."

He stiffens.

I know it's not fair of me to ask. They each want their pound of flesh from Aleksander for different reasons. The justice in our world is not ruled by man's laws or the judicial system. The only repercussions are those ordered by the Council. I'm at a crossroads of wanting a normal life and wanting to take back my father's legacy in order to punish those who betrayed him.

Aleksander deserves what's coming to him, but not

yet. There's a proverb by Sun Tzu that says keep your friends close and your enemies closer.

"You done sulking?" Hendrix says when he and Tristan come outside onto the balcony.

I guess my quiet time has officially ended.

Constantine rotates us around and holds me with a loose grip around my waist.

"I wasn't sulking. I just didn't want to get yelled at anymore. And you and I are going to have a seriously long discussion about your propensity to speak to me like a jackass."

I know I'm in trouble when I see the hot look he gives me. "I'd be more than happy to have that talk while you sit on my face."

I'm instantly wet. How the hell does he do that?

"Did you talk to Alana?" I ask Tristan with as much nonchalance as possible.

"She said she was turning in."

Relief rushes through me. She kept her word.

"Which is what I'd like to do." Hendrix takes off his shirt and tucks it into his pants, and yes, I stare. "We came all the way out here, to bloody fucking Texas, so you could confront your sister."

"When the fuck have I had time?"

"And can we stop with this Dierdre-Alana nonsense? The different names are confusing as hell. Pick one and stick to it." Hendrix bends to the side, stretching his obliques. All that inked skin stretched taut over lean muscle.

"Mine don't seem to bother you."

Syn. Aoife. Red. Firefly. Trouble. I kind of like having the various nicknames. Each one represents a different facet of who I am.

"You're special, baby girl," Hendrix replies.

Hearing the *baby girl* excites me because it sounds so much like *good girl*.

Tristan drops down onto one of the deck loungers and digs his palms into his temples. I extricate myself from Constantine and go to him. The stress, lack of sleep, and constant noise are a perfect recipe to trigger a migraine, and he doesn't have his medication. Everything we took with us to the Catskills is still sitting in the smoking remains of what's left of the Knight Estate.

When I straddle him, his knees bend to support me so I don't fall off the back of the lounger.

He sighs with pleasure as I rub clockwise circles from his forehead to the mastoid processes, the bony projections that are located behind the ears. The way he melts into the lounger cushions is like pulling the plug from an inflatable innertube and watching as it gradually deflates.

"Is it bad?"

"No headache. Just tired."

He pulls my right hand to his lips and sucks the tips of each finger with arousing whirls of his tongue that make my belly swoop and my pussy clench. I'm intimately aware of what that wicked tongue can do.

Those lusty musings evaporate when he says, "We're leaving first thing in the morning. Jax hooked us up with new phones, a laptop, and some cash, courtesy of your cousin."

I drop my hands from his face. I don't like that they made decisions without me, but it would be very hypocritical of me to get upset about it since I just did the same thing regarding Alana.

"We're going back to Darlington?" I ask hopefully.

"Hell, no. New York."

New York City is where the Ferreira family home is located. It's also where the Society gala used to be held every year during the second weekend in September, which is, coincidentally, this weekend.

"What about classes? I don't want to get behind. I also have work. I can't just skip out on Keith."

College may not be important to them, but it is to me. I got into Darlington Founders under false pretenses, but my dream of becoming a doctor hasn't changed. It's going to be a precarious balancing act of attending classes… and all the other stuff going on.

Tristan avoids answering me and instead says, "Tell me one more time what Aleksander said to you."

With a weary groan, I sit back, only to bend forward again when his knees poke into my spine. I've already told him a condensed, highly redacted version of what Aleksander said. I may have left out a bunch of stuff, including the part where Aleksander claimed to have killed Eva because Patrick told him to. I need Hendrix in a better headspace before I unload that ugliness on him. Hopefully, tomorrow, he and Tristan will have calmed down enough for us to have a conversation without the raised voices and male temper tantrums. Who am I kidding? Once I tell Tristan I sent Alana to Ireland with Cillian, he's going to explode.

"I'm sure you've memorized every word and could recite them back to me."

"This isn't a joke. You can't believe anything that bastard says."

Do not engage. Harder said than done.

"So, it's okay for you to take his word that your

parents, Patrick, and Gabriel are alive."

A muscle ticks in his jaw. He did not like me pointing that out.

"He's playing you."

"Obviously."

"He's using you."

I know that. I plan to use him, too.

"Of course he fucking is," Hendrix snaps, and I cut him an acerbic look. He's not helping the situation.

"He's obsessed with you," Tristan says next, and I choke back a laugh.

"That's ridiculous. If anything, he's obsessed *with you*."

He huffs out a sardonic scoff. "You're so damn clueless."

And we're back to that shit again, which means I'm done.

"At least you didn't call me stupid this time."

"Aoife."

"Syn," I correct him just to be difficult. "And I'm going back to Darlington."

I make it two feet past the French doors before the guys are right on my heels.

"We're going to New York."

If there was ever a time I'd want to pull out my hair and scream, it would be now. Instead, I go to the refrigerator to find something cold to drink. Spotting bottles of sparkling water, I grab one.

"You don't get how far he'll go, now that he knows who you are."

That's what he said regarding his father, then used it as the impetus to promptly move me into their house.

Twisting the cap off, I take a long, slow drink that

does little to help rid the tequila-induced cottonmouth I'm experiencing.

"How does Aleksander know who I am?"

Aleksander addressed me as Aoife. He asked if I remembered him. Even the guys didn't recognize me at first. Aleksander surely didn't in the elevator or when I went to confront him at the bell tower. The damaged woman I grew into looks nothing like the blonde girl of my youth.

Constantine frowns at Hendrix and Tristan, apparently coming to the same conclusion I do.

"*You* told him?"

Hendrix is fast to refute. "Don't look at me."

"Thanks, asshole," Tristan tells him.

"That would've been useful information to know before I was ambushed in the restroom and Alana got a gun pointed at her!" I yell, incensed.

Those seeds Aleksander sowed begin to sprout.

"*Everyone lies to me.*"

"*I won't. But you'll figure that out soon enough.*"

Tristan comes around the island and without warning, lifts me onto the countertop and pushes himself between the vee of my thighs.

"I did it to save your life."

My recollection of what happened in the garden is disjointed, a jumbled assembly of blood-soaked screams and the weight of a gun in my hand.

"She saved herself. She saved us," Constantine intervenes, and I want to leap across the kitchen and kiss the hell out of him.

I try again to get through to Tristan. "Aleksander promised a truce."

"Aleksander can go fuck himself."

His anger isn't about me. It's frustration. He wants to protect me. I get it. I really do, and I love him even more for it. But it's my choice, regardless of whether he agrees with me or not.

And if truth be told, I'd rather deal with Aleksander than with Francesco Amato, Patrick Knight, and Gabriel Ferreira. If there is karma, I hope that bitch comes for the three of them.

Then again, what Aleksander said in the hallway makes me think he has other plans.

"Oh, they're still very much alive. I wouldn't want to spoil your fun."

"I'm going back to Darlington."

I feel like I'm on repeat, hoping the more I say it, it'll finally sink in how important this is to me.

"Not a fucking chance."

Internally, I let out the scream I've been holding. Reasoning with Tristan is like banging my head against a wall made of steel, not brick. But he's not the only stubborn person in the room.

Running my hands down the front of his shirt, I ask, "Do you remember telling me that you were my reason to stay?"

The night of the rainstorm was a turning point between us. It opened the door for what came after. Losing my heart to three dangerous men. Falling in love. Intimacy. Orgasms. *So many orgasms.* And rediscovery. Of them and of me.

"I do."

"Then please don't be the reason I go back alone. You promised you would help me find who murdered my parents. Don't prove Aleksander right."

With a provocative touch of his finger, he tips my face

up until I'm staring directly into his golden eyes. "Right about what, exactly?"

"That I can't trust any of you."

If silence was a bomb, I just tossed a live grenade into the room.

CHAPTER 24

That underhanded son of a bitch. Aleksander went right for Aoife's biggest vulnerability. Unfortunately, what he said was the truth. We are keeping things from her. Important things. Life-changing things. Secrets that have the power to make her walk away from me for good.

And I can't let that happen.

Aoife is mine. She's always been mine. I fucking love her with every dark, damaged part of my blackened soul. Aleksander may claim a truce, but he's going to get a war because she will never be his.

That beast I try so hard to contain breaks free from its chains and goes after the thing it wants most. Her.

I want to claim her. Fuck her. Possess her. Mark her body with my mouth and my cock and my cum. Hear my name screamed from her lips as she falls apart underneath me.

"You want to trust something, Red? Fucking trust this."

I'm not gentle when I fill my hands with her curves and roughly pull her to me. I'm not kind in how I viciously claim her mouth. And I'm not tender when I devour her moan with my tongue.

She sets me on fire when she immediately submits, and I'm tempted to lay her out on the counter island and feast, but her lips are too good. The kiss too perfect. The way her body writhes in my arms too damn irresistible.

"*Tristan*," Aoife protests and tries to pull me back when I break our kiss.

"We done arguing?"

Never afraid to challenge me, she replies, "You started it."

I love how strong and stubborn she is. How she'll fight for what she wants and for what she believes in, even if it goes against what the guys or I want.

"Yes, I did." I twist her words around, changing the meaning to all the debauched things I intend to do to her. "And I plan to finish it with my cock deep inside of you."

Her brows lift in sexy defiance, and it hits me for the first time that I didn't notice they weren't blonde. Like her hair, she must have dyed them, too.

Arching her back until her luscious tits almost spill out of the top I'll be ripping off her soon, she suggestively bites her bottom lip. "Who says it's only going to be your cock inside me?"

All the air gets siphoned from my lungs as instant lust funnels directly to my dick, but it's my conscience that taps me on the shoulder to get my attention. As much as I want what she's suggesting—god, how I fucking want it more than anything—she's only been with Con. In almost every way that matters, she's still innocent.

The energy in the kitchen alters into something more provocatively dangerous when I sense Hendrix and Con draw nearer, but Aoife never takes her eyes off me. With those soul-deep baby blues, she watches as the angel perched on one shoulder battles with the devil on the other. When she sees the devil win, her smile is so fucking big and beauteous, it captivates me with the power of it.

I don't resist when she pushes me back with a finger to my sternum. The skintight material of her painted-on leggings catch the kitchen light when she slides off the countertop, changing the color from black to an iridescent aquamarine, like the wings of a blue morpho butterfly, a shade lighter than the color of her eyes.

She bends over to pull down the side zippers of the ankle boots, taking her sweet time and torturing us with teasing glimpses of her perfect ass.

"I don't want to be your good girl tonight," she says to the three of us, straightening up and stepping out of the boots. "I just want to be yours."

Showing a confidence I haven't seen before, she curves one arm behind her and pulls at the bow tying her shirt straps together. They slip underneath her long hair and fall like ribbons down her chest, tugging the bodice of the shirt just enough to expose the top swells of her breasts. I'm rabid with the need to suck her pert nipples into my mouth. From how sensitive they seem to be, I have a feeling that we can get her to come from breast play alone, and I'm dying to find out if I'm right.

With a slow seduction that is as much torture as it is erotic, Aoife makes a show of undressing in the middle of the kitchen, knowing full well there are cameras everywhere in the suite. I have no problem with public fucking or voyeurism, but Aoife's gorgeous body is for Con, Hen, and me only. The thought of anyone else seeing her like this has me feral with murderous rage. *Mine.*

"Baby, there're eyes on us."

I want to tell my damn conscience to shut the hell up, but Aoife isn't one of the nameless women Hen and I play with for a night. We love this girl, and she deserves to be treated like the goddess she is.

A dirty smirk graces her lips. "About that. Andie may have mentioned at some point between shots of tequila that only the cameras at the elevators and stairwell door would be operating tonight."

She sheds the rest of her clothes like they're made of tissue paper until she's standing before us like a mouthwatering treat. At the sight of her bare breasts and pussy, my cock swells painfully against the constraints of my jeans.

"I've never seen anything more beautiful than you."

Color tints her cheeks. "You make me feel beautiful."

She thinks the evidence of what happened to her overshadows her beauty, whereas I see her scars as perfect brushstrokes on the canvas of a priceless piece of artwork.

Hendrix goes to his knees in front of her and skims his hands up the long lines of her legs. Her thigh muscles quiver, and the sexiest moan dances up her throat when he runs his tongue along the inside of her upper thigh.

"You have the control here, firefly. Tell us what you want, and we will give it to you, over and over." He sinks his teeth into her soft flesh, biting down just enough to bruise the skin.

"That. I want more of that," she answers with a hitch of breath.

Her sigh is dreamlike when Hendrix gives her a matching bite on her other thigh, then laps at the moisture that begins to drip from her decadent cunt. Aoife loves the pain that comes with pleasure. She gets off on it, and it's hot as hell to watch. Even hotter to see the evidence of what we do to her. Her torso and legs are covered in our marks, some fading and some more recent.

Licking her essence glossing his lips, Hendrix looks up at her from his lowered position. "You're so fucking perfect."

She blushes again. Another thing I've noticed. She likes being praised, *good girl* being her favorite. Strong and submissive. She really is perfect for us.

As if reading my mind, Con fuels my fantasy from minutes before as he quickly clears the counter island of the glasses left on it until its surface is pristine.

"Hold on," Hendrix tells her and lifts her by the legs as he stands.

With a delighted giggle, Aoife clings to his shoulders to keep her balance as he carefully sets her down on the granite countertop.

"Holy shit, that's cold… *Oh my god!*" she chants when Hendrix doesn't waste any time, buries his face between her legs, and fucking consumes her with ruthless abandon.

The sounds they make—her moans and his animalistic grunts—are pornographic and have my mind racing with all sorts of sybaritic possibilities. I didn't think my cock could get any harder, but watching them together has me struggling to hold back my own release, and I'm damn sure not coming in my pants like a horny pubescent boy.

Con moves in and curves his hand around the back of Aoife's neck to hold her in place, then takes a peaked, rosy nipple into his mouth. The few times he joined Hen and me with one of our random fucks for fun, he sat in the corner and observed. Never actively participated.

This just got very interesting.

"Tristan."

My gaze lingers where Con makes love to her breasts with open-mouthed kisses, then travels a leisurely path up her body to her gorgeous, flushed face.

"Yeah, baby?"

"I want... I want you..."

Her sentence goes unfinished. She lets loose a long, hedonistic whimper when Hendrix grabs hold of her ankles and drapes her legs over his shoulders, opening her wide, and starts fucking her with his tongue like it's his mission in life to make her come.

—And fuck, does she come spectacularly. It's like watching the crest of a wave in a tumultuous ocean build higher and higher until it collapses in on itself once it reaches the shore.

A crescendo of shudders overtakes her until her muscles lock, and her back bows in a lovely feminine curve. All that wavy red hair spills over Con's hand and cascades around her in a cerise waterfall. And then she shatters, plush lips parted on a scream. Con greedily steals it for himself, hungrily kissing her as Hendrix wrenches her dry of every last drop of her orgasm with punishing lashes of his tongue on her clit.

Mouths fused together, she falls limp in Con's arms, a sweaty, replete, magnificent, sexed-up mess.

Hendrix eases her legs from his shoulders, gently bending them at the knee so that her feet gain purchase on the edge of the counter. Kissing his way up her stomach, he bends over her and suckles each breast.

"I love making you come. Favorite fucking thing in the whole world."

She traces the outline of his mouth. "You're really good at it."

Hendrix full-on grins. "Damn straight."

Her head lolls to the side, and she gives me that smile again, the one that makes me stupid in love with her. I glance at my two best friends. My soul brothers. Three men in love with the same woman. Four childhood friends who were destined to be together, and no matter what the Society, or our parents, or Aleksander *fucking* Stepanoff try to do to tear us apart, they will never succeed. The four of us together are like catching lightning in a bottle, something that should be impossible, but we've managed to shape it into something extraordinary.

"I love you, Red."

Her features soften, as does her smile. "Love you more. *Grá agat níos mó.*"

Removing my shirt, I toss it to the side, not caring where it falls. "Ready to be ruined, pretty girl?"

Her gorgeous face lights up. "Do your worst, Boston."

CHAPTER 25

My heart pummels my chest with excited beats of anticipation when Tristan lifts me in his arms and carries me down the dark hallway toward the bedrooms. Wicked determination glints in his whiskey browns, the need behind them making all my feminine parts tingle with enthusiasm.

Hendrix scoots around us, heading into the bedroom first. Laying my cheek to Tristan's shoulder, I look back at Constantine, my dark fallen angel. He takes my hand when I reach out for him, his gentle smile soothing my anxious nerves.

This is really happening. Three men. One… *me*. How does that even work?

I should be frightened out of my ever-loving mind, but I'm not. I want this. I want Tristan's promise to be thoroughly ruined by them in every carnal way imaginable.

Unfortunately, guilt begins to roll in like a storm front as soon as Tristan lowers me onto the bed. I spoke of truth and trust, and yet, I'm keeping things from them. I haven't lied, but isn't my silence almost the same thing? I should tell them everything Aleksander said, not just the censored version I gave them. I should tell Tristan I sent Alana to Ireland and tell Constantine what she said about his father. Damn Aleksander for getting inside my head and filling me full of doubts.

I sit up and fold my legs under me. "I need to tell you something."

But my confession dies before it's ever fully spoken when Hendrix materializes from the darkened corner of the room, a men's belt held in his right hand. The biceps and brachialis muscles of his upper arm contract and tumefy when his fingers flex around the leather. My wide eyes flit from the belt to his face, and *holy shit*—the implication of Hendrix's intense, penetrating blue stare has wetness instantly gathering between my legs.

"She's not ready."

My head swivels back to Tristan. "Not ready for what?"

Then it dawns on me. The stuff Tristan said Hendrix was into. His sexual proclivities and how he chooses women like Serena to 'play' with. Fucktoys, Tristan called them.

I want to be what Hendrix needs but I'm terrified that I'll disappoint him. Hendrix likes to dominate. He's a sadist who derives pleasure from giving pain. Loving him means loving every facet of him, especially his darker parts.

Determined, I take a guess about what he intends to do with the belt and kneel on the bed, holding my joined wrists out to Hendrix. His responding masculine groan lets me know I guessed correctly.

In my submission with my hands outstretched as if I'm offering them the beating heart from my chest, I'm giving everything to them. My love, my fears, my strength, my weakness, my dreams and nightmares. My scars. Everything that I am is theirs.

At that moment, I'm more exposed, more vulnerable than I've ever been with them before. Not because they can see the ugly trauma inflicted upon my naked body but because Tristan, Constantine, and Hendrix have the power to destroy me in a way my heart would never recover.

"Make me yours."

"You've always been mine," Hendrix asserts, coming closer but still out of reach.

He hands the belt to Tristan, and I'm disheartened that I won't get to experience being tied up.

"I'm not afraid."

I am, but I refuse to show it.

Hendrix puts a knee to the bed and leans in until our mouths are mere millimeters apart. "You're fearless, firefly, but Tristan is right. We need to explore your boundaries. Slowly." He bites my bottom lip and pulls. Standing back up, he stares down at me with lust and want and something akin to a dare. "Now be a good girl and finger-fuck yourself."

I'm shocked speechless for a second time tonight. Doesn't mean that I won't do it.

The luxurious comforter cushions me when I lie down, and the energy charging the air shifts into a tangible, palpable thing, like an electric caress across my chilled skin. The cotton duvet feels like silk against my legs when I spread my thighs, exposing my most intimate area, and a small sound escapes me when the pad of my finger presses on the swollen, sensitive nub. My breaths are stolen from my chest as quickly as they're exhaled when I rub small circles over my clit, the sensation too good.

There's a hush of movement around me, of zippers being pulled and clothes being removed. Watching them undress while I touch myself heightens my desire. I'm overloaded with a visual cornucopia of hot-as-hell masculinity. Tristan's lightly bronzed skin and V-shaped swimmer's body of broad shoulders tapering to a lean, chiseled waist. Constantine's intricately inked muscular form, exotic features, and the way his inky eyes can see straight into my soul. Hendrix's deceptively angelic blond hair and blue eyes that are in contrast with the wickedly colorful tattoos that stand out against his paler skin. Each man is unique, yet their soul-deep bond of friendship makes them closer than brothers.

"You are the most beautiful fucking sight I've ever seen," Constantine says in that raspy, broken voice that makes me ache for him.

I absorb every time they say I'm beautiful like parched earth at the first raindrops after a long drought. That one word is part of the thread that stitches the broken pieces of me together.

Spurred on by his praise, my panted breaths singe my throat when I slip a finger inside me and pump it vigorously, chasing the orgasm I can feel building quickly. *So close.* I don't try to act sexy and put on a performance. I go after the pleasure my fingers are giving.

As I reach that glorious peak, my hand is ripped from my pussy.

226

"Wait, I was—*Oh, fuck!*" I scream when Hendrix slams his pierced, tattooed cock inside me, filling me completely just as my orgasm rips me apart.

I have no chance to prepare for the vicious way he takes me. His larger body engulfs mine, pressing me into the mattress with every punishing thrust of his cock. Constantine makes love to me like I'm precious. Hendrix fucks me like I'm unbreakable.

With teeth bared, he pounds into me, my pussy convulsing around his shaft, my orgasm never-ending because he won't allow it. It feels like I'm dying and being reborn at the same time.

"Look at me."

His warm hand grips my throat, and my eyes fly open as I struggle to breathe. Hendrix's face fills my spotty vision, but I don't fight him. Seeing my acquiescence, he kisses me almost reverently until my mind and body start to float higher and higher toward another orgasm that feels bigger than the others.

"Good girl."

The pressure around my neck eases, and I freefall back to earth on a whimper as I'm taken to the precipice of release, only to have it denied me.

I clutch at his chest, fingernails digging in. "Please," I beg. My need to come is almost unbearable.

Hendrix rubs along my neck, soothing the burn his hand created. "You beg so prettily."

His piercing drags along my tender walls when he pulls out, and I full-body shudder when he pushes back in. He sinks into me with his entire body, and I give my hands free rein to explore any part of him I can touch. Hard muscle, smooth, sweat-slicked skin, and a furnace of heat that burns my fingers as they roam.

I emit an embarrassing, high-pitched squeak when Hendrix suddenly rolls and flips our positions. His fingers bruise my hips when he grabs me and slams me down onto his cock. My head rocks back on my neck on a shout of "Yes!" when his piercing hits some unknown erogenous zone that has me seeing literal stars.

Following the instinctive demands of my body, I brace my hands on his firm chest and rock my hips.

"That's it, firefly. Take your pleasure. Fucking own me with your pussy."

That shouldn't sound as hot as it does, but damn if I don't love his dirty words.

Hendrix lets go of my waist to play with my breasts. My nipples are so sensitive, I jerk when he pinches them. He does it again, harder this time, watching me closely for my reaction. My body turns into a conduit where any stimulus travels directly to my clit and has me gasping.

"You feel that? The way your perfect cunt squeezes me."

Oh, yeah. I absolutely feel it. It's like being dipped in gunpowder, and he just lit the match.

"You going to come on my cock, dirty girl?"

My thighs burn with exertion as I ride him, hurdling toward blissful release. "Yes."

"Not yet."

What? No! Goddammit!

Before I can call him every crass name I can think of for denying me once again, arms band around me and lift me up.

"On your hands and knees, Red."

I'm drunk on the giddiness that consumes me at Tristan's voice. My only thought is *finally*. The sexual tension between Tristan and me was instant from the moment I crashed into him in the back hall at the Bierkeller. Every time he's touched me, every argument we've had and every time our stubbornness butted heads, has been foreplay leading up to this. I know how his mouth and hands feels on my body, but I won't be complete until I know what it feels like to be fucked by him.

Hendrix stays where he lies, and I get a perfect view of his gorgeous, smirking face when I hover over him, trembling arms outstretched on either side of his head, knees straddling his midsection. I suck in a harsh breath when Tristan molds his wide palms over my ass, digging his thumbs into the crease, so close to that forbidden area.

Hendrix smiles up at me and blows me a kiss, but I'm too tense to smile back, all my attention focused on what Tristan is doing. I want them to claim me in every way a man can claim a woman, but I'm also a little terrified. This is all new to me. I'm not experienced like they are. I don't know the rules or the expectations. I feel like I'm trying to run when I haven't even learned how to crawl yet.

Hendrix raises up and kisses the apprehension from my face with feathery brushes of his lips.

"Breathe, baby."

I release the torrent of air clogging my throat. "I'm scared," I admit.

The hairs on Tristan's legs and chest tickle my backside as his body conforms over mine, a blanket of warm, sexy man. He peppers the softest kisses down my spine, pausing every few inches to nip the skin.

"It's going to feel so good when we're both inside you, me taking your ass while Hen ravages your pussy. But tonight we just want to love you."

I'm completely inundated with emotions that feel bigger than anything I've experienced.

Constantine appears at our side, and I blindly grab hold of his hand. My balance gets thrown off center, but Hendrix holds me up just as Tristan hooks one arm under my shoulder to steady me. I'm teetering on that precipice of heart-stopping expectation when I feel the head of his shaft nudge my entrance. I've been up close and personal with his impressive cock, gagged on his immense girth when I went down on him in the shower. I know how big Tristan is, and how small I am. He's going to render me in two when he fucks me, and I'm going to love every second of it.

"I need you."

My plea is the thing that cracks his control. He stretches me to the breaking point when he enters me, inch by excruciating inch that feels like an eternity. I'm anchored in place, intimately connected to him while also physically holding onto Constantine and Hendrix. There's a symbolic meaning to it that I don't analyze because it just is. The four us, bound together. The way it should be.

"So fucking tight. So perfect. You were made for me," Tristan grits out.

His muscles strain against my back as he pushes past my resistance. Once fully seated, he doesn't move, allowing me time to adjust to the pressure. *So much pressure.*

"You good?"

I nod.

Hendrix tweaks a nipple, and Tristan grunts when I bear down around him.

"He needs your words, love."

My throaty hum is the best I can do.

Tristan gathers my long, tangled mass of hair and twists it around his free hand. The bite of pain is exactly what I need when he uses the leverage to angle my head to the side. Our kiss is sloppy and messy and wonderful because it's us. And then he moves. Slowly at first. A slight jerk of the hips that sets off a deluge of explosions.

My world tilts on its axis when he lets go of my hair and pulls me upright, my back to his front. He cups a breast in one hand and goes straight for my clit with the other.

"Fuck, that's hot," Hendrix says and takes his cock, jerking roughly.

I'm transported back to his bathroom where I not so secretly watched him masturbate. How he groaned my name as he came.

I turn my head, and he eagerly seeks my mouth, kissing me as sensuously as the way he's making love to me.

"I can't hold back. You feel too good."

"Don't hold back," I pant, joining my hand with his between my legs.

Rapture sings through me as Tristan pumps into me fast and hard, taking me higher and higher until I can barely breathe. When my orgasm hits, it comes in a blinding rush of sweet oblivion. White static obscures my vision, and I think I pass out for a split second.

"Aoife," Tristan rasps against my neck as he comes inside me, filling me with pulses of warmth that set me off for a third time.

Wetness trickles down my legs and my stomach,

which confuses me, until Hendrix starts rubbing it into my skin. He's painting me with his cum again. It's debased and territorial, but I love it.

All too soon, Tristan pulls out, and I collapse forward on top of Hendrix. He holds me until my body stops convulsing, and I go lax in his arms.

His chest rumbles with a light chuckle. "I think we broke her."

I stir up enough energy to bite his nipple. He smacks my ass.

Not wanting to move, I nuzzle my face to his neck and lick at the salt of his sweat. God, he smells good. Like sex and musk and sandalwood.

"Syn," he growls in my ear. "You need aftercare."

"I don't know what that means."

Tristan kisses my shoulder and rubs up and down my back until I liquefy into a starfish-shaped puddle. "It means we take care of you."

I think they took care of me very nicely.

"*Noooo*," I mumble a bratty whine when Tristan slides me off Hendrix, then trip over into happiness when Constantine cradles me in his arms. I'm a mess, sticky, sweaty, sore in so many places, and need a shower. Oh, shower sex with Constantine would be really good.

"Give me five minutes," I sigh into his chest and wrap every part of myself around him—then promptly pass the hell out.

CHAPTER 26

Phantom tingles coax me out of the dream I was having. I was surrounded by a sky full of stars, anxiously searching for the pattern I know now belongs to the man who took everything from me and destroyed my life.

Awareness kicks in slowly when I blink my eyes open. Dewy early morning light paints the room a soft, pale yellow. I'm lying on my stomach, my face smushed into the pillow. Lips coast along my left shoulder, and I smile into the pillowcase.

Constantine kisses his way down the burns on my arm. The nerve endings have long been dead, but I swear I feel him.

"What time is it?" I ask when I notice Tristan and Hendrix aren't in bed with us.

He pauses at my elbow. "Seven."

Hendrix must be making breakfast, and Tristan must be... I listen for running water coming from the bathroom but don't hear anything.

Pushing up onto my elbows, I search the floor for a pallet and find none.

Rolling to face Constantine, I ask, "Did Hendrix sleep in the bed all night?"

He loops an arm over me and pulls me close until our noses touch. "He did."

I play with the coarse stubble along his jaw. He'd look sexy as sin with a short beard.

"Nightmares?"

"No."

Hearing that Hendrix slept through the rest of the night makes me absurdly happy.

"You interrupted me," Constantine says, his voice huskier than usual.

Muscles I didn't know existed protest when he rolls me back over, then continues where he left off.

Desire blossoms as he lightly kisses along the fine lines of where the man plunged his knife into my side. Constantine is a hardened man. Unemotive, stoic —brutal and deadly when necessary. He was forced to become what the Society demanded. After all the ugliness he survived, there shouldn't be a scrap of love or softness left in him, so it makes it that much more special when he lets me see it. Shows me in the gentleness of his touch and tells me with his broken voice that he loves me.

"That feels so good," I moan deliriously when his strong fingers dig into the muscles of my legs.

He kneads the tightness until the tension releases and I'm a blissed-out husk made of goo.

"I could get used to wake-up massages. Your hands should be classified as the ninth wonder of the modern world."

"Just my hands?" he teases.

He shifts to reach my other leg, and his morning erection prods my outer thigh.

Embarrassment comes swiftly when I realize that he watched me have sex with Tristan and Hendrix and didn't join us, then I literally fell asleep in his arms right after.

"I feel awful about last night." I correct myself when his hand stills. "That came out wrong. Nothing about last night was awful. Last night was amazing. What I meant…" I hate when my thoughts and my tongue misalign, and I can't say what I really mean. "It's just that you didn't… I mean, we didn't—*you know*," I finish on a whisper.

I feel his smile curve on my spine when he kisses up the valley of my lower lumbar. "Last night was about you and them."

"But—" I try to lift up but flop back down like a useless wet noodle when his thumbs press into my trapezius muscles near my shoulder blades.

"No buts. It was your time to be with them. Don't ever feel guilty about that. And don't ever be afraid to put us in our places if we demand too much from you or if you just want some time to yourself."

He positions my arms above my head and massages his way down each one to my fingertips while his mouth gets busy licking and kissing me everywhere, leaving me in a state of Zen but also incredibly turned on.

"I'm still unsure about how a relationship between all of us will work."

He covers me with his body, his mouth on the tendon at the base of my neck, and my very sore pussy perks right the hell up.

Clearing his throat, he says, "It'll work because it's us."

I would love for it to be that simple, but I know there'll be complications, jealousy, arguments, the usual relationship stuff—times three. Will it be okay if I want to be with one of them for a night? Do we all sleep in the same bed, or do I bed hop? Do I need to schedule my week to ensure that each of them gets equal time? What if I just want some 'me' time or want to do something with Raquelle?

He nips my ear. "You tensed up again. Stop overthinking it."

Wiggling to indicate I want to turn over, he lifts off me, giving me enough room to maneuver onto my back.

"I can't help it," I reply, pulling him back down. "I can't lose you all again."

His weight, so solid and warm, feels wonderful. My fingers immediately dive into his thick, dark hair, brushing the wavy, wayward locks out of his face.

Tears puddle without my permission, but I don't wipe them away. The months I spent in Ireland without them when Papa forced me into hiding broke my damn heart. I missed them so much, it hollowed me out until there was nothing left but anger and loneliness.

Constantine lowers his head and puts his ear directly over my heart, listening to its steady beat.

"You won't," he promises and kisses the side of my breast; however, I know all too well the fleetingness of life, especially the life we live where betrayal and death are the norm. And isn't that the saddest fucking thing?

"The morning you came back to the house still wearing the same clothes from the night before, you said you were out doing stuff. Did you kill someone?"

Cillian insinuated over the dinner table that Constantine had killed one of his men. It's been niggling me since.

"Yes."

I smooth away the frown line wrinkling his brow. "Why?"

I wait.

And wait.

Until finally...

"He was the man who attacked Tristan in the alley. He'd been following you. I found him in your apartment."

I don't ask why the man was in my apartment. If he worked for Cillian, then I get why he was following me based on everything I've learned of Cillian's role in my life once Papa asked him for help. I don't like it, and the next time I speak with him, he and I will definitely have words about it. I refuse to be stalked by a shadow everywhere I go.

"What were *you* doing in my apartment?"

He had come with me to help me pack when Tristan didn't give me a choice about moving in with them. There was no reason for Constantine to return. I didn't ask him to get anything for me. So why was he there?

Constantine's eyes narrow just a fraction, like he's trying to think up an explanation. When Aleksander's voice begins whispering those stupid doubts in my ear, I turn the volume down and tell it to fuck off.

I move my hands from Constantine's face to his chest. Every stunning, inked inch of this man is perfection. Even his blackened soul.

"Constantine."

The bedroom door cracks against the wall when it flies open, and Tristan appears in the doorway.

"Where the fuck is my sister?"

Oh, boy.

Naked with Constantine on top of me is not how I expected to have this conversation. With a quick kiss to his cheek, I gently push Constantine off me and sit up.

Tristan charges over to the bed, grabs my legs and slides me toward him, then shoves a phone in my face.

"Your cousin was kind enough to drop this off for you. Said to make sure to give it to you as soon as you woke up."

My stomach takes a nosedive when I see the text message from Evan on the screen.

Evan: Tell Syn that I just heard from Cillian. He and Dierdre should touch down in a few. I'm back at DF. Have her call me as soon as she can.

"I can explain."

Tristan tosses the phone on the bed. "You bet your sweet ass you're going to explain."

Hendrix walks in holding a cup of coffee I would sell my soul for right now.

None so gracefully, I clamber off the bed and head into the adjoining bathroom. "Let me take a quick shower, then we'll talk."

Tristan follows me and blocks the doorway. "We'll talk right fucking now."

I knew it wouldn't be that easy, but I did hope. I also really need a shower. My skin feels tight. The guys seem to love covering me in their cum.

Turning the shower on, I step under the spray, not caring that the water is icy cold, and grab the bottle of liquid soap from the shelf. Every movement hurts.

The water stings my abraded skin, chafed raw by their coarse stubble. My nipples are swollen and red from their mouths, and I turn around so the water beating down from the showerhead hits my back and not my front.

"T, what's going on? What did Andie give you?" Hendrix asks.

I assume Tristan shows him the message because Hendrix loudly exclaims, "Why the fuck is Evan texting you?"

I hiss under my breath when I gingerly soap between my legs. "Just give me a damn minute!"

I tune them out and do a brisk hair wash. Great. No conditioner. My hair is going to frizz like mad.

Finished, I turn off the water and get out. The memory foam bath mat soaks up the droplets that sluice down my arms and legs.

"Thanks," I tell Constantine when he engulfs me in a large white towel.

The bathroom is cavernous—double vanity sinks, expansive shower stall, and a large garden tub that sits in front of a frosted glass window—but with the three of them crowded in here with me, it feels the size of a matchbox.

I twist away from my naked reflection in the wall-length mirror. It's still hard to look at myself and see the burns that cover my left arm, hip, and thigh.

"I was going to tell you last night but then..." I blush thinking about what happened.

Tristan's arms cross at his chest, his biceps stretching the short sleeves. "Where's Dierdre?"

I puff out a breath. "With Cillian."

The muscle in his jaw ticks. "Where exactly is she

with Cillian?" he asks ominously.

"He's taking her to Ireland."

"Why?" he snaps, getting angrier.

"Because I told her to go."

I jump when he barks, "Why?"

"Please don't yell at her," Constantine says, but the way he says it is chilling and has Tristan transferring his glare from me to him.

"I asked Evan to take her to Cillian because I needed to get her someplace safe before Gab—"

I don't get to finish. Tristan uncrosses his arms and fists his hands at his side.

"You asked Evan?"

Getting irritated from his constant interruptions, I run my hand through my wet hair and try again. "After she told me about Gab—"

"You had no right asking that fucker for anything! She's *my* sister—"

I don't feel bad cutting him off since he has no problem doing it to me.

"And she's *my* mother."

Apparently, that was the wrong thing to say because he erupts.

"For the last fucking time, Dierdre is not your mother! Your mother is dead!"

Shock punches a hole through my chest, and I blink at him, frozen in place as that night replays in my mind. My mother was injured, too weak to fight off the man as he raped her right in front of me.

"Don't look, baby. Close your eyes and don't look. It'll be okay."

But the constellation man forced me to watch. Wouldn't let me look away. Her pleas for my life excited him. The malicious way the other man defiled and hurt her excited him more.

Hendrix pushes Tristan against the wall and away from me. "Jesus, man. That was uncalled for."

"Syn."

Constantine lifts my face, but I don't really see him, even though I hear his voice. I'm too far gone in those memories and react unconsciously when he touches me, grabbing his wrist and torquing it.

His grunt of pain brings me crashing back, and I let go, horrified that I've hurt him.

"Oh god. I'm sorry."

"It's okay."

"It's not okay!" I yell more at myself.

Constantine has been hurt by too many people, especially his father. *And now me.*

I sprint out of the bathroom. Blindly putting on pants I find lying in a heap on the floor, I grab the shirt hanging off the footboard, slipping it over my head as I hurry out of the room and race down the hallway.

"Aoife, stop."

I can't. I don't trust myself right now. I'm too angry. I'm not in control, and I fear what I'll do if pushed too far.

"Dammit, will you fucking stop?"

I run barefoot to the stairwell exit, no patience to wait for the elevator to arrive, and burst into the stairwell, startling the guard stationed on the landing. Once I pass through, the steel door closes and locks almost immediately.

"Holy shit, you scared the crap out of me," the guard says, his hand covering his gun holster.

Pound. Pound. Pound. Fists hammer against the

reinforced steel as Tristan's enraged shouts carry out into the stairwell.

The guard looks over at the door, then at me.

"Do you want me to open that?"

"No," I reply, sweeping my wet hair over one shoulder. I love Tristan but fuck him for what he said. "Could you tell Andie I'd like to speak with her?"

CHAPTER 27

"What on earth are you wearing?" Andie asks as soon as she sees me.

I peer down at the baggy men's clothes hanging off me. I didn't take much consideration on what I was throwing on as I left the room. I think I'm wearing Tristan's shirt and Hendrix's pants.

Not missing a beat, she asks, "Hungover? I can make you a banana smoothie."

Should I be hungover? I would think so after the shots of tequila I drank.

"Thank you, but surprisingly, I feel fine," I reply.

Some guy I haven't met yet gives me a brief once-over and a chin jerk hello from the couch and goes back to watching an MMA fight taking place on the living room television. Jax sits across from him, completely focused on the screen of his laptop. If he didn't have blond hair and glasses, he would be Constantine's twin.

"Have you eaten breakfast yet?"

I walk into the kitchen where Andie is transferring

pastries and donuts to a long serving platter and follow my nose to the freshly brewed coffee I smell.

"Not yet, but I'd love some of that." I point to the still steaming mug sitting on the counter next to her.

"Be my guest. Cups are in the cabinet above the maker."

"Where's Sarah?" I ask as I take a crossword puzzle print coffee mug down from the middle shelf.

"Still with Declan. She usually doesn't wake up until about nine."

Andie looks completely different than she did yesterday. Her hair is pulled into a high ponytail, she's dressed in form-fitting yoga capris and a pink tank top, and she's sans makeup. She looks like the girl next door, or perhaps a soccer mom, but definitely not a mafia queen.

"You have the most stunning eyes," I let slip as I study her while sipping my coffee.

She looks startled at my compliment. "Thank you. So do you. I've never seen that color of blue before. Guess unique eye color is something that runs in the family."

Family.

Finding out about this family of cousins I never knew existed has been surreal. It's a bit mind-boggling, to be honest. Papa and Mama didn't have any siblings as far as I know—but that doesn't really mean much since I apparently don't know a lot about the people who gave birth to me.

"Grab a donut if you want and follow me," Andie suddenly says and doesn't give me any choice but to follow her.

I'm not a dainty coffee drinker. I guzzle it down, wanting that kick of caffeine as quickly as possible.

I set my mug in the sink, eye the chocolate-covered donut sitting on top of the pastry pyramid, then decide against it.

"Moving in?" I inquire.

The layout of this floor is similar to the one we've been staying on, just different furniture and color scheme. There are a scattering of moving boxes lying around, some taped up, some half-filled.

"Moving out, actually. We bought some land and built a house out in the countryside away from everything. City life isn't for me, and I wanted someplace Sarah could run wild."

We enter a bedroom with the biggest four-poster bed I have ever seen taking up most of the space. It's easily twice the size of a California king.

"I grew up on a farm, so I hear ya. Darlington isn't much different. Very quaint and quiet and lots of stars at night."

"How are you liking college?"

"Love it. I wear my nerd badge proudly."

She comes out of the walk-in closet with an armful of clothes and dumps them on the bed. A metallic clatter draws my attention up to the metal rings dangling from each of the bed posts.

"What are those? Tristan has them on his bed."

Andie bursts out laughing.

"What?" I ask, confused.

She flicks one of the rings, and it clanks like a door knocker. "I'm sure you'll find out soon enough."

That isn't an answer, but I drop it.

"How long have you been with them? And those are for you," she says of the clothes she just tossed onto the bed.

I finger the dark blue material of the shirt sitting on top of the pile. "We were friends as kids. The sleeping with them is new."

I don't know why I admitted that but if there was anyone who would understand, it would be her. It's also nice to have another female to talk with about this stuff —and thinking that makes me miss Raquelle. I can't wait to see her when we return to DF.

Andie bounces a few times when she flops backward onto the mattress. "Best friends to lovers. I love that. Do those hurt?"

She's staring at my neck, not my burns, and I pull the collar up a smidge to hide the hickeys.

"No," I lie because of course they do. It's a good hurt that reminds me I'm alive and desired and loved. "Hendrix likes to mark me."

Why the fuck did I say that? Shut up, Syn.

Eyes bright with mischief, Andie eagerly rubs her hands together. "Do tell."

"That's a huge no." Changing subjects, I ask, "Do you have an extra phone I could borrow?"

She pops off the bed and disappears into the bathroom. "Didn't Tristan give you the one I dropped off?" She comes back out carrying bottles of nail polish.

"He kind of went ballistic when he saw the text message from Evan, then went supernova when I told him Dierdre was heading to Ireland with Cillian," I answer truthfully.

"I was wondering. You looked upset when you walked in. Will you tell me what happened?"

"Nope." I smile, hoping it lessens the severity of my rebuke.

"Didn't think so." She smiles back.

Climbing on the bed once again, she gestures for me to join her. I play along, even though I have no idea what's going on. I sit crossed-legged in front of her. She takes my hand, inspects the state of my nails, and *tsks*.

"Pick a color while I fix this disaster." She takes the nail clippers and starts giving me a manicure. "I'm not going to get all up in your business. I hate when people do that. Just know that I'm here if you ever want to talk."

My first instinct is to shut down. People can't hurt you or disappoint you if you don't give them the ammunition to use against you. It's best to seal yourself off, never let anyone get close, and guard your heart behind an impenetrable wall made of steel.

"I appreciate that. This is all new to me, and I don't know you, so please understand my wariness. I don't trust easily."

She nods. "Understood. And I get it because I'm the same. Offer still stands, though."

I hand her the bottle of black polish that looks almost navy blue when the light hits it. "I've never had my nails done before."

She flicks her violet eyes up at me. "My best friend Tessa and I used to do each other's nails all the time. I'm surrounded by guys and testosterone twenty-four-seven and need something feminine to help keep me sane. Manis, pedis, makeup, perfume, clothes."

Ah, the infamous Tessa who was supposed to do… *something*… for Tristan.

"I never had any friends growing up, but I did have a pet rooster."

Her laughter has me suppressing a smile.

"No shit?"

I shrug a shoulder, a little embarrassed.

"That's awesome." Once she's done with the clippers, she vigorously shakes the nail polish to mix it. "Liam says he wants a dog."

"Which one is Liam?" I ask as she carefully swipes polish over my thumbnail.

"The guy on the couch next to Jax."

Gray eyes. Dark hair. Gorgeous in a way that would have any woman stop in her tracks to take a second look.

Taking her up on her offer to listen if I wanted to talk, I ask, "How do you manage it?"

She finishes, and I blow on my nails to dry them, admiring how the color changes from dark blue to black and back again.

"Manage what? The guys?"

As if she can't sit still for more than a minute, she's up again and back within seconds holding a hairbrush and elastic hair bands.

"How do you handle the arguments? Ouch!" I yelp when the brush gets caught in a nasty tangle.

"Sorry. You have a shit-ton of hair. I love the color. As for arguments, we have them all the time. No way to avoid them when you have five people who are all stubborn as hell." She gathers my hair on top of my head and secures the ponytail with a hair band.

"What do you do when what you want conflicts with what they want?"

She does some twirly thing with my tresses and uses another band to hold them in place, then lies on her stomach and props herself up on her forearms.

"Depends on how badly I want it."

A bit disappointed that she didn't shower me with

sage wisdom, I accordion through the pile of clothes and select the blue shirt and a pair of jeans. Andie's clothes fit me last night, so these should as well. I take them with me inside the closet and change.

"Grab whatever shoes you want from the shoe rack."

As soon as she offers, I spy a pair of slip-on black Skechers and slide my feet into them. Fully dressed, I come out with my dirty clothes bundled under my arm.

"I don't like fighting with them. We lost so much time together, and I don't want to waste what time we do have left arguing."

Andie props her chin on her closed fist, her gaze shrewd and introspective. "If it's important to you, then they'll support you, regardless of whether they agree with you or not. That's what loving someone entails."

"What I want could be dangerous," I tell her.

The grin that takes over her heart-shaped face is dazzling. "Strong women never back down from danger. We thrive on it. We also back each other up. You need me, I'm there."

It hits me as she says it. The sincerity that can't be faked. She really means it.

"I've been known to kick some major ass when I need to," she adds.

I don't doubt it. I see her darkness, probably because she doesn't bother to hide it. Andie is just as dangerous as the men she's married to.

"Does having my back include helping me catch a plane back to Darlington?"

There's something I need to do without any interference from the guys. They're going to be livid with me.

Jesus, Synthia, you really are out of your mind.

CHAPTER 28

Hendrix tries to pull me away from the door after another round of futile pounding and shouted threats.

"She's been gone for almost two goddamn hours!"

I kick the shit out of the door because I'm pissed that she left us here, trapped like caged animals. Fucking mafia and their stupid paranoia, locked doors, and biometric security systems. If Con had the right equipment, he'd be able to bypass their system.

"She'll be back once she calms down."

I'm far from calm. Aoife sent my sister away without discussing it with me. We've been in Texas for little more than a day, for fuck's sake. It makes no sense.

"You shouldn't have gone off on her like that," Con not-so-helpfully says.

He's been going through the burner phones we were given, checking each one out, looking for tracking software or anything else that may have been installed.

"Fuck you," I reply, even though he's right.

I'm not proud of what I said in the heat of the

moment. Aoife didn't deserve having the reminder of what happened to her mother thrown in her face like that.

Hendrix goes into the kitchen, opening and shutting cabinets as he hunts through their contents.

"Bloody hell, all they stock is Irish whiskey," he grouses and holds up a bottle.

It's not even ten in the morning, but what the hell. I take the glass Hendrix pours. It burns like fire going down, leaving behind a smoky-sweet aftertaste.

"Since Dierdre is gone, there's no reason to stay here any longer."

I scowl at my friend. My sister was the only reason we came. I never got to talk to her. I barely got to look at her. I spent the last ten years mourning her death, only to find out she's alive, and I still don't know why.

"We need to find out where Cillian lives in Ireland."

"Why don't you ask Evan?"

I hit Hen with a withering glare.

"Besides," he goes on, "you said we were off to New York. I'm not flying to fucking Ireland."

I skim my hands through my hair and grip the ends. When did everything get so messed up?

"Syn wants to go back to Darlington. Wherever she is, is where I'll be." Con drops a phone in front of me and hands one to Hendrix. "They're clean."

Con's voice has been getting stronger the more he uses it. He'll probably never lose the gravelly, scratchy timbre, but I don't care. It's so good to hear him talk again.

"Are you sure?"

Taking affront that I would question his tech skills, he flips me off.

"I connected them to our network. Didn't want to piggyback off their Wi-Fi."

We have extra phones back at the house, but these will do for now. There are a multitude of things I need to do, including reaching out to the board members. My life might be in chaos and my parents might be dead, but that doesn't stop the wheels of the business from turning.

Putting my phone on speaker, I dial Dad's private number. When no one answers, I try Mom's number. Nothing.

Aleksander, you lying son of a bitch.

"Try phoning Malin," Hendrix suggests.

The mere mention of that scum sucker's name sets me off. "Fuck no!"

Hen fires back, "Well, fuck you very much. It was just a suggestion."

Thankfully, Con doesn't say anything. I haven't told Hendrix what Con figured out about Malin being the man who attacked Aoife and murdered her parents, or that my father is likely the one who ordered the hit. I want to hear my father confess it. Look him and Malin right in the eye, let them see their deaths coming, beg me on their knees to spare their lives, then do to them what they did to her. They deserve nothing less. But all of that hinges on Aleksander's word that they're still alive.

"I'll reach out to some of my contacts and see what I can find out. Hen, can you try to get hold of Serena?"

I know better than to ask him to call his father, which would be a more logical choice.

He tosses the rest of his drink back. "Why in the hell would you want me to talk to her?"

"She's Society and may have heard something."

It frustrates me to be in this position, and I curse Dad for keeping me on such a tight leash. All our fathers, actually. It's ironic that Hen, Con, and I were born around the same time. Three sons who became a threat to their fathers' ambitions. They could have killed us when we were children. Hell, Gabriel almost did kill Con. Instead, they tried to control us through fear and abuse.

Maybe they sensed we would turn on them. Felt it as each day drew closer to the date when, according to bylaws, they would step down and relinquish their seats on the Council to their sons. We knew they weren't going to do it and had been preparing to take it by force. But then fucking Aleksander and Aleksei had to mess up everything we had planned. And Hendrix—he never said a word that he wanted out until the other day.

Hendrix shakes his head. "Nope. You want to talk to Serena, you call her. Not touching that ever again. Syn would castrate me if she found out. She wouldn't care about the reason."

He has a point, especially after seeing what she did to Melissa just for flirting with him.

"I'll try to get in touch with her father first."

Politicians are a dime a dozen because their terms are short and fleeting. And then there are families like the Worthingtons who are career politicians with staying power. Serena's great-grandfather and grandfather were congressmen. Her father started out as one for the state of New York, then became a senator, always with his eye on the White House. If things go the way everyone predicts, Chester Worthington will be the next POTUS.

Con rubs the scruff covering his jaw, his expression as serious as I've ever seen it.

"Aleksander isn't going to stop coming for her. The fact that he traveled here and tracked her down at the bar worries the hell out of me."

"He could've taken us out but didn't. I don't trust the bastard, but I think his offer of a truce may be real," Hen says.

It causes me actual pain to agree with him, so I don't say a fucking word.

Con is somber when he says, "He's going to tell her, and when he does, we'll lose her."

The fuck we will because I won't let that happen. I will chase after her to the ends of the earth if she tries to leave us.

"Not if I kill him first."

Con drops his head to his folded arms and groans. "You can't. She told me last night not to go after him."

Before I can lose my shit for the umpteenth time, the elevator sounds its arrival, and I'm up and moving, ready to throttle Aoife for telling Con that and for leaving us stuck here. Then I'm going to fuck her senseless while I apologize for being an ass.

But it's not Aoife who walks off the elevator.

Dropping a duffel bag to the floor, Keane uses his foot to slide it my way.

"Good thing I brought clothes," he says when he notices Hen in only a pair of boxer briefs since Aoife ran off with his trousers.

"Where is she?" I demand to know.

"Gone."

Keane winces when Hen, Con, and I shout various versions of "What do you mean she's gone?"

Tired of all this bullshit, I grab Keane by his neck and slam him up against the wall next to the fireplace mantel. I don't give a crap that he's the new head of the Rossi syndicate, and I don't care that Andie is related to Aoife.

"Where. Is. She?"

Keane and I have similar builds, but I'm taller, which thrills me to no end because it means I get to look down on him.

His hazel eyes burn hellfire, and I'm disappointed he doesn't fight back.

"I'd suggest you back the fuck up."

Not happening. Keane Agosti doesn't scare me. His Grim Reaper, Jax, doesn't either, nor does Liam Connelly or Rafael Ortiz. Their tiny slice of power is nothing compared to the global reach of the Society.

"Look, I don't know exactly what's going on, only that Andie said to tell you that your girl has gone back to Darlington. Honestly, the sooner you assholes are out of here, the better. So I'd suggest you get dressed and haul ass to the airport to catch the next flight out."

Screw that. Our families have their own planes; however, it'll take a few hours to get one down here. It's either that or a charter. No way are we flying commercial. Takes too long, and I'd like to avoid the security checks.

I release Keane and pick up the duffel. "We'll be ready to leave in ten."

"Good. And a word of advice."

"Yeah?" I ask, wishing he'd get on with it.

"Trust me when I tell you that the tighter you try to hold onto her, the easier it will be for her to slip right through your fingers."

CHAPTER 29

The late afternoon sun warms me as I traverse the quad on my way to the bell tower. There's a crispness in the breeze that ruffles the loose wisps of my hair and gives hints that fall will soon arrive. The tips of leaves fluttering on the branches of maples and oaks that dot the campus are already starting to change color. The transition from summer green to autumnal reds and golds is subtle, and I can't wait to see the explosion of color in a few weeks when the fall foliage is at its peak.

I step out of the way of a couple of guys that get too close. I'm suspicious of everyone who walks by me. Are they from families tied to the Society? Are they the enemy? Remembering my past has tainted my view of the present. Walking around campus doesn't hold the magical appeal it did just last week. Syn looked at this place with hope and amazement, whereas Aoife sees Darlington Founders for what it truly is. There is no blade of grass, no single brick, no molecule of air that isn't steeped in the stench of the Society's influence and money.

When I pass the library, there's a new flicker of recognition when I see the dedication plaque mounted to the side of the red brick: *Named in Honor of Julius Wentworth.*

I glance around at the other buildings that surround the quad, seeing them with new eyes. A few surnames I had long forgotten now greet me on the front façades of lecture halls, carved into the stone of the triangular pediments. Where are the Amatos, Knights, Ferreiras, and Fitzpatricks, the founding members of the Society? On my walks through campus before classes started, I don't remember ever coming across buildings named after our families, and it makes me wonder why not. The university runs on Society money and donations, and wealthy, narcissistic megalomaniacs love to see their names plastered everywhere.

When I get to the fountain in the middle of the quad, I stop and take out the new phone Jax set up for me. It's much nicer than my old phone and untraceable, or so Jax said. Hitting the camera icon, I switch it to front-facing and snap a picture of myself to send to Raquelle. I had memorized her number the first day of classes when she programmed it into my old phone.

Me: Proof of life. I'm back.

Her response is instantaneous.

Raquelle: Ahhh! I've missed you! I can't wait to hear about your trip.

There is no way in hell I can tell her what really happened. Knowing I'm going to have to keep secrets from a girl who I consider a friend makes me second-guess everything all over again. It's an exhausting perpetual loop of uncertainty.

Me: I missed you, too. Trip was uneventful. Nothing really to tell.

Raquelle: Sure <wink emoji> I'm stuck in an art lecture until 6. <eye roll emoji> Want to meet up after? You didn't miss much in class, but I made copies of my notes for you.

I check the time and see that it's half past four. My internal clock still thinks it's three thirty because of the one-hour jump from Texas time to Darlington time.

Me: You are too sweet. Thank you.

Me: I have something I need to do. Rain check? Meet up for breakfast tomorrow morning?

Raquelle: Text me when you get up. <smile emoji> <paintbrush emoji>

I send her a quick thumbs up, pocket my phone, and force my feet to start walking.

On the almost four-hour flight back to Darlington, I questioned what I was doing a million times, and at one point, I almost demanded the plane be turned around.

"Burn girl!" someone shouts.

My head snaps around to find the source of the voice, and dread pools low in my belly when I see Serena and another woman striding my way. Who the fuck calls someone that, out loud, in public?

I don't need this right now. Pretending I don't hear her, I increase my walking speed.

"Hey, burn girl! Wait up!"

The high-pitched volume of her voice ensures everyone in the quad knows she's talking to me as evidenced by all the heads turning to look in my direction.

I have a feeling that she'll continue to pursue me, calling me that stupid name, if only to embarrass the hell out of me. I wouldn't put it past her.

Resigned to give her one minute of my time, I reluctantly pull myself to a stop in the middle of the walkway and turn around. Serena's light blonde hair is secured in an elegant bun, and her complexion looks much better without all the caked-on makeup. The dress she's wearing is a simple black A-line, and elegant pearls adorn her ears and around her neck. She looks tasteful and refined, vastly different from the girl Hendrix spent the night with who stumbled half-naked into the kitchen wearing only her lacy underwear the next morning.

The woman with her has long, straight ebony hair, and porcelain skin. She's tall with a willowy frame and very pretty. Her beauty is dampened by the mean look in her brown eyes, and that hateful look is aimed right at me.

Serena's overpowering floral perfume arrives before she does, and I wrinkle my nose to stop the sneeze that threatens to escape.

"Your face is fucked up."

Tactless as ever.

I forgot about the bruising on my face, so it slipped my mind that others would notice. At least the blue shirt Andie gave me to wear has a high collar and covers the hickeys on my neck.

"Ran into a door. I almost didn't recognize you with your clothes on. How's life at Kappa Cunt?"

It's immature to lower to her level, but she called me burn girl, so I couldn't resist using the name Hendrix called her sorority.

Her head tilts to the side like a dog's when it's trying to understand what a human is saying. It's impossible not to think about Hendrix fucking her when she's standing right in front of me. It makes me physically nauseous.

"Have you seen Hendrix? I've been trying to call him, and I stopped by the house last night and this morning, but no one was there."

Jealousy and possessiveness rear their ugly heads, and along with them come the compulsion to lash out. It would be so easy to break her thin bones, preferably all ten fingers so she never tries to touch what's mine again.

"Haven't seen him."

"What about Tristan?"

The other woman's contemptuous gaze sears into me with unbridled hostility at the mention of his name. I'm tempted to ask her what her problem is.

Being obtuse, I shrug. "Haven't seen him either. I have somewhere I need to be, so if you'll excuse me."

If it were only that simple.

Serena huffs and rolls her eyes like talking to me is exhausting. "You're fucking Tristan and Constantine and staying at their house. How could you not know where they are?"

Damn Tristan for telling her that.

"Doesn't mean I'm their babysitter," I reply as nicely as I can when all I want to do is throat punch her Botoxed face.

I don't stick around. My manners only go so far.

"Tell Tristan that Katalina would like to talk to him."

Katalina. Where have I heard that name before?

As I keep walking, she tacks on "ugly bitch" loud enough for me and everybody else to hear. God, I can't stand her. How Hendrix could even tolerate being around her, let alone stick his dick in her is beyond my comprehension—and repulsive.

After crossing the quad, it takes another five minutes before I arrive at the bell tower. The angle of the sun hits the glass windows and creates a blinding glare. Shielding my eyes, I look up at the old clock face. I thought I'd be more nervous, but my mind is calm, and my heart rate is steady. I don't even know if Aleksander is here. I didn't really think that part through. The security cameras would have already alerted him to my presence, so it's not like I'm going to surprise him.

"Alright, Aleksander. Game on," I mutter and open the front entrance door.

A gust of cold air hits my face, caused by the pressure difference between the warmer outside temperature and the air-conditioned indoors. The lobby is empty and dark, but the elevator doors are open, just like the last time I was here. With every step I take, the rubber soles of my borrowed Skechers squeak across the polished floor and echo around the cavernous space.

As soon as I step inside the elevator, the doors close, and the lift starts moving without me doing anything. Oh yeah. He's definitely here.

Expecting Aleksander to be standing on the other side, I brace when the elevator stops and the doors slide open. What I'm met with is mute darkness.

The outlines of furniture sharpen once my eyes adjust. Blackout curtains cover the window, not letting through even a sliver of afternoon light. Just when I'm about to turn around and leave, thinking no one is home after all, the hairs on the back of my neck and arms rise, warning me I'm not alone. It's then I see a silhouette across the room. Aleksander is watching me.

There's a clink of ice against glass as he raises his drink to his lips, those pewter eyes never leaving me as I warily enter his apartment.

"You came back."

His voice sounds different. Coarser.

"You knew I would."

The questions and doubts he left me with guaranteed I would come.

Recessed ceiling lights turn on as Aleksander saunters over to the coffee table and sets down his drink. He pulls one end of the men's tie he's wearing through the knot, then slides it from under the collar and drops it onto the table.

"Have you told Gabriel about Alana?" When his brow furrows, I clarify, "Dierdre."

"Not yet."

Meaning that he plans to, which makes my split decision to get her out of the country the right one.

Aleksander removes his cufflinks and rolls the sleeves up to his elbows, showing off thick forearms covered in intricate designs. "Would you care for something to drink?"

I find it somewhat comical that a man who is so brutal can be so polite.

"Water would be nice."

As soon as the plane landed, I called up an Uber and came straight here. Since I don't have the keys to my apartment and I can't get into the guys' house, I'll need to find a place to stay for the night. Andie gave me enough cash to last a while, but without ID, getting a hotel room isn't an option. Maybe Evan will let me crash at his place.

Aleksander is gone and back in less than thirty

seconds, holding a glass filled with ice and a bottle of water. He doesn't offer them to me, merely places them on the coffee table.

Dropping to the couch, he undoes the top buttons of the shirt, exposing a wide vee of his tattooed chest and neck, and reclines back into the cushions, making himself comfortable. He looks exhausted. There's noticeable fatigue and weariness carved into his face.

"Aleksei's wish was to be cremated, and his ashes spread over a field of sunflowers. He never told me why he wanted it that way." He roughly scrubs his palms over his eyes and looks at me. "I did what he asked. I said goodbye to my brother this morning."

I shouldn't feel bad that Aleksei is dead, but for some reason I can't explain, I feel bad for Aleksander. No matter what he has done, he lost his twin brother. His parents are dead. Aleksander has no one now. In a way, we're kind of the same.

My right hand automatically goes to the Sig Sauer Andie gave me that sits snuggly against my back.

"If you lured me here to kill me for what happened to your brother—"

"I meant what I said last night. You have nothing to fear from me."

"You said a lot of stuff I find hard to believe." I increase my grip on the gun, my posture rigid. "I'm sorry about Aleksei but I'm not sorry about what happened. He was going to kill Constantine. He was going to kill me. I had no choice."

Aleksander suddenly sits up, and I whip the gun around, training it on him.

"I told him not to touch you."

My thoughts travel back to the garden. With Aleksei

looming over him, I can see Constantine on the ground, blood dripping from his mouth, his eyes full of love and regret as he accepted his fate, hoping by sacrificing himself, it would save me.

"Well, he clearly didn't listen." I tap the side of my face where Aleksei punched me with the butt of his gun.

And why tell his brother to spare me? I was nothing to him. Just some random girl who he thought was sleeping with his enemy.

"I'm so sorry, *pevchaya ptitsa*. I didn't know—*fuck*."

I don't get him. If there ever was an enigma wrapped inside a riddle, it would be Aleksander Stepanoff.

"I killed your twin brother, and you're apologizing *to me*?" I ask with a hefty dose of skepticism.

His head tips back on the sofa cushion, and he closes his eyes. I'm at a loss. This exchange is nothing like I expected. Lowering my weapon, I chance a step forward.

"What does *pevchaya ptitsa* mean?" I butcher the pronunciation.

"Songbird."

That's actually very lovely and increases my confusion over this man even more. I take another tentative step closer. There are so many things I want to ask him. So many questions I want answered.

"I lied before. I do remember you. The gala when we were children. You asked me to dance."

Aleksander smiles, popping twin dimples that completely transform his face. As if lost in the same memory, he says, "You look completely different now, but your eyes are the same."

"Well, you look... bigger," I stupidly reply.

His smile widens.

With a shit-ton of trepidation, I take a seat in the armchair across from the couch, but in no way lower my guard. Not taking my eyes off him, I reach for the bottle of water and twist the cap off one-handed since I'm still clutching the gun.

After a few swallows, I boldly inform him, "I'm taking back my father's seat on the Council."

His sharp nod precedes, "Good."

Good? He murdered Eva to get Patrick's vote, then staged a coup, and I'm supposed to believe that after killing his brother, he's just going to let me waltz in and take over?

I set the bottle of water down too hard, and droplets splatter on the glass of the coffee table like rain. Tristan was right. Aleksander is playing me.

"This was a mistake."

I abandoned the guys in Texas to come here because I thought… what in the hell was I thinking?

I leap to my feet. When Aleksander follows suit, I shift my weapon toward him once again, a warning not to make any sudden moves.

He ever so slowly raises his hands in front of him, but it does little to alleviate my distrust.

"Aoife, please don't go."

Retreating toward the elevator, my footsteps falter momentarily at the desperation I hear. I jab at the button to call the lift. *Come on. Come on.* Fucking elevators. I'm never taking one again. I'd rather suffer the agony of climbing up and down flights of stairs.

"You promised a truce if I came back to Darlington. Well, I'm here. You also swore no harm would come to Tristan, Constantine, or Hendrix. If you or anyone else from the Society so much as breathes on them, you'll be joining your brother in hell."

"I will never break a promise to you, *pevchaya ptitsa*," he vehemently declares.

Is he for real?

"You and Aleksei went to Hendrix's family estate with one clear goal. You were going to kill them. Why would I believe that you won't try again?"

As soon as I hear the *ding*, I hop in the elevator. When Aleksander lunges forward and blocks the door from closing, I shove the nozzle of the gun to his forehead. It would be so easy to kill him right now. Squeeze the trigger and be done with it. But something stops me.

"I didn't know you were alive, and that changes everything. And I won't touch them because their deaths would only hurt you."

"Back up," I warn him, and he immediately complies.

Just as the elevator door shuts me safely inside, Aleksander's parting words cut me wide open.

"You can't trust them, Aoife. They're lying to you."

CHAPTER 30

"She's not here."

I quietly approach where Aleksander stands at the window, hands shoved deep into the side pockets of his dress slacks, looking very much like a man with a lot on his mind. The curtains are half drawn on one side, and the light coming in outlines his profile in stark relief as he stares off into space.

"But she was," I reply.

I knew as soon as Keane said she was gone that she would come here.

Aleksander turns away from the window to face me, his head tilted to the side. His silver irises gleam in the soft aura filtering through the window. His head tips downward, slowly and deliberately, cloaking his features in a shadow. The bold outline created around his body, like the ring around the moon during a solar eclipse, shudders as he directs his gaze to me once more, a note of ice-cold menace evident in his voice.

"She's magnificent, isn't she?"

"She isn't yours," I snap, glaring intensely at the man I have despised for years and who has despised me in return.

Aleksander breaks out in a smile. A smug, sickening grin which stretches from ear to ear beneath his predacious eyes.

"She's not really yours either," he retorts, sliding his right hand from the interior of his pocket and pulling at his open collar. After a moment or two of absentminded adjustment, he lets his arm fall back to his side. "I saw how she kissed Constantine and Hendrix at the bar. I have to admit, it was hot as fuck to watch. How does it feel to know the woman you love wants your best friends more than she wants you?" he murmurs, his expression a display of mock sympathy. "It must piss you off."

I don't want Aleksander to have the satisfaction of seeing how much he's getting to me. My fists clench and unclench at my sides as I desperately try to control my rage. It takes every ounce of self-restraint I have not to cross the room and choke the life out of him.

"If you laid a fucking finger on her—"

Aleksander scoffs. "So damn dramatic. You know I wouldn't. You counted on it when you told me who she really was."

And I regret that split-second decision. At the time, I thought I didn't have a choice.

Aleksander's leather-soled shoes are silent on the polished hardwood floors as he walks to the middle of the room. With a graceful, almost choreographed motion, he effortlessly sweeps up a men's tie lying on the coffee table, drawing my attention to the two drinking glasses sitting there. Drinking glasses filled with half-melted ice, fresh condensation perspiring down their sides. How long was Aoife here?

Aleksander quietly observes me as he slips the tie around his neck, letting the ends dangle on either side of his unbuttoned shirt. "In case you're interested, Aleksei's ashes were scattered in Maybach Field this morning."

I experience a fleeting pinch of regret before I lock it down.

"Aleksei was a sociopath."

Aleksei was unhinged. Violent and unpredictable. A rabid dog who had to be kept on a short leash by his twin brother. I wish Con had killed him and not Aoife. She shouldn't need to be burdened with his death haunting her conscience.

Veins pop on Aleksander's forearm when he picks up his drink, his grip crushing the glass until it cracks.

"Show some goddamn respect. He was your brother."

Hating the reminder that we share anything in common, I reply, "Just because Francesco made the mistake of fucking your mother once upon a time doesn't make either of you my brothers."

"Half of my DNA says otherwise."

Aleksander and I found out about Francesco's affair with Nina Stepanoff at the same time. It was the night at the gala where Aleksander asked Aoife to dance, and he and I got into a fight. While waiting in a back room for our fathers to come and deal with us, Mom let the familial secret slip just as Dad walked in. She was drunk on wine and doped up on pain meds from her last plastic surgery after finding Dad screwing his new mistress in their bed. He took the whip to both our backs once we got home. I had to sleep on my stomach for almost a month.

I never knew for sure if Aleksander told Aleksei, but I'd always wondered. Knowing the truth wouldn't have made a difference. Aleksander and I had been enemies for far too long. Too much bad blood existed between us that couldn't be erased by the knowledge that we shared a father. A man I loathe and wish dead more often than not.

"What do you want, Aleksander?"

"What I've always wanted."

Taking a seat on the couch, he props a leg over a knee, and his fingers tap rhythmically on the side of his lower thigh. *Middle, ring, middle, index. Middle, ring, middle, index.* He follows that pattern, over and over, as I wait for him to continue. He seems to revel in the anticipation, the slightest hint of joy creeping into his dark, soulless pupils.

"I find it interesting that you haven't asked about him," he comments after a beat.

I don't admit that I tried calling Francesco, several times.

"Probably because I don't give a fuck," I reply.

He and Aleksei were lucky that Francesco never claimed them as his children, illegitimate or otherwise. Nikolai Stepanoff may have been a hard, cruel man, but at least he wasn't an abusive sadist.

When I don't take the bait, he says, "Francesco and Helena are at the Society compound, alive and well. Patrick is at his estate. What's left of it." He grins. "But I doubt Knight cares about that... or his dear, sweet mother."

I hold back the *fuck you* I want to hurl at him.

"Cops? Media?" I ask because the last thing any of us

need is an investigation into what went down at the Knight Estate.

"Being handled by friends of the Society."

Meaning that they're on our payroll.

I'm reluctantly impressed that he was able to control the situation so well, considering he caused half the fuck up.

"You seem to have made new friends. Never thought you'd be besties with the mob. The bomb was a nice touch, by the way. Wasn't expecting that."

I say nothing and keep my mouth shut. Let him think whatever he wants.

"And Gabriel?" I inquire.

Aleksander makes a thoughtful hum. "I thought I was seeing a ghost last night. Our sister has been a very naughty girl. Faking her own death. I wonder what could have driven her to do such a drastic thing?"

Aleksander loves to talk in nuances, leaving behind tiny breadcrumbs for the listener to catch, like his quip about Dierdre right after I asked about Gabriel.

Turning attention off our sister, I say, "I want to speak to Francesco."

"You'll see him at the gala this weekend when he names me as the new head of the Council."

He looks so pleased with himself. What a fucking douche. That was his grand design? All the shit he's pulled and the people he's hurt was just to get Francesco to acknowledge him and push me out of the way? The juvenile, petty jealousy rolling off him stinks up the room.

"I'd still like to speak with him. *Now.*"

"His phone privileges have been revoked. Besides, you know there's no cell reception in the catacombs."

Aleksander places his phone on the coffee table and spins it a hundred and eighty degrees, showing me a live feed on his screen of my father pacing a small room that I recognize immediately. It's one of the cells the Society uses to detain people. My eyes briefly alight on the figure standing in the corner. Malin. I only get a glimpse before Aleksander blacks out the screen, but it's enough.

"Where's Helena?"

"Enjoying better accommodations." Aleksander has been staring at me the entire time, his gun-metal gaze never wavering. "Did Aoife tell you that she wants her father's seat at the Council? I think it's a fantastic idea, don't you?"

His round-and-round is giving me a damn headache.

"You went to a lot of trouble to take over the Council. You expect me to believe that you'd really give up that position so easily?" I counter and watch his reaction.

Flicking imaginary lint from his dress slacks, he drapes a casual arm over the back of the couch, looking nonplussed.

"I'd do it for her. Would you?" he challenges.

My knuckles pop when I flex my fists. "I'd die for her."

Aleksander emits a sharp boom of laughter. "I can't wait for her to find out what a lying sack of shit you are." Rising from the couch, he cuts the distance between us. "I promised Aoife I wouldn't lay a hand on you or Knight or Ferreria, so here's my proposition. Why don't we let her decide at the gala? If Aoife wants me gone, I'll go. If she wants to burn the entire organization to the ground, I'll be the first to light the match."

That imagery hits too close to home with Aoife's scars, and I'm sure Aleksander used the metaphor deliberately.

272

I don't believe a word that has spewed out of his lying mouth. But I'll play along only because it serves my purposes. He's actually making it easy for me. Him, my father, Malin, Patrick, and Gabriel all in one place, under the same roof, vulnerable and unsuspecting.

What had Aleksander said to me? Oh yeah, *"I did warn you that you had no idea what was coming for you."*

Endgame, motherfucker.

"Agreed," I reply.

He holds out a burly hand, waiting for me to shake on it. I don't.

Hopping on the elevator, I punch the ground floor button. "Stay away from Aoife. She doesn't need you fucking with her head. She's been through enough."

That stupid grin returns. "What if she can't stay away from me?"

The doors thankfully shut, and I take out my phone to text the guys.

Me: Still nothing?

Con: No. Checking her friend's dorm, the girl from her calc class.

Hen: Just left the Bierkeller. Shelby wasn't working, so I'm going to check out her place. No sign of our girl at the fucktwins?

Me: She was gone by the time I got there. Had an interesting conversation with Aleksander. Will fill you in later. Heading to the house.

Aoife, where are you?

CHAPTER 31

"Baby, wake up."

A Bostonian accent rouses me, but the nightmare doesn't want to let me go.

"Sweet girl, open those beautiful blue eyes for me."

I jolt awake and wipe away the dried tears crusted to my lashes.

"Tristan?"

As soon as his handsome, concerned face comes into view, I burst into tears. I can't help it. When I used to dream of that night, I would wake up with fuzzy recollections that I'd write down in my journal. Not now. Now, when I dream, I'm forced to relive every horrific thing that happened in stark detail.

"*Shhh.* I've got you," he promises, pulling me to him and holding me tight. "Why are you sleeping on the ground?"

I didn't know where else to go after I left the bell tower, so I came to the house. To the spot in the backyard where Tristan likes to sit next to the fragrant flowering bush. As soon as I rounded the back of the house, I swear I saw him sitting on the grass, knees bent to his chest, his figure bathed orange from the fiery light of the setting sun. But it was a trick of the mind, and once I blinked, he was gone.

I had laid down in Tristan's spot and stared up at the clouds, thinking about what Aleksander had said. I must have fallen asleep at some point.

"I wanted to feel close to you."

The outdoor security lights are on, and I search the backyard but don't see Constantine or Hendrix. No lights shine from inside the house. It's early evening, maybe eight o'clock or so.

"How did you find me?"

The screen of his phone glows light blue when he takes it out of his pocket. "Took a guess. Let me tell the guys. As soon as we landed, we split up to look for you."

A mountain of guilt consumes me when I see the message he sends.

Found her in the backyard. She's safe. Come home.

"I'm sorry."

Tristan drags his gaze away from the phone and locks those mesmerizing whiskey eyes on me.

"Me too, Red." He kisses my cheek, my lips, then buries his face in my hair, inhaling deeply.

His hands touch me everywhere, almost as if he's reassuring himself that I'm okay, and that's when he finds the gun tucked away at my back.

Warmed metal scrapes my skin when he slowly slips the pistol out from my waistband. Checking to make sure the safety is engaged, he carefully sets it on the ground.

"You went to see him." It's a statement, not a

question, which means he already knows.

I give him a shaky nod yes.

"Dammit, Aoife."

He sounds disappointed. I'd rather take his anger. Anger I can fight.

"How mad are you?" It's an idiotic thing to ask.

"Pretty fucking mad, but we can yell at each other tomorrow. Hop on," he tells me and pats his back.

Like an emotional yoyo, I go from sad to worried to amused. "You want to give me a piggyback ride?"

He glances over his shoulder, a slight curve to his lips that's not quite a smirk but close enough.

"If I recall, you used to love my piggyback rides."

I did. Any chance I could get, I would jump onto his back and have him cart me around.

Sweeping a hand down from my head to my stomach like a game show hostess, I inform him, "I'm not a little kid anymore and about a hundred pounds heavier."

More like a hundred and twenty, if I'm being honest, and all of it went to my boobs and ass.

With an impatient eye roll, he replies, "You're a feather. Now get the fuck on."

Once I climb on, he circles his arms underneath me, locking his hands together at his wrists. I keep my grip loose around his neck—don't want to choke him—and enjoy the ride as he carries me to the house.

"Hold tight," he says, stopping at the patio steps.

I'm tilted almost upside down when he bends over and picks up a rock half buried in the mulch of one of the plant beds.

"Spare," he says, showing me the detritus-covered silver key he retrieves. "You don't want to know how many times Hendrix forgets his."

"You can install a biometrics panel—*Ow!*" I shriek when he pinches an ass cheek.

"Not funny. We were stuck in that godforsaken place for two hours before Keane finally showed up."

"I really am sorry." I stifle my giggle when he pinches me again.

Unlocking the back door, he says, "Memorize this."

Propping my chin to his shoulder, I pay attention to the sequence of numbers he enters to turn off the alarm.

"You hungry?" I ask because I'm starving. The air still carries the buttery smell of the croissants Hendrix had made.

"Yes." But he walks us right out of the kitchen.

I look up at the stained-glass windows perched above the front door. Their patterns are haphazard and don't create a coherent picture. More like a collage of colored glass.

"I can make us something," I offer, as he climbs up the stairs. "Tristan," I say when he doesn't answer me.

Going into his room, he lets go, and I slide off his back until my feet hit the floor.

"Will you please say something?"

Shutting the door, he turns unexpectedly, and the air gets knocked out of me when he shoves me against the pressed wood.

"Don't ever leave us again."

The man in front of me looking like danger and filthy promises is the Tristan from the thunderstorm.

"I won't—"

I lose my breath once again when his mouth goes deep over mine, shutting me up. Hands possessively bracket my face, angling my head to control the kiss. When I reach for him, he pins my arms above my head.

"I don't want your fucking apologies. Now keep your hands up and don't move," he commands, tugging at the collar of my shirt. The material falls away with one hard yank, and my nipples instantly bead at the rush of cool air.

His gaze heats with a predatory hunger as it roams over my exposed skin. "You're mine, Aoife."

His roughened fingertips brand a trail along my collarbone, and I tremble with excitement. If this is how he wants to punish me, I'm all for it.

My breathing grows labored as those fingers quickly caress their way between my breasts, over my stomach, and under the hem of my jeans. With a flick of his fingers, the button comes undone, as does the zipper. He pushes the denim down to just above my knees and cups my pussy, sliding a thick finger through my folds to find me already wet and needy. Bringing his finger up to my lips, he paints them with my essence, then kisses me.

My arms are beginning to numb but I don't dare move as I watch him pull the zipper of his jeans and take out his cock. The head glistens with pearls of precum, and I lick my lips, only to taste myself when I'd rather be tasting him.

Tristan's hungry eyes never leave mine as he moves closer until our bodies are flush.

I cry out when he enters me, the pressure and sense of fullness unimaginable because I can't spread my legs apart.

"Tristan, I can't." My vision glazes with a haze of pleasure and pain.

He sucks my tongue into his mouth, kissing me into submission. "You were made for me, Red. You'll take it all."

He pushes in even deeper, which shouldn't be possible. I feel his cock pulse inside me like a heartbeat, and my core tightens around him.

Resting his forearms against the wall, he grabs my face between both hands. "Swear you'll never leave. No matter what. Swear it."

It's an easy promise to make. They own me. Body, heart, and soul.

"I swear," I gasp.

And then, Tristan fucks me, hard and fast, until I explode on a long, convulsive moan that echoes around the room. White obscures my vision when the coil of tension breaks, and I come harder than I ever thought possible.

Our eyes remain tethered as I ride out my orgasm and feel the warmth of his release penetrating deep when he follows right behind me. Absolutely spent, I go limp against him, a quivering mess of satiated woman who just got savagely taken against the bedroom door.

"I love hearing you moan my name."

He caresses my breast, pinching and pulling at the nipple, then takes the tight rosy nub into his mouth, sucking hard.

I play my fingers through his hair and kiss the top of his head. "I love feeling you come inside me."

I almost jump out of my skin when someone bangs on the door.

"That was pathetic. You lasted less than two minutes," Hendrix shouts.

"Fuck you!" Tristan shouts back when Hendrix starts laughing. "A man who can give his woman an orgasm in under two minutes knows what he's doing."

"I bet I can beat that. Now open the fucking door."

"Hold on!" Tristan brushes a kiss on my lips. "I know we have a lot of things we need to talk about, but are we good?"

"Yeah, we're good."

I shudder when he pulls out, and promptly pull my jeans up. I may love how it feels when the guys come inside me, but I don't care much for the mess it makes.

The door bumps against my ass when Hendrix pushes on it. "Hurry up."

Tristan mutters a few choice expletives as he moves me out of the way.

Hendrix's blond head pokes through the gap. When he sees we're clear, he flings it the rest of the way open.

"Come here, Trouble."

It takes two steps before I'm in his arms and kissed senseless.

"I'm sure T's dick made it clear, but don't ever do that again."

I don't mean to laugh, but it splutters out of me. "I won't. I'm so sorry."

Apologizing to them isn't enough for what I did, but it's a start. And there's one more person who needs to hear it.

"Where's Constantine?"

As soon as I say his name, I hear the thud of footsteps coming up the stairs. Hendrix sets me down, and I rush out of the room.

Constantine stops at the top of the stairs when he sees me. His hair is mussed and sticking up all over the place, and he's wearing an aggravated scowl.

I'm sorry, I sign.

One sexy black brow arches.

Please forgive me.

He studies me intently for a few moments before the corners of his lips twitch. "What happened to your clothes?"

I look down at my bare breasts and unbuttoned jeans.

"I apologized to Tristan, and this is what happened."

Constantine's scowl gives way to a naughty grin, and he strides forward with purpose. Before he gets to me, Hendrix's arms come around my waist, and I'm hauled back into the bedroom.

"We're just getting started, firefly."

CHAPTER 32

"That's... not... very... sanitary," I moan as Hendrix eats the strawberry he just shoved into my pussy.

He lifts his head from between my thighs and licks the juices from his lips. "But it's delicious," he replies and crawls up my body to kiss me, giving me a taste.

Tristan pushes him off me. "Let her eat her damn breakfast."

I sit up when Constantine hands me my coffee. I'm going to need an infusion of it today to stay awake after being kept up all night being fucked within an inch of my life. I smile against the rim of my mug.

"That's a good look on you, Red."

I take the bite of toast Tristan holds out for me.

"What is?" I ask as I chew.

Constantine gets situated on the bed at my feet and digs into the scrambled eggs and sausage Hendrix made.

"Seeing you smile," Tristan replies.

"I'm happy."

It's the last thing I should be feeling right now, but it's the truth. Everything else may be in chaos, but this right here—breakfast in bed, laughing—makes all the bad stuff not so important.

Unfortunately, my inner voice decides to speak up. *You need to tell them.*

"Where'd you go?" Hendrix offers me a plump strawberry from the bowl of fruit he's holding. I bite it in half, but all I can taste is his kiss.

"Just thinking." Lifting a leg, I point my big toe at one of the metal rings on the bedpost. "What are those for?"

I've been wondering what they are since I first saw them, and Andie wouldn't tell me, saying I'd find out soon enough, whatever that means.

Hendrix grins. "Those are for playtime."

When I still look confused, Tristan says, "Bondage, baby. They're used to tie someone up."

Huh? *Oh.* I try to imagine what that would feel like, having my hands or feet bound. Not able to move while the guys did very dirty things to me.

Hendrix laughs. "The look on your face. So damn cute."

I playfully smack his chest and steal a cube of cantaloupe. "I'm curious. How would it work with the belt?" I ask, still a little disappointed about last night.

Consider me a kid in a candy store, wanting to sample every tasty treat. If the past week has shown me anything new about myself, it's that I really like sex.

"We'd use ropes." Hendrix swirls the tip of a strawberry over my nipple. I'll never look at fruit the same way again. "Do you know what a butt plug is?"

My nose wrinkles. Just the name sounds unappealing. "No."

He waggles his eyebrows. "You will."

Hearing him talk about sex toys has my mouth running before I can stop it. "I ran into Serena on campus. Lovely as always."

At the mention of his ex-lover, fucktoy, whatever the hell she was to him, Hendrix's mood shifts from playful to agitated in mere seconds.

"What did she say to you?" he asks in a terse tone, his blue eyes glacial.

I can feel the tension radiating off all three of them. This isn't going to be a pleasant conversation. I really need to learn to keep my damn mouth shut.

"Nothing important."

He's quick to argue. "We both know that's not true."

Seeing as I started it, I relent. "She said she was looking for you." I peer over at Tristan. "And she wanted me to tell you that Katalina wants to talk to you. She's staying with Serena the rest of the week."

My stomach knots itself into a pretzel as Tristan's scowl takes over his face.

"Jesus fucking Christ."

"Who's Katalina?" I ask.

"She's no one."

Hendrix tenses when I softly utter, "That sounds familiar."

"Aoife, don't go there. I swear Katalina is no one you need to worry about. She's not an ex or someone I was remotely interested in. My father wanted me to pursue her for a fucking business arrangement. I didn't."

I teethe my bottom lip and nod my head, relieved. "Okay."

"Is that all Serena said?" Con asks.

It's scary how well he can read me.

"I have a new nickname. Burn girl."

Saying it out loud hurts just as much as hearing that bitch shriek it for everyone on campus to hear.

"Are you fucking kidding me?" Tristan shouts.

"God, firefly. I'm so fucking sorry." Hendrix lets out a slow breath before pulling me close and wrapping me in his arms. "I'll take care of it. She won't bother you again."

"I can take care of her on my own." She got a free pass because I was preoccupied and didn't want to deal with her skanky ass. "You really have shitty taste in women."

He grips the back of my neck and forces me to look at him. "I love you, which makes me pretty damn smart."

My heart stops. Literally stops. *Oh my fucking god.* He said it. The biggest smile breaks free and lights up my entire face.

"I love you, too."

Hendrix's eyes close when he touches his forehead to mine. "That's the best fucking thing I've ever heard."

"I told you before."

"When?"

"On the plane. *Tá mé i ngrá leat.*"

"I want to hear you say it just like that while I'm buried deep inside you," he says against my lips before kissing me.

This man and his beautifully filthy mouth.

Tristan goes over to his chest of drawers and shucks on a pair of black boxer briefs.

"Hen and I are dropping out of DF," he announces like it's no big deal when it's anything but.

When did they decide this? I'm caught off guard for the millionth time, and I'm getting sick and tired of it.

Hendrix chucks a pillow at his head. "Thanks for

being the Debbie Downer in the room, asshole."

Not understanding the logic, I say, "But you'll be graduating in May."

It makes absolutely no sense to me why they would waste almost four years only to say "fuck it" months before graduation.

He scratches his chest over the flower and heart tattoo that represents his sister. "Never wanted a degree or to go to college. The only reason we're here is because it was expected of us."

It's funny how I wound up in the same place I'd be anyway if my parents were still alive. And as much as I didn't care for my public high school in Dilliwyll, I would have hated the all-girls academy I would've been forced to attend even more.

Tristan brings me one of his shirts. It smells like him. I hope he doesn't expect me to give it back because it's mine now. I lift my arms for him to pull it over my head. The soft cotton feels comforting as it slides against my abraded, sensitized skin. Several new marks—some of them fingerprint bruises where the guys' hands held my hips when they took me from behind—adorn my body.

Taking the pillow Tristan tosses back, I hug it to my chest. My fingers anxiously dig into the goose-down filling as I struggle not to freak out.

"So you're leaving?" I ask, slightly panicked.

It's inevitable that they would leave once they graduated. New York would've been my guess since that's where their families' businesses are headquartered. However, I thought I had at least another eight months with them before that happened.

Constantine grabs my ankle. "I'm staying at DF. Might as well finish my bachelor's in computer science."

"We're dropping out, baby, not leaving you. Where you are, we are. You're our home, Aoife."

Tristan's words melt over me, sweet like honey. They also worry me. I don't want to be the reason that binds them to a place and a life they don't want. Relationships are destroyed when one person loves another so much that they give up everything, become someone who they're not, just to conform to what the other person wants. Our parents did that to us. We had no choice and no free will. I won't become another shackle that keeps the guys chained to the ground when all they want to do is fly.

I stretch forward and kiss his full mouth. "And you're mine. No matter where we go or where we are, *gheobhaidh mo chroí do chroí*. My heart will find yours."

Needing a moment to process, I finish my coffee and get up.

"I'm going to take a shower and get ready for class. Alone," I add when Hendrix looks like he's going to follow me.

CHAPTER 33

Inspecting my overall appearance in the bathroom mirror, I apply another layer of liquid foundation to better camouflage the bruise on my face. I feel almost normal after taking a long, scalding-hot shower and putting on my favorite Seamus Knox tee, but until the bite marks heal on my thighs, I'll have to wear either jeans or leggings.

Finished with the makeup, I remove the headband holding my hair back and store it in my cosmetics bag. I left my hair down today after taking the time to blow it dry. My blonde roots are beginning to show, but I'm thinking of letting it grow out a little more before I decide if I'm going to color it again.

Picking up my phone where I propped it on the vanity, I take it to the bench seat next to the window in my bedroom. The sun rose a little while ago, and the sky outside is painted a pastel watercolor.

Rearranging the throw pillows, I recline back against the wall and text Raquelle.

Me: I'm dressed. Meet up at the SU?

While I wait, I open the internet browser and search for any mention of Hendrix's family estate or Eva and find nothing. I didn't expect to. One thing the Society does well is protect itself.

My phone chirps, and Raquelle's reply pops up.

Raquelle: Just got out of the shower. Give me 30?

Me: Sounds good.

She attaches an image of a painting with the message: **What I've been working on**. **Your hair inspired me.**

I laugh when I open the attachment to see a canvas filled with vibrant red slashes of paint.

Me: I love it. Glad I could be your muse. Can't wait to see you.

I usually write something in my journal in the mornings, and it feels weird not to. Its absence reminds me of my clover and pressed flower I keep inside the front cover. Unique, sentimental items that can never be replaced. I also don't have a laptop or my textbooks. I took everything with me in my backpack to the Catskills.

"Well, shit," I grumble.

I'll see if the guys have a laptop I can borrow until I can get a replacement. I'll have to purchase new textbooks, though. I like having new books that no one else has marked up or highlighted, but new ones cost two hundred bucks or more each. When we were hanging in her dorm, Raquelle showed me the online store where she rented used copies of her textbooks. May as well take a look and save some money.

Gazing out the window, something in the backyard snags my attention—or the lack of something. The flowering shrub is gone, and in its place is a fresh circle of dirt where it used to grow. It was there last night. I search the ground. Where's the gun?

About to head downstairs and ask Tristan about it, my phone vibrates with an incoming call from Unknown. No one other than Andie has this number since it's technically her phone.

"Hello?"

"Synthia?" Alana says from the other end. "Andie gave me this number. What the hell is going on? Where are you?"

Profound relief is the first thing I feel at the sound of her voice.

"Are you at Cillian's?"

She must be walking because I hear muffled footsteps on the other end.

"We got here a couple of hours ago. Now answer my question."

I'm not used to her speaking to me with a biting tone. "I'm back at Darlington."

Her footsteps stop. "Did you explain things to Tristan?"

My relief morphs to guilt. "Not yet."

She doesn't say anything for a full minute, but when she does, I have to hold the phone away from my ear.

"Dammit, Synthia! You promised."

This isn't my adoptive mother Alana talking. This is a very pissed-off Dierdre Amato.

"I tried but he wouldn't listen. He was too busy yelling at me about Evan. And then other stuff came up and—"

She hangs up on me.

What in the hell just happened?

Maybe we got disconnected. I wait for her callback and when it doesn't come, I hit redial. Busy signal. I try again. Getting the same annoying busy signal, I give up and drop the phone on the bed.

"Well, that's just peachy."

"You okay?"

I don't ask Hendrix how long he's been standing there. I saw his reflection in the window glass and know he heard everything.

I puff my cheeks out and release the air with a quiet *pop*.

"Francesco was going to force Dierdre to marry Gabriel. That's why she faked her death. She felt that it was her only way to escape. Aleksander recognized her the other night, and he's going to tell him."

Hendrix walks into the room with a sinful swagger. He doesn't do it on purpose; it's who he is. He exudes natural masculine sex appeal. His stunning face, his body, his larger-than-life arrogance. The way he talks and the things he says. He's the forbidden bad boy every father warns his daughter about.

"And that's why you sent her to Ireland with Cillian," he finishes for me. "You did the right thing. You were protecting her. T will understand."

My eyebrows raise incredulously.

"Okay, yes, he'll bitch and complain, but he'll understand."

He lifts my left arm, resting my hand on his shoulder, then clasps my left hand, holding it out to the side. Curving his other hand around my waist, he steps forward.

"See if you can keep up, Trouble."

I look up at him curiously, then fly into a fit of

giggles when he starts dancing me around the room in a simplified waltz—another thing we were forced to learn as children, but I loved to dance, so it didn't bother me. My first dance instructor was a mean bitch who loved smacking me with her cane whenever I made a mistake. I broke both of her hands. Her replacement was much nicer.

It's been forever since I waltzed. I keep count of the triple beats in my head, trying valiantly not to step on his feet as he twirls me around and around. My hair flies out in a pinwheel the faster we go, and then he finishes by dipping me low to the floor.

"Not too shabby, Mister Knight." My cheeks hurt from smiling.

Gently raising me up, he takes a step back, brings my hand to his lips, and bows low at the waist.

"Soon we're going to take a trip to Hawaii, and I'm going to dance with you on a black sand beach."

Astonished, I can only splutter, "You remember that?"

Dancing on the beach and going to Hawaii were two of the things on a silly list I created when I was eight. I think I called it, "Stuff I Want to Do by the Time I'm Twenty-Five." To an eight-year-old, twenty-five was very grown up and ancient.

"I remember everything," he says with such gravitas, my heart squeezes inside my chest. "I'm not good at relationships, and I know I'm going to fuck up often because I can't help being an asshole, but I want this. Us. You and me."

Not knowing why he suddenly became sentimental, I cup his clean-shaven jaw and kiss him.

"You have me, Hendrix."

"Then please don't leave like that again. You left before, and it fucking broke us when we thought you were..." He drops his gaze and lets the rest of what's unsaid hang between us. "Just remember that you're not alone anymore, okay?"

He's right. It's not only me now. It's me and them. We stand together, fight together, and love together.

I slip my hand into his. "You think you're no good at this relationship stuff, but I think you're pretty darn perfect."

"I'm far from perfect. Except my cock. And the way I fuck."

Lord, save me from men with big dick energy.

"How about we go downstairs and tell him together?" He gives my hand a yank and leads me to the door, but I pull him back.

"Tristan isn't the only one I need to talk to. There's something I need to tell you about Eva. Something Aleksander said."

Hendrix covers my mouth. "I don't want to know."

With his hand muffling my speech, my "but" comes out as "woof."

With a grave seriousness he rarely shows, he says, "I really don't want to know, especially if it came from that motherfucker. There's a lot of shit that went down when you were gone. Stuff I may not be able to ever talk about. I'm glad she's dead. I know that sounds horrible, but I don't feel sorry about the way I feel. They all deserve to rot in hell."

I bury myself deep into his solid warmth. "I hope one day you'll tell me what happened."

Laying his chin to the top of my head, he replies, "If there's anyone I would trust enough to tell, it would be you, love."

Hendrix has nightmares and sleeps on the floor. If Eva's death helps him find any semblance of peace, then I'm not sorry Aleksander killed her.

I wanted to kill Gabriel. It was a week after he attacked Constantine and choked him. Papa caught me sneaking out one night with the sniper rifle hard case I stole from his private armory. The thing was as big as me and heavy as shit. When I told Papa what I intended to do, he promised that he would take care of it. Just another lie I was force-fed.

I wonder how I'll feel seeing Gabriel again. In order to protect Alana, would I still want to kill him given the chance? Which side of me would win out—Aoife or Syn? My darkness or my light?

CHAPTER 34

Finding an unoccupied bistro table outside the student union, I text Raquelle to let her know where I am, then sit back and enjoy my iced coffee. A light breeze lifts the ends of my hair as I look up at the cloudless aqua sky. I take a quiet moment to soak in the sun's warming rays, but that moment is fleeting because it's interrupted by Aleksander's smooth baritone.

"No bodyguards today?"

Without an invitation, he takes a seat across from me, all grins and dimples. The band tee that fits his muscular chest like a second skin is not his usual attire of dress slacks and button-up shirt. Tristan has a similar fashion style, but I don't voice my comparison for obvious reasons.

After I told Tristan and Constantine about Alana and Gabriel, Tristan said he was going for a run. He hadn't returned by the time I left the house—without

Hendrix or Constantine, who made it crystal clear they were not happy about me walking to campus by myself. I didn't give them a choice. I'm done with the mandated babysitting and compulsory escorts. Besides, this morning I was taking a page out of Andie's book and having some girl time with Raquelle.

"We both know I don't need one," I coldly reply, wishing I had my knife Hendrix finally returned to me this morning.

He looks amused at my rebuke. "No, you most certainly do not."

Sitting back in my chair, I mask my interest in why he's here with a practiced resting bitch face. "What do you want, Aleksander?"

"I thought you'd like to have this back."

He drops my backpack onto the tabletop, and I snatch it from his grasp, not waiting for him to leave before checking its contents. Not only is my journal there, so is my laptop, textbooks, the dresses and heels Raquelle gave me to wear, and Tristan's prescription bottle of migraine medication. I double check the zipper and interior pockets. No cell phone.

I gape at him and can only manage a bewildered, "How?"

His mouth tips up at the corners with a pleased grin. It's disconcerting how charming he looks when he smiles.

"I have my ways."

He stands up, making like he's about to go, even though he just got here. With the sun directly behind him, his tall stature is outlined in a rim of golden yellow.

Acting as if he's suddenly shy, he slips his hands

inside his pockets and rocks back on his heels. "You look very pretty today."

My eyes widen at the unexpected compliment, and I unconsciously touch my hair.

"Thank you?" I reply more as a question.

"You're welcome." He places a torn piece of notebook paper in front of me.

"What's this?" I ask, picking it up.

"My private number. See you around, songbird."

He walks off before I can open my mouth to tell him I don't need or want his phone number.

What. The. Fuck?

When the guys find out Aleksander sought me out again, they're going to flip.

I take out my journal and check the front inside cover.

"Oh, thank God," I whisper when I see Tristan's pressed flower and my clover.

I jump when Raquelle exclaims, "Hey, girl!"

She bends to give me a quick hug, smelling like paint fumes and jasmine, and sits down in the chair Aleksander just vacated. Her hair is pulled back with a yellow flower-print bandana and braided in pigtails that reach past her shoulders. She's swapped her usual pastel coveralls with a cute sundress and cardigan. Raquelle looks like springtime and sunny days.

I hide the slip of paper Aleksander gave me inside the front cover with my pressed flower and put my journal away. Getting situated, Raquelle places her bag on the ground and the to-go cup of her drink on the table. I follow suit and set my backpack securely between my feet, hooking my foot through a strap, just in case. Not risking it disappearing again.

"You look fantastic," she comments, and I mentally

high-five myself for doing a good job with my makeup.

"I was going to say the same about you, but you always look gorgeous."

She flashes me one of her effervescent smiles that shows off her perfect teeth.

"I'm so glad we could meet up before class. Did you switch phone numbers again? I didn't realize it was you who texted me, otherwise I'd have been here ten minutes ago."

Constantine didn't want me using the phone Andie gave me. There are some understandable trust issues between the guys and my cousin. I didn't argue.

"It's no problem," I reply, thankful for the delay, otherwise, she would've shown up at the same time Aleksander did.

I get distracted by the man trying his best to blend in but doing a horrible job at it. I'm pretty sure it's the guy Cillian sent to keep an eye on her. I'll add him to the list of things I need to speak with Cillian about.

I hold up my new phone, pretending to show it off when what I'm really doing is taking a picture of the man in the DF hoodie wearing shiny black leather loafers, dark gray suit trousers, and black aviators. I mean, come on. At least try to do a better job of fitting in.

"How are you?" Raquelle asks.

"I'm good. Tired. I foresee another nap in the quad after calc."

Thin tendrils of steam rise from the small opening on the lid after she sips her drink to test the temperature, apparently finding it too hot because she puts the cup back down. Her head disappears below the table for a second, then she pops back up holding her refillable glass water bottle.

"Fill me in on your trip. All the juicy details, please," she says, unscrewing the lid.

I don't like how I'm instantly on alert. I'm pretty certain Raquelle isn't Society, but I'm not a hundred percent sure. My gut tells me she isn't. She's too nice, too chipper, too happy; personality traits the Society sucks right out of you at an early age.

"The Catskills are pretty."

She flutters her hand at me. "Get to the good stuff. The S-E-X stuff," she whispers.

I use my straw to absentmindedly stir the ice in my cup, hoping to steady my nerves. "You already know I'm officially deflowered."

I glance around to make sure no one is watching, including the guy in the hoodie who is now leaning against the outside of the SU and looking at his phone, before pulling down the collar of my shirt and giving her a glimpse of a few of my love bites.

Raquelle's eyes bug out, and she slaps a hand to her mouth to stop from spewing her water everywhere.

"Holy shit, those look painful."

"They're not so bad. I hardly feel them."

She accepts the napkin I offer and cleans up the spilled water, then reaches across the bistro table, covering my hand with hers.

"Are you good? No regrets?"

My thoughts stray to the first night with Constantine, then to last night, and the burn I can feel growing in my cheeks becomes a full-body flush of arousal.

"I'm more than good. Zero regrets."

Raquelle's honey-brown gaze transfixes on me with rapt attention. "Who took it?"

I burst into laughter. "You make it sound like someone broke into my vagina and stole my virginity. And it was Constantine."

Leaping from her seat, she does an excited shimmy, waving her hands in the air like a lunatic. "I knew it!"

I flap my hands, trying to hush her when we get a few curious looks. I don't want a repeat of yesterday with the whole 'burn girl' thing.

Raquelle sits back down and leans in conspiratorially. "What about the other two? Mr. Handsome Glare and the Greek Adonis?"

I tuck my chin when I feel my face heat a tomato-red.

"So, it's like that, huh? Good for you. And don't you dare be embarrassed. You are the envy of every woman on the planet." Raquelle giggles as she dramatically fans herself. "Three hot men and all those fabulous orgasms."

I gulp down a long sip of my iced coffee, hoping it'll help cool me off. They were really fabulous orgasms. I'm forced to cross my legs to help relieve the sudden ache that fires to life.

Emboldened by her positive reaction, I ask, "Has Drake ever tied you up?"

She snort-laughs and pushes her glasses back into place. Today, the frames are a bright blue. "Other way around."

Drink forgotten, I gawp at her beaming, girl-next-door face.

"What? I may look like a Taylor Swift, but I'm all badass Beyoncé in the bedroom."

I absolutely love this girl.

"You are very badass."

She produces a square plastic container and pulls the

lid off to reveal red seedless grapes and apple slices, then hands me a toothpick. "Convenient for when you haven't washed your hands."

I take it and spear a grape. "How was your weekend?"

"Went to a Greek party with some girls on my floor on Saturday. Discovered a little off the beaten-path art supply store on the other side of campus off Carver Street. Pretty boring compared to your weekend... and you're blushing again."

Damn my stupid fair skin.

"Oh, before I forget," I tell her as I unzip my backpack.

Aleksander must have taken the dresses to the dry cleaners because they're neatly folded in sealed clothing bags that carry a fancy name scrolled in gold lettering. Raquelle's eight-hundred-dollar pair of high heels are also in their own silk drawstring bag.

Just when I think I have him pegged as the bad guy, he does nice stuff that only confuses the hell out of me.

"I, um..." I hold the items out for her. "Thank you so much. The guys loved the blue dress," I flat-out lie since I never got to wear any of the items she lent me.

"You're very welcome." She shoves everything into her bag and sits back, a diabolical grin overtaking her face. "So, you want to be tied up?"

CHAPTER 35

The auditorium lights are dimmed, and the professor's voice is hypnotically dull as he explains derivatives in the most boring way possible.

"Wake up."

Raquelle elbows me when I start to nod off. It's been almost impossible to keep my eyes open during class.

Hiding my yawn, I check the time on my phone and see a text message waiting from Constantine. No actual message, just an attached image. Grateful for the distraction, I open it. Constantine is standing in his bedroom, holding a large white poster board with the message "**Will you be my girlfriend?**" written in big black letters.

The biggest, goofiest smile blooms across my face. Raquelle leans over to see what I'm looking at and sighs dreamily.

"That's so sweet. Just like the movie *Love Actually*." At my blank look, she says, "The scene where the guy stands at Keira Knightley's door and tells her that he loves her even though she's with another guy. Have you seriously not watched that movie?"

"Nuh-uh," I reply and text Constantine back.

Me: YES!

"It's a must-see. I'm calling movie night. I'll invite some of the girls from my floor, and we can make it a thing. Watch a movie, get drunk, do each other's nails, gossip about guys."

Sounds exactly like what Andie and I did.

"I'm in. Just no tequila shots. Tequila makes me do bad things." Like dance on bars and make out with three guys in public.

"Someone's got a story to tell," Raquelle sing-songs.

Cacophony erupts when the professor dismisses class, and everyone rushes to get out. I gather my stuff and move into the aisle to let the people in our row get past.

"What happens in Texas, stays in Texas."

"Texas? I thought you went to New York?"

Backtracking, I reply with a conciliatory shake of my head, "That's what I meant. Brain fatigue." I fake yawn to prove my point.

Thankfully, my phone vibrates in my hand. Another attached image from Constantine. The new poster says: **Will you go out with me?**

Butterflies, the good kind, come to life and flutter rapidly inside my chest. I've never been on a date or had a boyfriend. Pathetic, I know. If I were a romance trope right now, I'd be the nerdy and unpopular bookworm being asked out by the super hot bad boy at school. Or would it be grumpy-sunshine? Maybe friends to lovers.

Getting impatient, Raquelle elbows me again. "Will

you tell the poor guy yes already?"

My thumbs fly across my screen as I reply, **I would love to go out on a date with you**.

Constantine: Come outside.

He's here?

Raquelle nudges me to get me moving. "Don't make him wait."

"You are so bossy," I tell her, but she just laughs and pushes me up the aisle and out of the auditorium.

The main hallway is jammed with people who have nothing better to do than to stand in everyone's way and block the flow of traffic trying to get to the exit.

"Do you have work tonight? I've been meaning to drop by the Bierkeller."

"I'm off for the rest of the week," I reply as we push on the glass doors when they start to shut.

As soon as sunshine hits my face, I'm eagerly searching the crowd milling about for one in particular.

When dark eyes meet mine from across the way, I lose the ability to breathe. Standing under the red oak tree, holding his guitar by the neck in one hand and what looks like a picnic basket in the other, is a devastatingly handsome Constantine. Black shirt, black-washed jeans, and a ball cap pulled low over his eyes. He smiles as soon as he sees me, and my damn knees go weak.

"That man is so gone for you."

"Other way around."

She snickers at my use of what she said when I asked her if Drake ever tied her up.

Looping her bag strap over a shoulder, she hip-bumps me. "I'm off to art class. Call me later?"

"Will do."

After a side hug goodbye, I'm skipping down the steps toward my boyfriend.

My boyfriend.

Constantine's dark gaze never strays from me as I walk toward him. I don't like being anyone's focus of attention because it's usually for the wrong reasons, like yesterday with Serena or when people ogle my scars. It's different with Constantine. I enjoy how it feels when he watches me with feral-like intensity. It's the same with Tristan and Hendrix. I'm not damaged in their eyes. I'm beautiful. Sexy. Strong.

High on giddiness, I stop in front of him, my smile as big and bright as the late morning sky.

"Hi."

"Hey, sweet girl," he says in his raspy voice that sends millions of goose bumps scuttling over me from head to toe.

Needing to touch him, I grab hold of the front belt loops of his jeans. I feel like an idiot to be acting this way, but tell that to my pounding, ecstatic heart.

"How was class?"

"I kept nodding off. Wonder why?"

Constantine's cocksure smirk could outrival Hendrix's. It also makes my clit tingle.

"What's the basket for?" I ask.

He looks down as if suddenly reminded he was holding it. "Lunch date."

A soft puff of air escapes my lips. "I'd love that."

Constantine never ceases to amaze me. Behind his dark, dangerous exterior is a man who is romantic, sweet, and thoughtful.

"There's a small butterfly garden in the back of the biology building."

Excitement percolates. The small garden is gorgeous and would be the perfect spot for a picnic.

"I know where that is. I found it on one of my walks through campus when I first moved here."

He hands me his guitar and takes my backpack, then grabs my free hand and leads me away from the quad.

"When did Aleksander give you this?"

His grip tightens when my feet trip over themselves. I should've known he would have noticed the backpack. Nothing gets past him.

"He dropped by the student union while I was waiting for Raquelle. He gave me my backpack and left."

I don't pontificate further, simply because there's nothing more to say about the matter. That's literally all that happened. I still don't fully comprehend the rivalry between Tristan and Aleksander, other than it's an instant dislike that stems back to when we were kids. There's a deep hatred that exists between them, and hatred like that just doesn't spring forth from the ether. Something big caused it. Something I'm not aware of. Something that made Aleksander go down the path of destruction he's now traveling.

"Do you mind if I look through it?"

If any other man said that to a woman, she would think it's because he didn't trust her.

"Of course. There's also something I want to show you, but it can wait," I say.

Even if Cillian confirms the man I saw at the SU works for him, I'd like for the guys to see his face and know what he looks like.

Taking a shortcut around the library and past the front entrance of the two-story, red brick biology building, Constantine leads me through an arbor gate and into a small botanical garden enclosed within wrought iron fencing. Monarch butterflies flit among the pink cluster flowers growing at the tops of the stalks of marsh milkweed, gorging on nectar needed for their long migration to their overwintering habitats in Mexico.

Choosing a clear spot in the grass, Constantine sets down my backpack, then unpacks a soft, blue blanket from the picnic basket. He spreads it out over the ground and gestures for me to sit. Propping the guitar in my lap, I lightly strum the melody to Fleetwood Mac's "Landslide" while I watch him carefully remove the stuff from my bag. He takes his time feeling around the pockets and the straps. Seeming satisfied that Aleksander didn't plant anything, he puts everything back.

"Don't use your laptop until I can run some software on it," he says and scoots behind me, slotting me between the vee of his legs. Removing his ball cap, he rests his chin on my shoulder and watches as I pluck the chords. "I'm impressed with how well you play."

"Even when I didn't want to remember, I kept parts of you with me," I tell him.

Taking ASL classes, learning how to play the guitar. Constantine was always there. Just like he and Hendrix kept parts of me in the images they had tattooed all over their bodies.

I'm engulfed in his warmth when his arms come around me. His fingers line up and cover mine on the fretboard. He does the same thing to my right hand, manipulating my thumb to strum different strings.

I laugh when our fingers fight against each other. "I feel like a marionette at the control of its puppeteer."

"Stop trying to lead. Let me do it," he says next to my ear. His breath caresses over my cheek and neck, and I shiver.

I force myself to relax and let him guide me as he presses my fingers into different chords.

"What do you think is going to happen now?" I ask, knowing he'll understand what I'm referring to.

He lets loose a sigh. "I honestly don't know. Clearly, Aleksander has the backing of Patrick and my father."

"And Francesco?"

I lose his warmth when he pushes away from me and lies back on the blanket. I set the guitar to the side, and he repositions his long frame, so his head rests in my lap, those brown-black eyes looking up at me.

"We'd been biding our time, waiting for graduation when we'd officially be inducted into the Council. We knew our fathers had no plans of relinquishing control, so we were going to take it from them."

I glide my fingers through his hair, letting the soft strands weave between my fingers. "Kill them?"

"Yes."

To any other person, the notion of patricide would be horrific. But I know what kind of men Francesco, Patrick, and Gabriel are. I witnessed what they were capable of and the horrors they inflicted on the boys I loved. The lash marks that cover Tristan's back and the more recent burn on his hand. Hendrix can't find peace, even in sleep, because of the nightmares that haunt him. Constantine's shattered voice that acts as a daily reminder that his father almost killed him.

"Dragon."

Startled out of my morose thoughts, I follow where he's pointing and peer up at the puffy white clouds in the sky that weren't there earlier today.

"Where?"

When Council meetings would go long, and we got bored, the guys and I would sneak to the roof and play this game, except it would be with the stars hanging in the night sky, not clouds.

Failing to see a dragon anywhere, I bend over as far as I can with his head in my lap. The breeze fans its florally perfumed breath over my face, but it's his subtle cologne and the scent of his citrusy shampoo that invades my lungs.

"That one, right there. It's a dragon," he says.

"It's a pickle with feet."

He barks out a laugh that does crazy things to my insides. "It's not a pickle, woman. Look. There's the head and wings and fire coming out of its mouth." He traces the shape of the cloud with his fingertip.

"Still a pickle."

"It's not a damn pickle."

I yelp when he reaches back and digs his fingers into my ribs, knowing exactly where I'm most ticklish.

"Con! Stop!" I giggle-snort and hearing it makes me laugh even harder.

Constantine abruptly rolls over and pushes me back onto the blanket. My breath catches as sparks of desire shoot straight between my thighs. Unable to stop them, my hands explore every bulge and dip of his impossibly toned arms. The weight of him is heavy and enticing as he pins me beneath him, his chest rising and falling against mine with labored breaths.

"I missed hearing you laugh," he quietly says, his face filled with a myriad of emotions. "I love you so fucking much."

Those butterflies I had felt inside my chest when he sent me the texts in class explode into bombs of confetti.

"I love you more."

Is that my voice, all wispy and needy?

Just like with the clouds, he draws shapes over my skin. A heart over my jugular notch. The rounded loops of flower petals across my cheek. I can feel the power of his gaze on me when his finger moves to my mouth and he begins spelling out individual letters over my parted lips. M-I-N-E.

"I am, and I always will be," I reply when he finishes. "Constantine?"

"Yeah, baby?"

"Do you think they're responsible for my parents' murder?"

Wrinkles appear on his forehead when he frowns. "Who?"

"Francesco, Patrick, and Gabriel."

It's a question that I can't seem to stop pondering. If anyone had the resources to orchestrate the attack on the cabin in Ireland, it would be them.

I stare up at him expectantly, wanting to know what he thinks about my new theory. What I get is an unexpected declaration.

"I swear on my life I will never let anyone hurt you again."

His lips take mine with urgency, and it's like I'm both falling and flying at the same time, a feather at the mercy of the wind. As soon as I open for him, his tongue slips inside on a quiet moan that could have been from him or from me, maybe from both of us. I expect his kiss to be hard and demanding, but Constantine devastates me with softness, delving deep to tangle his tongue with mine, then gently sucking and pulling, before sinking into me again. Every stroke causes my body to tense and twist until I'm practically squirming underneath him.

I whimper from the loss when he pulls back just far enough to flutter butterfly kisses over each eyelid and the tip of my nose.

"I love the way you kiss me," I profess, entranced by him.

Clouds pass overhead, casting shadows on us as Constantine delicately brushes his hand down my scarred arm before replacing his fingers with his mouth, and those phantom tingles return. I know it's psychosomatic and in my head, but it doesn't make the sensations of his lips on my scarred skin less real.

"And I just love you," he eventually replies.

CHAPTER 36

By the time my last class of the day dismisses, I'm exhausted and barely able to string two thoughts together, so it shouldn't be a surprise when I barrel straight into someone as soon as I exit the lecture hall.

"Oh, my gosh, I am so sorry," I apologize, quickly looking up—only to meet agitated hazel eyes behind black-rimmed glasses. "Oh, hey!" I say when I realize it's Evan.

"Why didn't you call me? Andie said you left and came back here."

Getting out of the way of the mass exodus from class, I move to the other side of the doorway.

"I don't have your number." Which is the truth, but with so much going on since I got back yesterday, I also completely forgot.

"I called you, several times."

The strap of my backpack rubs against my shoulder where the bullet grazed it. It hasn't bothered me at all until now. Switching my bag to the other shoulder, I waggle my replacement phone at him.

"Constantine gave me a new phone. What's your number?" After he rattles off his digits, I text him and hear a notification chime from his back pocket. "I was heading back to the house. Want to walk with me?"

His rigid posture visibly relaxes. "I have a major assignment due that I haven't even started. I was going to the library, but I wanted to check on you. Proof of life."

His lopsided grin has me impishly rolling my eyes. "Don't expect me to send you selfies."

"I wouldn't mind if you did," he replies.

That sounded almost flirtatious, but I brush it off as him being playful. Evan has a friendly and open demeanor, kind of like Tristan, but nowhere near as cocky.

"Have you spoken to your father or Alana today?"

Evan leans a shoulder against the wall. "Spoke to Dad this morning. Why?"

"Just checking," I reply.

I still can't believe Alana hung up on me.

The hall has mostly emptied out, making it easier to hear one another. The acoustics in the building are horrendous, same as the lecture hall. Voices reverberate and bounce off one another. Sitting in the back of the auditorium, it was hard to understand the professor, especially when the girl in front of me wouldn't shut the hell up the entire class. I got an earful about the blowjob she gave to someone at a frat party this past weekend. Probably the same party Raquelle said she went to.

Pulling up the picture I took with my phone, I show it to Evan. "Is he one of yours?"

My hand gets trapped under his when he raises my

phone higher. "Yeah. That's Ian. Christ, he's not very inconspicuous, is he?"

"With those shoes, no." I laugh and pull free from his grasp.

"Come on. Since the library is on your way..." He trails off as he pushes from the wall and starts walking toward the front doors.

I catch up with him just as he asks, "Did Hendrix tell you that Patrick is back at the estate?"

Trundling down the steps, my head cocks sideways, so I can see his face better. "I doubt Hendrix knows. What is Patrick doing back there?"

A couple of girls sitting on the grass wave, and I know it's not me they're waving at. Evan holds his hand up in acknowledgment, but otherwise, doesn't stop to chat.

"Rebuilding would be my guess," he replies. "The explosion didn't cause much damage. It was more of a distraction."

I want to point out that the *distraction* knocked my ass out.

Glancing over my shoulder, I find that the girls are still watching. "They're cute."

Evan turns to see who I'm talking about. "Not my type."

"What is your type?" I probe.

"Not them."

There's a flash of pale blonde hair in my peripheral, and without looking, I know it's Serena. If she shouts 'burn girl,' I'm going to kick her ass. Almost daring her to, I slow my pace and turn my head. Next to her is Katalina, looking as refined and porcelain as she did yesterday. But it's the person they're talking to who I lock eyes with. Aleksander sends me a subtle chin lift and a small smile. I don't return it. I can't deal with either of them right now, so I herd Evan down the paved sidewalk that cuts right through the center of the quad.

Serena and Hendrix. Serena and Aleksander. She must be Society. Katalina, too, especially after what Tristan said about his parents pushing him to get with her. No wonder she kept giving me bitch eyes yesterday. I don't recall ever meeting them growing up, not even at the annual galas. Their families must be newer members, which means I'll have to deal with them at some point.

Fuck me.

"What?" Evan says.

Did I say that out loud?

"Just me talking to myself. Can I ask you a question?"

"Go for it."

"How did Cillian know Aleksander and Aleksei were going to be at the Knight Estate?"

It's something I've asked a few times now and one I still don't have an answer for.

Evan rubs the back of his neck. "I don't know. Dad has a habit of not telling me shit other than ordering me around. Sometimes, I feel more like one of his lackeys than his son."

I know all too well the pressures a parent can place on their child to become who they want them to be.

When we reach the large fountain, I abruptly stop.

"Do you happen to have a penny handy?" The wind blows spray into my face, misting my hair and making a few loose strands stick to my mouth.

Evan fishes inside his pocket and pulls out a couple of quarters. "Are you seriously going to make a wish? I'm pretty sure it's not allowed."

Tossing pennies into wishing wells was something Papa and I would do. He used to call me his lucky penny because of my middle name, Penelope. I think he did that because I hated my middle name. Aoife Penelope never sounded right to me, but Mama insisted on it when I was born because it was her middle name.

"Can I keep this one?" I ask, holding up the quarter that was minted the year I was born.

It's nice being able to remember it now. December twenty-fifth. I'm a Christmas miracle—something else Papa used to call me.

Evan nods, and I drop it in the side mesh pocket of my backpack, then take the other quarter and cup it between my joined hands.

"Seeing this will buy us twenty-five wishes, make a wish with me."

He side-eyes me when I twist around and hold my hands in front of his face.

"Now, close your eyes."

"You gotta be fucking kidding me," he mutters, but does it anyway.

I close my eyes at the same time, my lips wordlessly moving as I say my wish. When we're done, I drop the large silver coin. It hits the shallow pool of the fountain with a small splash and promptly sinks to the bottom.

"What did you wish for?" Evan asks.

What did I wish for? To come face-to-face with the constellation man. I want to carve his flesh from his bones, bit by bit, while he watches. I want it to hurt. I want him to suffer. Then I want him to die.

"If I tell you, it won't come true."

The front door opens with a loud creak as I step into the warmly lit foyer. Patterns of color projected through the stained-glass windows decorate the eggshell-painted walls in various hues of reds, yellows, blues, and greens.

"Hey! I'm home!"

No one answers back. The house is quiet.

Closing the door behind me, my sandals make hushed thumps on the floor as I slip them off. I dig my toes into the soft, worn threads of the foyer rug, a trick I learned from the movie *Die Hard* that helps you to de-stress. Checking to make sure the alarm is disengaged, I enter the code just in case, then head upstairs. After dropping my backpack in the doorway of my room, I peek inside each of the guy's bedrooms. Nothing. Not even a shower running.

Leaning over the top of the banister, I call out, "Hello?"

Silence greets me once more. Where is everyone?

When I get back downstairs, I poke my head into the living room, expecting to see Tristan asleep on the couch with a football game playing on mute on the television or Constantine reclining back on the cushions, looking at something on his phone. When I don't find them, I go to the kitchen, already knowing Hendrix isn't there because I don't smell any delicious aromas of dinner cooking.

Just as I'm about to take out my phone and text them, I'm halted in my tracks by a strange noise. Dormant instincts kick in and before I realize what I'm doing,

I reach for the knife block on the counter. My senses become hypervigilant, but the hard pounding of my heart overwhelms my ears until all I hear is a loud *whoosh, whoosh, whoosh.*

Keeping my back to the wall, my bare feet are silent as I take one careful step after another. The noise comes again, muffled but close, and any semblance of calm evaporates into vapor when I hear an enraged Bostonian cadence coming from the backyard.

My hand tightens its grip around the handle of the knife, and the haunting voice that used to plague my nightmares chants its destruction inside my brain. I give in to my deadly impulses, letting that dark part of me take over.

Tristan can't be shouting at Aleksander since I just saw him in the quad. Doesn't matter. I'll kill anyone who touches my boys.

Time seems to slow to the incremental flow of glacial ice, the five feet it takes me to reach the back door feeling more like hundreds of miles.

Trying not to make a sound, I slip outside onto the patio.

"Ow! You evil little fucker."

A flurry of orange and black blurs past, with a dirt-streaked Tristan chasing after it, cursing up a storm.

Is that—?

I carefully set the knife down on the patio table. Hands on my hips, I survey the backyard and find Constantine and Hendrix sitting on the ground, laughing their asses off as they watch Tristan run around like a deranged idiot, chasing after my pet rooster.

My heart absolutely melts into a ball of goo when I see

the wooden chicken coop that now stands in the place where the bush used to grow. Tristan wouldn't tell me why he cut it down.

The coop is adorable. Made out of gray wood, it looks like a small house on stilts with chicken wire enclosing the perimeter.

"Surprise," Hendrix says, finally seeing me standing on the patio.

I look over at him and Constantine with tear-glossed eyes. I don't know how they did it, but they did this for me.

Fuck, I love them so damn much.

Tristan stumbles when he skids to a stop at the base of the steps. Bent in half with his hands on his knees, he breathlessly grumbles, "That thing is an asshole."

Taking in the sight of him, I burst out laughing when I see a feather sticky out of his messy hair.

Hearing me, Cocky Bastard makes an ear-splitting squawk and changes direction. When he gets to me, he struts a happy dance back and forth at my feet. I crouch down, pick him up, and snuggle the shit out of him.

"I've missed you so much," I coo into his soft feathers.

Tristan glares at me. "I love how we did all the work, and the damn demon bird gets all the fucking hugs."

I set Cocky B down and leap from the top step into Tristan's arms, then proceed to pepper kisses all over his dirty, sweaty face.

"I think I can do much better than hugs."

CHAPTER 37

After noticing I've re-read the same paragraph five times without absorbing any information, I use my highlighter as a bookmark and close the biology textbook. Uncrossing my legs, I straighten them out in front of me and reach to touch my toes. My back and butt ache from sitting on the floor for too long.

"You can save a tree if you went digital," Constantine says from the couch.

"I like having the physical book."

He hauls me off the floor and pulls me into his lap, then proceeds to render me catatonic when he begins massaging my neck and head. He works on the tightness in my trapezius, and my head droops forward like a wilting flower as I go boneless from his ministrations.

"I still can't believe you kidnapped Cocky B and flew him up here."

"It was either a one-and-half-hour flight or an eleven-hour car ride stuck in a pet carrier," Tristan says as he shuts his laptop.

When we talked this morning about Alana and Gabriel, I had mentioned in passing that Alana asked our neighbor, Mike, to take care of Cocky B and the hens. I didn't ask how they were able to locate my rooster so quickly or what they did to get him here. Some questions are best left unanswered.

Tristan lifts my feet to prop them on top of his thigh, and I go from catatonic to moaning like a whore when his fingers dig into the arch of my foot.

"I'm going to have to go to New York next week for a board meeting. Elias has things handled for the time being."

My relaxed state of bliss disappears at the mention of his family's shipping company. In a perfect world, we'd be four regular college students with boring lives who have nothing more important to think about than studying and which party to attend on the weekends.

"No one has heard from Francesco or Helena?" I ask.

Tristan's thumb pauses its circular motion. His whiskey browns flick to me, then away. "Uh, no."

Constantine's hands slip from my neck when I sit up and slide my feet off Tristan's lap.

"I know this is a hot button for you, but maybe you should ask Aleksander."

"No."

Shocker.

"Hear me out—"

"I said no," Tristan bites out.

Stubborn, pigheaded pain in my ass.

When he gets up from the couch and storms out of the living room, I'm right on his heels. All the mind games from Aleksander and prevarication from the guys are beginning to drive me nuts. I feel stuck, and I'm frustrated that I can't move forward in my life until I find who killed my parents.

"You said you wanted all this to be over, so why aren't you doing anything to end it? Aleksander alluded knowing where they were, so make him tell you... or I will."

The more I thought about what I mentioned to Constantine earlier about the possibility of Patrick, Gabriel, or Francesco being responsible for what happened in Ireland, the more I think I'm right.

Tristan pivots around and gets up in my space. "Stay away from him."

"You know I can't. Not now. Not if he knows something that will help me find who—"

The air gets knocked out of me when I'm lifted and tossed over a shoulder.

"It's too late for that shit, and I'm horny," Hendrix says, taking the stairs two at a time.

"I'm told cold showers work wonders."

He smacks my ass, hard, and a bloom of warmth spreads where his hand made contact.

Using his back as leverage, I push up to reduce the pressure of his shoulder on my stomach.

"Thanks for interrupting."

I say it sarcastically, but Hendrix flips it to mean the opposite.

"You can show me your appreciation by wrapping those luscious lips around my cock."

I make an embarrassing squeal when I encounter nothing but air when Hendrix flips me over onto Tristan's bed. Raising up on my bent forearms, I blow the hair out of my face and scowl at him.

"Stay right there. Don't move," he says and leaves the room.

"I'm not a dog!"

I hear him laugh. "You'd look hot as fuck wearing a collar."

Oh, hell no. After looking up butt plugs online, I now know enough about BDSM to positively say that collars, whips, paddles, and nipple clamps are four things on my 'never in this lifetime' list.

Tristan's disembodied voice comes from out in the hall. "I thought we were waiting to give that to her this weekend."

My ears perk up. "Give what to me?"

Hendrix comes back, clearly hiding something behind his back. "Get naked, and we'll show you."

"No." I beam a stubborn, victorious smile at Tristan when he walks in with Constantine. He's not the only one who can say that word.

Hendrix hits me with what he knows is my kryptonite. "Good girls get presents and orgasms."

And just like that, my body immediately responds. Arousal pools deep in my core, my breasts grow heavy, and my pussy aches to be filled by them.

"You don't play fair, Mister Knight."

"Master Knight," he playfully admonishes, and I treat him to the biggest roll of the eyes I can make.

Standing, I walk to the end of the bed and curl my hand around the top of the post. Nothing outside this bedroom matters. Not our argument or the Society or Aleksander.

"Are you going to show me what's behind your back?" From my vantage point, I try to see what Hendrix is hiding.

"Pick. Right hand or left hand."

"Left."

I think my mouth makes an 'O' of surprise when he produces a slim, satin-black jewelry box. Other than the plastic watch I sometimes wear and my belly button stud, I don't own much jewelry.

Tristan takes the box from Hendrix. "We have a lot of birthdays to celebrate that we missed out on." He opens the case, and my eyes widen at what looks like a diamond necklace. "We wanted you to have this so you would always remember that you are loved... and wanted... *and ours.*"

Heart swelling with emotion, my fingers tremble when I reach down to accept the exquisite gift. Small round diamonds adorn a long, delicate filigree chain.

"Thank you. It's a beautiful necklace."

"It's not that kind of necklace, baby. It's a belly chain," Tristan informs me.

Constantine steps forward, lifting it from its cushioned nest and circling it around my waist. His hands brush against my side as he secures the clasp. The diamonds sparkle in the waning light, which perfectly complements the effulgent happiness radiating from within me.

"Silver?"

I coast my fingers along the links of the chain. Even though it seems to pulse with an inner luminosity, the metal feels cool against my flushed body.

Hendrix makes a disgusted scoff. "Hell, no. Platinum."

I don't want to cry during such a lovely moment, but dammit, I can't stop the tears when I look at them.

"I love it. Thank you so much."

Constantine grabs my waist and slides his long-fingered hands around to my ass, then down the backs of my thighs. The height of the bed with me standing on it puts his mouth almost level with my belly button piercing, and my stomach muscles quiver when he bumps my shirt up with his nose and kisses where the belly chain has settled at my navel.

"Fuck, your skin smells good."

Every thought flies right out of my head when his soft lips travel along the hem of my yoga pants, then move lower when he hooks his thumbs under the nylon-Lycra waistband and pulls. My skin turns to goose flesh as he slides the silky, stretchy fabric down my legs.

His breath fans over my mons, and I rasp, "It's my gardenia body wash."

The mattress sinks when Tristan comes up behind me.

"No, Red, it's all you."

Constantine braces the curvature of my torso to hold me steady when I let go of the post and raise my arms above my head for Tristan to remove my shirt. I'm not wearing a bra, and my nipples instantly pucker as soon as cold air kisses them.

"Can I touch you?"

He knows he never has to ask for my permission, but it's his way of apologizing for our earlier argument.

"Please touch me," I entreat.

The pads of his fingertips sweep across my nape like an artist's paintbrush. Sliding my hair out of the way, he runs his tongue up my neck to my ear, and I shudder. The chill on my skin intensifies when he molds his hands over my breasts, tweaking my nipples between his thumbs and middle fingers. The electric sensation travels straight down to my clit, and I bite my bottom lip to hold in my whimper of need.

Constantine shatters that composure when he inserts a finger into my wet heat.

"Fuck yes!" I cry out.

His groan of satisfaction when I spasm around him tells me that he derives as much pleasure from touching me as I get from what he's doing.

"So fucking tight."

He adds a second finger, scissoring them to stretch me wide. I try to hold off the orgasm that quickly builds, but as soon as he puts his mouth on me, sucking my clit between his lips, I climax within seconds. It's a quick explosion of rapture, one that takes me by surprise but leaves me hungry for more.

"So beautiful," Tristan says when I'm nothing more than a twitching mess.

"Want to play, baby girl?"

My eyes find Hendrix, and my insides tingle with excitement when I see the long, red silken sash dangling from his fingers. The second present he was hiding behind his back.

I nod enthusiastically.

"I fucking love how eager you are to be corrupted. On your knees, firefly. Submissive position."

Finally able to speak, I reply, "I'm not calling you sir."

Grinning wickedly, he coils the sash around his hand and pulls the end taut. "Never say never."

Tristan nuzzles my neck. "No matter what, if there's something you don't want or are unsure of, you say stop."

I love how protective they are of me, but I'm not

fragile.

"I won't break, but I sure as hell want you to try."

"God, I love you." Bunching my hair in his fist, Tristan wrests my head back and kisses me until my legs deliquesce, and I sink to the pillowtop mattress.

As I kneel on the bed, Hendrix tips my chin up, his blue eyes sparking with feral desire. He shows me the red strip of silk before covering my eyes with it.

"I can't see."

"That's the point. With your eyesight occluded, your other senses will heighten," he explains, intertwining the fabric until it's secure at the back of my head.

I moan when firm lips settle over mine, the kiss pillow-soft. Constantine. I can tell by the shape of his mouth and by the way he kisses me like I'm precious.

I can hear them moving about the bedroom and want to know what they're doing, but I don't dare remove the blindfold.

I startle when someone grabs my left wrist.

"I'm going to bind your wrist and secure the rope to the metal ring."

Hendrix.

My pulse picks up speed. "Okay."

A strange current of desire courses through me as he wraps the binding around my wrist. There's something inherently erotic about giving them control over my body. I trust them. I know I'm safe with them. That knowledge is what helps me feel secure in pushing my boundaries and exploring the darker side of sex and intimacy.

There's a tug, and my left arm lifts to shoulder height. Hendrix talks me through what he's doing as he knots the binding on the metal ring, then repeats the same procedure with my right arm.

When he's done, he inquires, "Too tight?"

I test the ropes by twisting and pulling at them. There's enough give, so they don't cut off my circulation.

"They're good."

Hendrix feathers a kiss across my mouth. "All you need to do is feel."

My eyelids flutter close behind the blindfold when hands begin to touch me everywhere. A gentle trailing of airy circles over my clavicle, a graceful finger between my breasts, the backs of knuckles drifting over the scars on my arm, a hand flattened over my abdomen. My breaths grow labored and echo around the room as every caress tightens the coil of desire. When their touch disappears, the absence of their hands leaves an emptiness that just adds fuel to the inferno burning inside me.

"Please," I plead.

There's a rustle of fabric as clothes are shed, and I squirm against the restraints.

"You're dripping, baby," Tristan says, gliding his finger up the inside of my thigh.

Someone's hard cock prods my backside. I feel the cold metal of the piercing and know it's Constantine. Using gentle pressure on my back, he guides me down until my chest is parallel to the bed. With my arms bound and splayed to either side of me, I'm suspended in a half-plank position on my knees. The ropes cut into my wrists as they take most of my weight, but I don't complain. I know the pleasure they'll give me will be worth a little discomfort.

"Open," Hendrix says.

My lips obediently part. He uses the head of his cock to smear precum over my mouth, then roughly shoves his length to the back of my throat until I gag.

A hiss of pleasure rumbles out. "You feel so good."

His hand clasps the back of my neck, arching my head as far back as possible while he rocks into me. The sensations sharpen almost painfully as he moves against my throat, each snap of his hips becoming more punishing. He uses me for his own pleasure, and I finally understand the meaning behind fucktoy.

Kisses rain down my spine, and my moan vibrates around Hendrix's cock when Constantine lines himself up and pushes in. My excitement emboldens me, and I moan louder for them to take me harder. Every searing thrust of their cocks elicits hedonistic cries from deep within me. The magnitude of pleasure and pain is like lightning under my skin, the intensity unbearable. I'm hovering on the edge of insanity, desperately needing to come but never wanting this to end. I'm tied up, blindfolded, and being fucked my two men. It's depraved and filthy, and I love every second.

Constantine slides his hand under me and between my legs, strumming my clitoris like I'm an instrument he's skilled at playing. He whispers things in Portuguese I don't understand, but I can feel their meaning, and it's his words that fling me over into bliss as my orgasm splinters me apart.

Hendrix's movements grow more and more erratic, and I'm given no time to catch my breath. His groan of release is the only warning I get before he unloads hot pulses of cum down my throat.

"Oh, fuck. Your mouth, perfection. Take all of me. Swallow every fucking drop."

I try to, but it's a lot, and I wind up choking on most of it.

Constantine holds still to allow Hendrix to pull out, and I gulp in much-needed oxygen as soon as he slips free. There's a tug on the sash, and the blindfold falls away. Even with the room mostly dark, it takes a second to acclimate.

Hendrix's blue eyes come into focus, and he smiles as he wipes himself from my mouth.

"*Tá mé i ngrá leat.*" His piercings scraped my throat raw, and it came out raspy and quiet, but he heard it.

"Love you more, baby girl. I'm going to undo the ropes. Con, hold her."

The tension on my right arm releases, followed by my left, but with Constantine's grip on my hips, I thankfully don't fall forward on my face.

Hendrix rubs circulation back into my hands, but my arms are dead weight and flop to my sides when Constantine turns me over and lays me on the bed. Settling on top of me, he combs through the sweaty strands of my hair, and I become enthralled by the deep abyss of his gaze.

"Hi."

His mouth quirks. "Hey, sweet girl."

Our fingers thread and hold, and he raises our joined hands above my head. I tip my face back and smile at Hendrix, who is watching from the foot of the bed while stroking his beautifully inked cock. Damn, that's hot.

Returning my attention to Constantine, I whisper, "Love me."

"Always."

Wrapping my legs around his waist, I welcome him inside me once again. My heart pounds wildly in my chest at the feel of him. Warm. Solid. *Mine.*

Our sweat-slicked bodies melt together then tear apart. Constantine makes love to me slowly, spending long, wonderful moments kissing my lips, my breasts, my face. Our fingers untangle, and his hands brush along my curves. Every nerve ending lights up under his touch. When the next orgasm takes me, it doesn't come as an explosion but in gentle waves that are never-ending.

"Happy?"

"Very," I reply and sigh into his kiss.

However, there is one more man I need before I feel complete.

"Boston?"

When Tristan takes Constantine's place, I know there will be no gentle or slow. His eyes burn whiskey fire as his full lips find their way up my body, exploring every inch of me until I'm consumed by him.

Heat radiates through my skin as he plays with my belly chain. "We're going to fuck you in every way imaginable so you know exactly who you belong to."

His lips capture mine, his tongue slipping inside, claiming, devouring. I grope his ass, pulling him to me, and shout my elation when his thick cock thrusts deep.

I lose all sense of reality as they take me again and again. By the time we collapse in a heap on the bed, my jaw aches, my clit throbs, and I'm sore in a way that I'm sure I won't be able to move for days. I've never been happier in my entire life.

CHAPTER 38

"Shut the fuck up!" the man snarls in my face, his spit splashing across my nose and mouth.

A harsh hand grips my long hair and wrenches my head back. I couldn't look anymore as the man, the other one with a jagged red line down the left side of his face, defiled my mother in the cruelest of ways.

When my eyes find her again, her body is unnaturally contorted, bent at an odd angle on the living room's red floral Chateau rug. Her head is turned in my direction, her once beautiful, clover-green irises are black, like a doll's soulless eyes. I think she's dead.

They already killed Papa. They killed him first. And I'm next.

Because the Society demands it. That's what the guy with the constellations drawn on his neck said right before he shot my father in the head.

A strange odor, both acrid and sweet, assaults my nose, but I'm not able to process it over the searing pain of the knife being shoved in my side. The pain comes again and *again, each time hurting a little less until there's no pain at all.*

I come awake gasping.

Cupping a hand over my eyes, I count backward from ten and try to breathe in more than a shallow, panted breath.

I hate having to relive what happened over and over again every time I close my fucking eyes. The sounds of my screams. The feel of the blade as the man plunges his knife deep into my side. The smell of smoke and burned skin.

Turning my head, I stare at Constantine's slumbering face and watch his chest rise and fall with his slow, even breaths. My safe place. My comfort.

I roll over when Tristan shifts behind me, mumbling something incoherent in his sleep. I can just make out Hendrix on the other side of him. He stayed with us and didn't move to the floor.

Usually their presence helps soothe me, but the longer I lie there, surrounded by the quiet of the house and their light snores, the more my skin prickles and tightens, until the constricting pressure is unbearable.

Knowing sleep will remain elusive, I decide I might as well catch up on my studying. It takes a monumental amount of flexibility to extricate myself from the tangle of arms and legs I'm trapped under. After some careful wiggling, I use the heels of my feet to inchworm down to the foot of the bed and slide off without waking them up.

Thankfully, the bedroom door is open, so it's an easy tiptoe out into the hallway. Using my foot to slide my backpack out of the way, I wince when the hinges squeak as I try to quietly shut the door to my room. The guys are usually light sleepers, especially Constantine. The last few days must have finally caught up to them. I wish it was the same for me. I'm so damn tired. Silver lining is that I have the rest of the week off from work and can catch up on my sleep this weekend.

After grabbing some clean clothes, I head straight for the bathroom. Shower first before anything else. Normally, I would ignore my reflection in the mirror, but I stop and take a good, long look at my naked body, trying to see the woman the guys see when they tell me that I'm beautiful. However, the only pretty thing I see is the delicate platinum and diamond belly chain the guys gave me. I finger a few of the small round stones, loving how they twinkle like stars under the recessed lights. Somehow, wearing it feels just as claiming as the bite marks and finger bruises that decorate my skin.

Turning to the side, I let my gaze travel over the half of me that isn't scarred, then twist to see the half of me that is. It's kind of symbolic in a way—the two sides of me. Aoife and Syn. Darkness and light. Damaged and flawless. Broken and whole.

After a quick shower to wash away the hours of sex that coat my skin, I slip into the shirt I never gave back to Tristan and pull on my softest pair of yoga leggings. I can't use the hair dryer without waking the guys, so I twist the wet mass into a bun.

Yawning widely, I contemplate whether to go downstairs and make coffee, but my attention gets drawn to my backpack and the front zipper pocket where I keep my journal. I didn't look at it after Aleksander returned it to me, other than to open the cover to make sure my pressed flower was still there. *And hide the piece of paper with Aleksander's phone number on it.*

I should have thrown it in the trash as soon as he gave it to me. Something I can rectify now. Taking my journal out, a photograph falls out from between the pages and lands at my feet. Then another, and another, and another, and another. I watch, dumbfounded, as they float to the floor one by one, like leaves flitting on the wind as they snap off their branches and drift to the ground.

Those aren't mine, which can only mean Aleksander looked through my journal. Despite how violated I feel that he read my private thoughts, my anger doesn't get a chance to form because something familiar in the images has me taking a closer look.

Bafflement gives way to curiosity, and I sink to the floor, spreading out the four-by-six glossies in front of me with trembling hands. There are five of them. Five photographs that rip me to shreds as soon as I recognize the pattern of stars inked on the side of the man's neck.

My nightmare has come for me. Constellation man. The man who so mercilessly killed my parents, tortured me, and left me to die as flames ate at my body.

But he isn't who tears my world apart and shatters me completely.

Because standing right next to him, looking dashing and so heartbreakingly gorgeous in their fitted tuxedos, are Tristan, Constantine, and Hendrix.

CHAPTER 39

The most godawful noise I've ever heard assaults my ears and brings me out of a deep sleep. Cocky Bastard crows again, and it's like listening to a thousand cats dying. Worse than fingernails down a chalkboard.

"What the fuck is that?" Hendrix startles awake, and I'm lucky he doesn't knee me in the balls.

"Rooster," Con groggily replies.

"Fucking hell," Hendrix grouses and pulls a pillow over his head. "Firefly, shut your bastard up."

Out of all the animals she could have chosen, leave it to Aoife to have a pet rooster and name it Cocky Bastard.

I roll over to wake her, only to discover she's not there. "Aoife?" I call out.

When she doesn't respond, Con sits up and drapes his legs over the side of the bed. "What time is it?"

I dig my palms into my eye sockets to wipe away the sleep and look over at the small digital clock on my nightstand. "Four."

Con stands and stretches. "Want some coffee?"

Getting up as well, I reply, "Coffee would be good."

Hendrix makes a grunting noise of discontent. "I'm going back to sleep. Make sure Aoife wakes me up before she leaves, so I can walk her to class."

I toss Con a pair of basketball shorts after I slip on some gray sweatpants.

"I was going to do that."

"I called dibs. Now fuck off."

"Fuck you."

Not the best comeback, but whatever.

Piano music starts playing from somewhere in the house.

"Do you hear that?"

Hendrix lifts up onto his elbows before collapsing back down. "It's someone's phone."

I stumble out into the hallway just as the music cuts off and starts up again.

"Sounds like it's coming from Aoife's room," Con says.

Why would anyone be calling her at four in the morning?

"Red," I say when we enter her room, only to find it empty. The phone stops ringing and begins again, but it's not coming from in here; it's coming from down the hall. "Hendrix, you jackass, it was your phone!" I yell.

He shouts something back, but I don't hear him through the sudden rush of white noise that fills my head when I see what's on the bed. A gust of air brushes my arm when Con edges up next to me.

"The fuck?"

Aligned in a straight row on top of the bedcovers are five photographs that look like they were taken at the Knight Foundation benefit in London last year. And each one has a dark red letter written on it in jagged slashes of what looks like blood.

L-I-A-R-S

CHAPTER 40

Darlington's familiar streets, bathed in the ethereal glow of the moon, take on an entirely new character in the early hours of the morning. The solitude is both eerie and peaceful, a stark contrast to the bustling life that envelops the town and its campus during the day. There's an undeniable darkness lurking beneath its charming façade, where every shadow holds its own secret—something I refused to see when I first moved here.

The rubber soles of my tennis shoes pad silently on the black asphalt as I round the corner into the alleyway. I watch my shadow elongate and shrink, then elongate again, as I pass under the dingy, yellowish light that shines down from the top of the building. The cooler night air helps dampen the stench of rotting garbage overflowing out of the trash receptacles, but the sour smell is pervasive and inescapable.

Approaching the back service exit of the Bierkeller, I trail my fingers over the coarse brick until I feel the circular indentation of a bullet hole.

Funny how you always end up right back where you started.

"I'm glad you called."

Aleksander steps out into the open, his face a harsh mask of trenchant angles created by the light of the waxing moon. The severeness of his face is softened somewhat by the slight Cupid bow shape of his mouth and the light pewter of his eyes.

"Cut the bullshit, Aleksander. How long have you known?"

He runs a hand through his short hair, mussing it up. "Not long. A year, perhaps."

His words from the bar make much more sense now. *"Oh, they're still very much alive. I wouldn't want to spoil your fun."*

"How long have *they* known?"

Alexsander's broad shoulders hunch as he breathes in deeply through his nose. "Malin is Francesco's fixer and right-hand man—"

He wasn't before. I would've remembered him.

"—so, I can only assume that Tristan has known all along."

Pain lances my chest, its blade sharp and hot. I remember Constantine's reaction in the shower when I told him about the constellation man. I point-blank asked him today about it. He fucking knew who I was talking about, yet he said nothing.

Betrayal sinks its fangs into me, delivering the bitter poison of their deceit straight to my heart. As my thoughts swirl in a maelstrom of doubt and anguish, I question every moment, every memory, every touch between us.

Meeting Aleksander's penetrating stare, I let the pain I feel erupt, molten and scalding.

"That's his name? Malin?"

I can barely say it out loud, the visceral pain so intense, I almost double over from the severity of it.

"Yes."

"There was another man. He had a scar on his face."

I hear my mother's screams echoing around the alley, and my vision obscures with the crimson tincture of vengeance.

Aleksander's brows knit with a confusticated downturn. "Another man?"

Without warning, I rush Aleksander and slam him against the wall of the building. By the time it takes him to recover, I have my knife out, the point of the blade cutting into the tender flesh of his neck.

"Do *not* lie to me."

He barely reacts when I press deeper, just a breath's-width away from where his pulse thrums rapidly. The gray of his irises blot black when his pupils dilate, but it's not fear I see. It's something else entirely.

"Don't," I warn, a tremor lacing my voice when he raises his hand to my face. His calloused fingertips are insistent, like a burning brand on my cheek, and yet there's a reverence in his touch.

"Let me help you," he implores. "Let me give you your revenge."

My gaze bores into him, the knife in my hand steady. One more inch, and I'll sever a major artery.

"I don't want your fucking help. Everything you've done has been to benefit yourself."

Aleksander has been playing me from the beginning. I'm little more than a mouse to his cat.

"Everything I've done," he retorts, his voice carrying an ache of unspoken regret, "has been for you."

Disgusted that he would lay the blame for what he's done on me, I hiss, "Don't you dare use me as the excuse to justify the bloodshed and destruction you've caused. We barely know each other. I am nothing to you!"

His mouth twists in pain as he whispers hoarsely, "You are not nothing, Aoife. You're my wife."

Revenge, redemption, and rebirth. It's time for the phoenix to rise. Are you ready for the end? Their story concludes in Beautiful Chaos (Beautiful Sin Series Book 3).

Keep reading for an exclusive sneak peek at Beautiful Chaos.

EXCLUSIVE SNEAK PEEK AT BEAUTIFUL CHAOS

CHAPTER 1
SYN

"I can control my destiny, but not my fate." - **Paulo Coelho**

A slow, steady rain starts to fall and pelts the window, creating tiny rivulets that drip down the glass like teardrops. My fingertip follows the haphazard patterns they create as they trickle down the outside pane. Chaos theory helps explain why their paths look random and chaotic, when in fact, they're not. Like everything in life, there are inherent repetitions, patterns, and feedback loops. Everything is interconnected in some way.

Wrapping my arms around myself, I try to chase away the sudden chill, but the cold that has embedded its icy fingers in me goes bone deep. As deep as the betrayal I'm drowning in.

The men I trusted lied to me. Alana lied to me. And my mother... God, I hate her for what she did. I was her daughter. She was supposed to love and protect me. Instead, I was nothing more than a business transaction. She sold me off just like Francesco sold Alana.

I glance down at the floor where the signed contract with my mother's elegantly distinctive signature rests at my feet in a crumpled ball, then lift my gaze to find Aleksander in the reflection of the glass, warily watching me from across the room.

"I may have been promised to you, but I'm not your wife."

I never consented. I never said, "I do." I was nine fucking years old when the contract was signed between my mother and Nikolai Stepanoff.

In the eyes of the Society, it won't matter. The legalities of things mean little to an organization that thrives on doing whatever the hell it wants with no repercussions.

Was this the betrayal my father spoke about that night?

When Aleksander doesn't say anything, I cross the living room and take a seat on the coffee table in front of him. I shouldn't feel an iota of sympathy for this man. He may not have had control over the things that happened when he was younger, but he's an adult now. Everything he's done, he did so by choice. Yet, I can't help but feel sorry for him. In a way, Aleksander and I are very similar.

"Let me take a look."

Bright crimson blots the white terrycloth he's holding to his neck.

"I'm good. Just a scratch."

Just a scratch my ass. I shove his hand out of the way. The blood hasn't clotted yet and slowly weeps from the wound.

"Where's your first aid kit?"

"I'll get it," he says and tries to stand, but I none-too-gently push him back down.

"I'll do it. Just point me the way."

He motions with a tilt of his blond head in the direction of the kitchen. "There's one in the cabinet underneath the sink."

On my way to the kitchen, I study the layout of the place. Nice, modern décor. Clean. There are maybe two bedrooms down the hallway that leads from the living room. The kitchen is small and utilitarian. Hendrix would hate it.

I miss them.

For fuck's sake, stop thinking about them.

Opening the bottom cabinet at the sink, I immediately spot the first aid kit… along with a small revolver duct-taped to the inside of the cabinet door. My fingers itch with temptation when I lightly touch the hilt.

It would be so easy.

Ignoring it, I hastily grab the small plastic box and go back to the living room.

"I hope you're up to date with your tetanus booster."

"I am."

His eyes briefly fall to my right hand when I kneel in front of him and something akin to relief flashes over his face. He knew damn well the gun was there when he told me where the first aid kit was. He'd been testing me.

"If I was going to kill you, I'd have done it in the alley. No cameras. I don't play games, Aleksander, so don't play them with me."

The side of his mouth curves in a bemused half smile. "Noted."

I roughly jerk his chin up so I can clean and dress the wound. "Speaking of games, you're an asshole for leaving those photographs in my journal for me to find."

Ripping open an alcohol wipe, I clean away the crusted blood and inspect where I sliced into his neck with my knife.

His vocal cords vibrate under my fingers when he replies, "You would have never believed me without proof."

I don't disagree because he's right.

After dabbing antibiotic ointment over the area, I use two butterfly strips to keep the cut closed so it heals properly, then choose a large, waterproof adhesive pad instead of gauze and gently smooth out the edges to make sure it stays secure.

"You'll live," I tell him when I'm done.

He covers my hand with his, and softly says, "Thank you, Aoife."

Aoife was the girl I used to be. The woman I am now is someone entirely different. In order for me to begin taking back my life, I have to make a choice. Be the naïve girl whose life wasn't her own or become a strong woman who will never let anyone control her again.

"It's Syn," I reply intentionally. I pack everything back into the first aid kit and move over to sit on the couch across from him. "And you can thank me by telling me where to find the man with constellation tattoos."

I refuse to say his name out loud. The next time I utter it will be the last thing he hears before I kill him.

Considering me, Aleksander props his elbow on the arm of the chair and touches his thumb to each finger, pinky to index and back again.

"Tristan hasn't told you anything, has he?"

My heart painfully slams against my chest. No matter how much they've hurt me, I can't just shut off my feelings or make myself stop loving them by flipping an invisible off switch.

"If there's something you want to say, spit it out."

He leans forward, and by the seriousness on his face, I know I'm not going to like what's about to come out of his mouth.

"Tristan came by looking for you last night. He also wanted to know where our father was."

Our father?

Whatever I was going to say abruptly dies on the tip of my tongue. And then I get angry. Fuck him. My tolerance for manipulative bullshit is at capacity.

Unable to listen to one more person lie to me, I'm off the couch and walking toward the elevator.

"Syn, don't leave."

"I won't let you use me for your stupid vendetta against Tristan."

"Don't go," he implores, sounding almost panicked.

Incensed, I stab at the down button.

Aleksander bounds out of the chair and makes the mistake of grabbing me. Twisting out of his hold, I spin around to his back and kick out his knee. The hard wood judders under my feet when he hits the floor.

"You don't ever fucking touch me without my permission."

He twists his body around and looks up at me. I'm taken aback by the visceral sadness that clouds his storm-gray eyes. Aleksander is twice my size, but right now, he looks so much like the shy boy I remember from the gala ten years ago.

Bending his legs to his chest, he cups the back of neck

with both hands and drops his face to his knees.

"I'm sorry. I just... please, don't leave."

I glare down at him. "Give me one good reason I should stay."

I said something similar to Tristan not too long ago.

His deep, gruff voice is muffled and barely coherent when he replies, "Because I have no one else."

Damn him for saying that. I know that pit of loneliness all too well. I've been submerged in it for the last ten years. The guys mentioned that Nikolai died a few years ago. I don't know what happened to his mother, Nina. And Aleksei... *fuck*.

I hadn't felt any remorse for what I did to Aleksei until this very moment. I took Aleksander's brother from him. *But Aleksei isn't his only brother.*

Before I can convince myself that this is a really bad idea, I lower to the floor and sit cross-legged, facing him.

"You said '*our father*.'"

Uncomfortable silence descends and smothers the air around us.

Just when I'm about to say *screw this* and plow over him to get to the elevator and leave, he says, "I found out the night of the gala when I asked you to dance." He chuckles quietly, but it's hollow and devoid of any humor. "Helena Amato has a big fucking mouth when she's drunk and high."

Warily, I scoot a little closer. "Tell me."

This is the last chance I'm giving him to be honest and real. A chance he doesn't deserve, but one my guilty conscience wants to offer him.

"Tristan was with me when Helena spilled the secret."

My heart breaks for the second time tonight. I search my memories, trying to wrap my head around it. Tristan never said anything, but I knew something was wrong when I couldn't find him after their fight.

The antagonistic relationship between Tristan and the twins makes more sense, but it also doesn't. They're not responsible for what their parents did, so why do they hate each other so much? And Alana—she's his half sister. She didn't do anything to him.

Aleksander pulls me from my thoughts when he says, "When I confronted Mom about it, she broke down. I'd never seen my mother cry before, not even when Dad beat her. She blurted out that Francesco had raped her. She swore me to secrecy." His biceps bulge as he grips the back of his neck harder. "I never even told Aleksei."

Compassion pushes my anger away, and my hand unconsciously wraps around his forearm in a gesture of comfort. What he said hits me hard because of what happened to my mother.

My rage flash-freezes to a bitter, icy cold when I think about how scared Nina must have been. Did my parents know that happened to her? Did they do nothing, just like Papa did nothing after Gabriel almost killed Constantine? I know damn well the Society wouldn't have lifted a finger to help her or to punish Francesco for what he did.

Aleksander's chest expands with a single, ragged breath. "She said it happened when Dad was away that summer. He'd been in Russia on business. She discovered she was pregnant right before he returned. Mom said he never suspected anything."

Nikolai Stepanoff must have been the most clueless man on the planet. Surely, he would've looked at the ultrasounds or gone to one of Nina's appointments and had questions about the date of conception.

"If Nina made you promise not to tell anyone, then how did Helena find out?" I gently query.

A snarled curse leaps from his lips. "Somehow, Francesco knew Aleksei and I were his. Admitted it to my face. Called me a dirty little bastard. Said I was nothing but the unwanted result of a bad fuck."

I still have questions, but I don't push for more.

Taking a chance, I cup the sides of his stubbled face and force him to look at me.

"From what I remember of Nina, she was kind and always nice to me. I'm so sorry. For her and for you. But it's not Tristan's fault. You can't blame him for what his father did. He hates Francesco."

Aleksander's cruel fingers claw into my wrists with an iron grip. "You're so fucking blind when it comes to him. He's the reason your parents are dead."

"No, he's not," I snap.

Outraged by what he said, I struggle against his punishing grasp, trying to break free.

He lifts my scarred arm between us. "He's the reason for *this*. Why do you think your father hid you in Ireland? James made a deal with Francesco. You were supposed to belong to Tristan. Your mother found out and made sure that would never happen. Francesco retaliated. If Tristan couldn't have you, no one else would."

"Shut up!"

With a strength born from rage, I use his hold on me to yank him closer. Wrapping my legs around his torso, I push forward and pin him forcefully to the floor, but he uses the momentum of his large body to flip us over and trap me underneath him.

"Get the fuck off me!"

Aleksander's weight presses down, trying to subdue my efforts to escape. "I promised you revenge. I can give you Francesco and Malin."

His words reverberate enticingly, quieting my struggles, their allure too much to resist.

"How?"

"Because I know where they are."

Our intense stare-off is interrupted by a loud chime. Aleksander slowly lifts off me and takes his phone out from his side pocket. Whatever it is has his brows drawing down.

I sit up when he turns his phone, allowing me to see the live video feed playing on the screen.

"You have a visitor."

Revenge, redemption, and rebirth. It's time for the phoenix to rise. Are you ready for the end? Their story concludes in Beautiful Chaos (Beautiful Sin Series Book 3).

LETTER TO READERS

Dear Reader,

Are you ready for Syn to embrace her darkness? *Beautiful Chaos* is going to be one wild ride, so buckle up.

I can't believe that it's almost the end. I absolutely adore these characters and will be sad to leave them. Hopefully, somewhere down the line, Syn, Tristan, Hendrix, and Constantine will pop up in another story, just like Andie and her men (from my Savage Kingdom series) did in this book.

Now for my thank yous.

Thank you to my sweet sista friend, Rita, for always being my cheerleader and my beta girl. And no, I'm not going to tell you how the story ends, no matter how much you beg ;-)

Thank you to Ellie, my awesome copy editor at My Brother's Editor, for your support and love for my stories, and for the hard work you put in.

Thank you to my readers who have given me daily doses of excitement about getting this series done and published.

Thank you to all the book bloggers who support me, and the supportive author community on Instagram.

Thank you, Nala, for our weekly author meetings where I can hash out ideas, get inspiration, and meet my goals. Your organizing skills are truly inspirational!

Thank you to Jennifer and Autumn at Wordsmith Publicity for all the hard work you have done to promote my books.

A huge shout out to my awesome ARC and Hype teams! You ladies and gents are the absolute best!

Thank you to my husband and family who support me one hundred percent every day. Love you so much!

And thank you, reader, for coming along this crazy journey with me and supporting independent authors like myself.

If you haven't read my other books, check them out. I have a reputation for drinking the tears of my readers and have been called the queen of WTF twists. My Fallen Brook Series (*All Our Next Times, Paper Stars Rewritten, Broken Butterfly*) is an angsty, twisty-turny emotional roller coaster that involves a love quadrangle between childhood friends. You'll definitely want some tissues for *Broken Butterfly*. The Montgomerys series of stand-alones takes place right after *Broken Butterfly* and each book focuses on one of the half siblings of Fallon Montgomery. *That Girl* is Aurora + JD's story; *Wanderlost* is Harper + Bennett's; *About That Night* is Jordan + Douglass's; and Sebastian's story will be up next. If you want something darker, check out my Savage Kingdom reverse harem/why choose series (*Savage Princess, Savage Kings, Savage Kingdom*). All of my books are packed with my signature WTF moments, strong women, and swoon-worthy men. You can find them on Amazon and Kindle Unlimited. You can also visit https://www.jennilynnwyer.com for a complete list.

Until next time,
Love and happy reading,

JENNILYNN WYER

ALSO BY THE AUTHOR

Under Jennilynn Wyer (New Adult & College, Contemporary romance)

The Fallen Brook Series

#1 All Our Next Times

#2 Paper Stars Rewritten

#3 Broken Butterfly

The Fallen Brook Boxed Set with bonus novella, Fallen Brook Forever

4 Reflections of You (Coming 2024)

The Montgomerys: Fallen Brook Stand-alone Novels

That Girl* [Aurora + JD]
* *Winner of the Rudy Award for Romantic Suspense*
* *A Contemporary Romance Writers Stiletto Finalist*

Wanderlost [Harper + Bennett]
* *Contemporary Romance Writers Reader's Choice Award Winner*
* *Contemporary Romance Writers Stiletto Finalist*
* *HOLT Medallion Finalist*

Carolyn Reader's Choice Award Finalist

About That Night [Jordan + Douglass]

The Fallen Brook Romance Series: The Montgomerys + bonus novella, Second Chance Hearts (Mason's story)

Savage Kingdom Series: A dark, enemies to lovers, mafia, why choose romance

#1 Savage Princess
HOLT Medallion Finalist

#2 Savage Kings

#3 Savage Kingdom

The Savage Kingdom Series is now available as audiobooks (Narrated by Keira Grace)

Forever M/M Romance Series (A Fallen Brook Spin-off)

#1 Forever His (Julien's POV)
A Contemporary Romance Writers Stiletto Finalist

#2 Forever Yours (Elijah's POV)

#3 Forever Mine (Dual POV)

Beautiful Sin Series: A dark, enemies to lovers,

reverse harem/why choose

#1 Beautiful Sin

#2 Beautiful Sinners

#3 Beautiful Chaos

Anthologies

Blue Collar Babes
My novella in the anthology is titled Tate and takes place in my Fallen Brook world.

Under J.L. Wyer (High School & Young Adult)

The Fallen Brook High School Young Adult Romance Series: a reimagining of the adult Fallen Brook Series for a YA audience

#1 Jayson

#2 Ryder

#3 Fallon

#4 Elizabeth

The Fallen Brook High School YA Romance Series

Boxed Set (Books 1-4) with bonus alternate endings

YA Standalones

The Boyfriend List
* *HOLT Medallion Award Winner*
* *A Contemporary Romance Writers 2022 Stiletto Finalist*

ABOUT THE AUTHOR

Jennilynn Wyer is multi-award-winning romance author (Rudy Award winner for Romantic Suspense, HOLT Medallion Award winner, Contemporary Romance Writers Reader's Choice Award winner, four-time Contemporary Romance Writers Stiletto Finalist, three-time HOLT Medallion Award Finalist, Carolyn Reader's Choice Award Finalist) and an international Amazon best-selling author of romantic fiction. She writes steamy, New Adult romances as well as dark reverse harem romances. She also pens YA romance under the pen name JL Wyer.

Jennilynn is a sassy Southern belle who lives a real-life friends-to-lovers trope with her blue-eyed British husband. When not writing, she's nestled in her favorite reading spot, e-reader in one hand and a cup of coffee in the other, enjoying the latest romance novel.

Connect with the Author

Website: https://www.jennilynnwyer.com

Linktree: https://linktr.ee/jennilynnwyer

Email: jennilynnwyerauthor@gmail.com

Facebook: https://www.facebook.com/
JennilynnWyerRomanceAuthor/

Twitter: https://www.twitter.com/JennilynnWyer

Instagram: https://www.instagram.com/jennilynnwyer

TikTok: https://www.tiktok.com/@jennilynnwyer

Threads: https://www.threads.net/@jennilynnwyer

Verve Romance: https://ververomance.com/app/JennilynnWyer

Goodreads: https://www.goodreads.com/author/show/20502667.Jennilynn_Wyer

BookBub: https://www.bookbub.com/authors/jennilynn-wyer

BingeBooks: https://bingebooks.com/author/jennilynn-wyer

Books2Read: https://books2read.com/ap/nAAgBb/Jennilynn-Wyer

Amazon Author Page: https://www.amazon.com/author/jennilynnwyer

Newsletter: https://forms.gle/vYX64JHJVBX7iQvy8

SUBSCRIBE TO MY NEWSLETTER for news on upcoming releases, cover reveals, sneak peeks, author giveaways, and other fun stuff!

JOIN THE J-CREW: A JENNILYNN WYER ROMANCE READER GROUP

Join link https://www.facebook.com/groups/190212596147435

Printed in Great Britain
by Amazon